Burlington

Heather Dixon

Text copyright © 2023 by **Heather Dixon**

Cover Illustration © **Nat Mack**
Distributed by Blackstone Publishing

ISBN: 978-1-998076-38-3
Ebook: 978-1-998076-39-0

FIC031100 FICTION / Thrillers / Domestic
FIC030000 FICTION / Thrillers / Suspense
FIC044000 FICTION / Women
#BurlingtonBook

RISING ACTION

For Mom.
I hope this makes up for how terrible I was to you when I was a teen.

Burlington

Chapter One

In Burlington, Vermont, a mother disappeared.

The day Mae Roberts heard the news, the air was crisp enough to bring color to her cheeks, and the sun shone down on the wet leaves that dotted the ground in reds and yellows. The kind of fall weather that gave her hope.

A few mothers huddled in clusters outside Riverpark Elementary School, rigid and stiff in their designer rain boots and tailored jackets, while others sipped coffee casually, wincing when steam escaped through the tops of their to-go mugs. Mae stood off to one side, a few feet away from most of the women. They spoke in muted voices and harsh whispers, but Mae couldn't make out what they were saying. She dipped her head and inched a little closer.

"She couldn't have just—*vanished*," one mother said. "That sort of thing doesn't happen around here."

Another woman reached for a lock of hair, examining

it as she wove it through her pointer and middle finger. "I think I need a new hairdresser."

"Lindsay. Did you hear what I just said?"

Lindsay dropped the lock of hair and placed her manicured hand into her pocket. "What? She's probably bored. Maybe she got tired of all the laundry, dishes, and school lunches."

That couldn't be it. Even Mae knew that once you were *in* at Riverpark, you didn't leave. It's a privilege you don't discard as easily as leftovers. Lindsay glanced in Mae's direction. Mae looked away, her neck warm at being caught eavesdropping.

The bell rang, signaling the end of morning social hour. Most mothers turned their slender backs and paired off, sauntering away to return to their empty, echoing houses. One woman threw her head back and laughed at something her friend said. Mae was struck by the casual air about them, their indifference. She should have tried harder to find out, but she was frozen in place. She should have asked how this could happen, a mother vanishing, and why nobody seemed very concerned. Did the woman leave, or did she disappear? Words like disappear and vanish were so sinister, though, so loaded with meaning. It didn't seem right to be using them while standing on the blacktop, watching small bodies with huge backpacks happily file into the building.

The truth, Mae thought, had to be hovering beneath the surface, but nobody was willing to admit it. Nobody insisted on answers, so her questions hung in the air like fog.

Burlington

And by the end of the month, another woman would go missing.

Chapter Two

Two weeks earlier

The neighborhood Mae walked through each morning could have been ripped from the pages of *Better Homes and Gardens*, and yet, she didn't feel quite right in it. Giant oak trees lined the sidewalk, their thick branches forming a canopy of dangling leaves overhead. Ruby and Isla bounced and hopped on the sidewalk up ahead on their way to school, picking up small sticks and kicking pebbles with their running shoes. The sun pushed its way through the treetops and warmed Mae's shoulders.

From afar, Burlington looked like something a model train might trundle through, all the homes with black rooftops lined up and encircled by lush, green trees. Mae and Drew's house was situated in the middle of one of the streets, on a quiet court. It was an elegant Victorian-style home that Mae still couldn't believe was hers, even after several weeks of living in it. The glossy hardwood floors and high-ceilinged rooms were a far cry from the small back-split starter home she and Drew had bought when they first married. And even further from the cramped town homes she had grown up in.

"Careful," Mae warned Isla. Her younger daughter, the wild card, always tested the boundaries. Now she walked as if on a tight rope along the edge of a stone wall, pointing her delicate toes, her arms outstretched at her sides.

"I'm fine, Mommy."

Isla. She was always so sure of herself. It's the little ones, the youngest of the siblings, who are certain they're invincible, isn't it? Mae knew better about the cold realities of life, but she didn't tell the girls much about it yet. She wanted to hold onto their innocence with a white-knuckled grasp for as long as she could. When they were born, Mae promised her daughters would never know what it was like to grow up the way she had.

Isla hopped down and raced ahead, then stopped and turned, smiling at Mae and Ruby while she waited for them to catch up. Isla had one chipped baby tooth on the right side of her mouth that showed whenever she smiled wide enough. She had decided to play tag with her eyes closed at the playground one day when she ran into a pole and nicked a corner of her tooth off—a clear sign that she wasn't as invincible as she liked to believe. Mae and Ruby caught up to where she stood, and Isla grinned again before turning and taking off at top speed.

"Isla!" Ruby called.

"It's fine," Mae said. "She'll wait for us." Mae could

sense that Ruby didn't want to rush. Mae didn't want to either. Time was another luxury that came with Burlington, and one Mae could enjoy now.

When Drew told Mae about the possibility of being transferred here for work, they left the girls with her mother and drove out for an afternoon to look around. At the time, Mae was hesitant to leave her old neighborhood. They were settled and happy in Montréal, Quebec. They lived on a nice street. There was a park with an old wooden playground and an outdoor public swimming pool down the road for the girls. It was only an hour and a half drive to Burlington, and even though it meant all the headache of a work visa and piles of paperwork that went along with moving countries, it also meant they could upgrade.

In the car on the way to the open house of their now-home, Mae had placed her hands in her lap as they passed the still waters of Lake Champlain and wound their way through streets lined with emerald-green lawns and well-shaped shrubs.

"Look at the size of that house," Drew said. He shook his head and laughed, his eyes wide.

A warm current of excitement moved through Mae's body as she caught a glimpse of what her new life could be.

It was a natural progression; Drew got a promotion to a higher-paid position as Operations Manager of a private engineering firm, which meant they could afford a bigger home. Drew even mentioned that Mae might not have to work anymore if she didn't want to. In Montréal, she only had a short commute by train to her office in the city, but she didn't love her job. Mae never felt like she fit into the flashy life of advertising. Expensive suits and buzz words, with people rushing from meeting to meeting asking her to "put a pin in it." It was a little too much for her.

Up until that point in life, Mae considered herself an independent woman, able to support herself. Even in marriage, as her life with Drew became more and more entwined in schedules and raising kids and their coupled-off friends, Mae always felt like her own person. Yet, when Drew first dangled the idea of quitting her job and staying home to manage their new house, it surprised her how much she liked the thought of it.

Now, the crown of Ruby's head shone in the early daylight as if a halo had settled on top of her freshly washed hair. Ruby spoke excitedly about rocks. *Sedimentary. Metamorphic. Igneous.* Her voice sped up, a constant stream of chatter in her nine-year-old manner. Mae listened, taking it all in. There was no rushing to work, no hurrying through the morning. She could be present for her kids all the time. She and Drew had moved up in life, and she finally got to appreciate every minute of it.

So why aren't you happier?

"Mommy," Ruby said. She glanced around as if she wanted to be sure nobody heard her. Ruby sometimes forgot to call Mae mom when she was around other people, but she was always mommy when it was only the two of them. Mae loved it.

"Yes?" She turned her head toward Ruby in acknowledgement. Her daughter had cheeks that were starting to thin out as she got older, a nose sprinkled with freckles, and giant teeth that looked awkward in her small mouth.

God, it was both beautiful and heartbreaking at the same time. To watch your children grow up meant they got both closer to you and also slipped through your fingers more and more every day.

"I'm going over there now, okay?" They had turned a corner and arrived at the school yard. Ruby pointed toward the vast field in front of them, where the footsteps of four hundred kids left it with spotty grass that struggled to grow.

"Sure. Have a good day," Mae said. She made her way to the edge of the blacktop where the parents usually gathered. Ruby and Isla dropped their backpacks with a thud into a growing heap of bags, and Ruby went back to the field, her head down, studying the grass. Isla stood face-to-face with a few other kids in her class, grinning, telling them things that made their eyes light up. Their faces bloomed with small smiles.

A mother walked across the blacktop as if on a mission, her long ponytail swishing back and forth with purpose. Her tanned, lithe body was emphasized by the workout clothes she wore. They were the kind of outfits meant more for fashion than exercise: leggings with strips of mesh along the thighs and calves that showed off a little skin, and a fitted, cropped sweater. When she leaned over to say something to her daughter, the bottom of her sweater rode up, revealing a slick, muscled lower back.

A Riverpark Mom.

That was the not-so-original name Mae had overheard about a certain group of women you couldn't help but notice around here. In the short time she had been in Burlington, Mae hadn't been able to miss the mothers who brought their kids to school and back, day in and day out. The ones who embodied perfection. They had long, curled hair that they wore loose down their shoulders and thin, taut bodies dressed in expensive clothes. They were beautiful and radiated popularity, as if they had always been this way. Mae couldn't help but stare whenever they were near. These women were just so ... put together. Did they not have bad days when they wore baggy t-shirts and didn't bother with their hair? Mae wondered if they looked that way when their children were babies, when it was impossible to find time to shower, let alone put on a full face of makeup every day.

Their presence oozed money—in the cars they drove, and the boots their kids wore. They lived on streets with gigantic houses that Mae and her kids passed when walking home from school. Mae deduced that most of them didn't work. If they weren't dressed in exercise gear and on their way to a mid-morning workout, they were checking their phones and discussing plans to have coffee in the middle of the day.

A few minutes later, another Riverpark Mom approached the school yard, her silky, white-blonde hair falling to the middle of her back. Her bum was perfection. *After two children*, Mae thought as the woman bent to kiss the top of her sons' heads. She had on a pair of wedge heels that looked uncomfortable and impractical for walking over a bumpy field and navigating hundreds of pairs of little feet.

A third mother—this one with dark hair twisted into a perfectly messy bun—walked up to the first and touched her elbow. The mom with leggings turned, kissing the side of the other mother's cheek and squeezing her shoulder. They stood in the schoolyard with their flawless and incandescent skin shining like metal.

Mae glanced down at the old Converse running shoes on her feet. They were the only pair she could wear because they were big enough for her orthotics to fit into. *Plantar fasciitis* was a bitch.

As she balled her hands into fists inside her sweater, she silently cursed herself for leaving the house with her old maternity hoodie on yet again. The thing was ten years old, and it was a *maternity* sweater, but she had taken to wearing it around the house. It was loose and comfortable but also made her stick out like a sore thumb here. Mae tugged at the edge of the thick hem to hide the soft rolls around her middle.

"Morning, you." Her friend Alice approached with her hands in her pockets.

"Hey," Mae said. Her shoulders softened. "How are you?"

"Not bad. It was a bit of an exhausting morning, though. Meltdowns over everything." She nodded in the direction of her kids, who were just out of hearing range, and sighed. "I worry so much about them, you know? Especially Hailey." Alice's daughter was Ruby's age. They watched Hailey say something to Ruby that caused Ruby to tip her head back and laugh, mouth wide open and eyes closed.

Mae and Alice exchanged an amused glance.

"She seems good now," Mae said.

"She sure does. Same with Ruby. All good with you guys?"

Mae touched the edge of her jawline. "I think so. At least, I hope. It's tough being the new kid."

Alice nodded and reached out to place a hand on Mae's arm. "Hey, you wouldn't want to come by for a glass of wine tomorrow night, would you? I could use some downtime after this week."

That sounded perfect. So far, Alice was the only friend Mae had made in Burlington, and it was probably because Alice was so outgoing. On the outside, she was like them—the Riverpark Moms. She was beautiful, her clothes expensive and exquisite, and she had a way about her that was extroverted when she needed to be—all laughter and loud talking—except she was also the type of person who was kind and quiet and could be introspective. Alice went out of her way to get to know Mae and include her in things, which caught Mae off guard at first. She hadn't had any close girlfriends growing up, and certainly not the type like Alice.

"I'd love to, but Drew mentioned some plans with his coworkers and their wives tomorrow. We're having dinner at his boss's house with a bunch of people I don't know," Mae said.

"Sounds awful." Alice smiled. There was a tiny mole just above her lip that made Alice look striking, like a model.

"Actually, you might know one of them? Drew said he works for a guy named Evan. His kids go to Riverpark. His wife's name is Eleanor, I think. Elizabeth?"

"Evelyn," Alice said. "I know her. Everyone knows her."

"And?"

"She's ... outgoing. You'll be fine." Alice's gaze flicked upwards.

"I guess you won't be there then?"

Alice squinted into the sun. "Uh—no." She brushed a piece of hair away from her face. Mae waited for her to elaborate, but she didn't.

"Anyway, be prepared for Evelyn," Alice said. "She'll ask you a million questions like she'll want you to divulge your entire life story."

Mae detected a hint of something in Alice's voice, but she couldn't pinpoint what it was.

"Thanks for the tip."

"Sure," Alice said. "I have to run. Text me when you're free for that glass of wine."

Mae waved at Alice and then made her way across the field toward the sidewalk. There was no way she would be telling anyone her life story tomorrow night. It was best left in the past. Mae had worked hard to get here, and she was proud of how far she'd come. She and Drew had a big, beautiful, shiny new home, and she had given up working to take care of her family. Aside from a little extra baby weight and the casual clothes, she was just like the rest of the women in this neighborhood.

Nobody needed to know anything else.

Chapter Three

NINE YEARS EARLIER, Mae sat upright in a hospital bed, cradling Ruby's delicate newborn body in her arms, baffled that her body had created and grown another living thing. Not only that, but she was now responsible for her. Everything from feeding and clothing to ensuring Ruby made the right choices in life. The weight of it was almost too much if Mae thought about it hard enough.

After a few weeks, Mae learned to keep her sight on short-term goals instead: first, it was ensuring Ruby gained weight as a baby, then it progressed to helping her learn to say her first word, working with her on her reading, and teaching her to ride a bike. Once each goal was checked off, she could move on to the next, and Mae could be certain she was doing enough for her daughter. Everything repeated itself when Isla came along.

As Ruby got older, Mae could already see the beginnings of hormones at work. It was the first sign that the naked baby with soft, downy hair on her shoulders in the hospital was no longer Mae's alone. Ruby was becoming her own person with big emotions. Her friends were starting to matter more and more, and Mae was no longer the center of Ruby's universe. As Ruby's sense of self was really starting to establish itself, Mae had a deep need to give her daughter everything she required to feel good in her skin. Everything Mae didn't have at that age.

THE NEXT MORNING, before the bell rang, a Riverpark Mom wearing jeans with aggressively large holes in the knees and a tight black t-shirt arrived at the schoolyard. She had a large, bulky, cloth bag slung over her forearm. After digging inside for a minute, she pulled a small canvas painted with bright colors out of the bag and scanned the little group of girls that had gathered in front of her. Their faces were pointed up at hers, grinning, expectant.

The mother smiled and reached over the crowd to hand the painting to one of the girls. A budding willow tree grew on a bright background of pinks and yellows. It was impressive artwork for a nine-year-old. The mother dug into the bag again and pulled out the next one. Another willow tree. Same pinks and yellows as the first. She handed it to one of the girls and then passed out another one and another until she had no more. She handed out nine identical willow trees, all on pink and yellow backgrounds, to nine smiling kids. It dawned on Mae that they were birthday party favors from one of those kids' art parties, and all the girls in Ruby's class had one. Except for Ruby.

Mae's chest tightened. She spotted Ruby standing off to one side, leaning against the brick wall, her hair hanging like a curtain down one side of her face. Ruby kicked at a rock with her flower-patterned running shoe, then leaned down to adjust her sock. That morning, she had chosen bright blue socks with a giant llama face wearing glasses. Ruby thought they were hilarious when Mae first brought them home. Now she pulled at the edge of the sock and then pushed it down, scrunching it over her ankle, so you could no longer make out what was on it.

When Mae was in school, standing alone waiting to be included was a regular occurrence. But Ruby was different. Ruby was easy-going and well-liked back in Montréal. It made Mae swell with pride that her daughter could be so different from her. Being the only one not invited to a birthday party must have felt so odd for Ruby. Mae couldn't help but wonder if this was somehow related to her.

"Shit," she said out loud. A few startled mothers next to her looked over with a gaze of disapproval. Mae shifted her weight from one leg to the other. Maybe she needed to make more of an effort to belong with the parents around here so she wouldn't be so overlooked, and her kids wouldn't be overlooked by association.

She went to take a few steps toward Ruby but then stopped. There was nothing Mae could do at that moment to fix it, and she was hit with the weight of how much work Riverpark Elementary School was going to be for her daughters. Every friend and club and group and activity would need to be earned.

When the bell rang, Mae quelled the urge to rush to Ruby's side, to wrap her in a hug and kiss the top of her head, to rest her nose on Ruby's scalp and breathe in her lavender shampoo. She would have loved to brush a piece of velvety hair off Ruby's face and ask her how she felt before she disappeared into the school for the day, but Ruby would be mortified. She didn't like public displays of affection, especially in front of her classmates. Instead, Mae watched Ruby walk into the building with her head hung. Mae pressed her hand into the side of her thigh and tried to ignore the hard pit in her stomach. Eventually, she turned on her heel to leave. The ache stayed with her all the way home.

———

BACK IN HER EMPTY KITCHEN, Mae sat at one end of their large wooden table surrounded by white cupboards, white drawers, and white walls. She picked up her phone.

"Hey," she said to Drew. "Is that thing still on for tonight?"

"With my boss?" Drew said. "Yeah. Why?"

The morning sun illuminated the tiny particles of dust hanging in the air. Dust light. That was the way Mae described it. The appearance was beautiful, but if you thought about it, you were only looking at shiny dirt.

"I was talking with my friend Alice yesterday, and she invited me over for a drink," Mae said.

"Sorry, hon. We really need to go to this."

Mae sighed. "I know." She had hoped by some odd stroke of luck it had been canceled. Mae would much rather have a drink with the only woman she had connected with here than make small talk in a room full of strangers.

When Alice and Mae first met, Alice was on the quiet side. She was polite but bordering on the edge of distant. They met in the schoolyard. After several mornings of showing up and standing in the same place, nodding and smiling at one another, but neither one venturing to make that first stab at conversation, Isla broke the ice for them.

"Mommy," Isla had said. "You look different today."

Mae didn't have time to put on any makeup, not that she ever wore much, but she left the house without even slathering on her tinted sunscreen.

"I was in a rush this morning," Mae said. Alice's eyes flicked to Mae's. She nodded when Mae looked back.

"You look tired," Isla said. She narrowed her small eyes and studied Mae. "No, wait. You look sad. I think you need more of that creamy stuff you put on under your eyes."

Alice erupted into laughter. Mae's head shot to the right, her eyes locking on Alice, and then her shoulders rounded in on her body, and Mae laughed, too.

"I also have a little truth-teller," Alice said. She turned her body toward Mae. "At least she didn't tell you your bum was squishy like Jell-O. I get that on a regular basis."

Mae laughed again. Alice moved closer and stuck her hand out.

"I'm Alice. Nice to meet you."

After that morning, Alice and Mae met at the same

spot almost every day and chatted for a while before walking home together. Soon after, they exchanged numbers and started going for coffee mid-morning on Mondays or meeting up to take the kids out to play. It was an easy friendship, one that built slowly. Mae had never had one happen so naturally before.

"It won't be *that* bad." Drew's low voice brought Mae back to her kitchen.

"I know." Mae moved one hand over the top of the table, back and forth, feeling the cool oak under her finger-tips. She could picture the way Drew was likely shrugging on the other end as he spoke. He was the constant optimist. Drew didn't want to see the negative in anyone or any situation and was always certain everything would be fine. It was a quality of his she normally liked.

"What's the matter then?" Drew asked, his tone filled with concern.

"Nothing." It was a lie, but Mae kept talking. "I don't know. I'm awkward sometimes. I worry about getting to know new people. It's so uncomfortable, and you know how I am." They weren't all like Alice. Mae could already tell most of the other women around Riverpark were vastly different from her and likely wouldn't be as accepting or as easy to get to know. They probably had no idea what it was like to be a lonely outsider as a kid. That feeling of not being good enough dimmed, but it never completely left, even into adulthood.

"You're the best the way you are. I love you," Drew said.

"Well, I know *you* do."

Drew laughed. "Maybe you need to keep busy. With a

project or something. Like organizing the basement." He was joking, trying to make light of the situation.

Mae scanned the room. There probably *was* something that required organizing or planning today. Even before leaving her job, everything with the kids fell into the realm of Mae's responsibilities and household duties. Doctor appointments, birthday parties, after-school activities, and summer schedules. When December rolled around, Mae would keep an elaborate spreadsheet with each girl's Christmas gifts and who they came from. She did it all because if she didn't, it wouldn't get done. Mae didn't mind, either. Drew did his stuff. She did hers.

The truth was, Mae didn't know what she needed. This was what she wanted—the house, the neighborhood, the better life. She had come so far, but now that she had it, there was a part of her that had trouble allowing herself to be fully immersed in her new life. What if she gave off signs that she was a fraud?

She should call Frankie. Mae always talked to her mother when she was uncertain about something. When Mae was a teenager, she pulled away from her mother the way most daughters do, but now they were incredibly close. After having Ruby and Isla, Mae could recognize how good her mother was, how much she sacrificed. Back then, Frankie's love was enough to keep Mae from noticing that they didn't have much in terms of material things. It was almost enough to shield Mae from the fact that she hadn't developed many close friendships as a child. Mae was a lonely kid, especially at school, but at least when she was at home, Frankie would make Mae feel safe. In the evenings, when Frankie was tucking her in, Mae would ask to hold onto Frankie's hand in the dim of her bedroom, feeling her mother's thin fingers and the warmth of her palm until she could feel them no longer, until Mae was fast asleep. It didn't matter what happened that day or how wrong Mae felt, Frankie knew how to right it.

But in this case, Frankie might not understand Mae's hesitation. She would have trouble comprehending the issue because Burlington was every dream Frankie had for Mae.

Yet, what Frankie didn't know was that there seemed to be so many unwritten rules to follow in Burlington. Here, you were supposed to care a lot about how you looked, your house should be well-decorated, your lawn manicured, and your car flashy. There was a trifecta of things you must possess if you wanted to be let in. You had to be rich, beautiful, and thin. It was sometimes okay if you were only rich and beautiful, with a little extra weight. However, you could never be *not* rich. It didn't matter how gorgeous and tight your body was; if you didn't have money, or at least pretended you did, you were an outsider. Not everyone followed all the rules, but those who didn't were the ones who didn't matter—the people on the edges.

Mae made her way over to the coffee maker, pushing it back so it lined up with the other appliances on her countertop. The smell of wet coffee grinds flooded her nose. The filter needed cleaning. "I'm not so sure I belong here."

Drew's voice lowered again. "Hon, you'll be fine. I know you will. You just need to give it a little time."

He truly believed it. Mae could understand Drew's

thoughts so well. They were only teenagers when they first met. Since then, they had grown up together with the same values and similar goals. She knew every inch of his body, every thought he was likely to have in any given situation. Drew knew the same about her.

"Anyway, most of the time when we don't want to do something or go somewhere, it ends up being fun, right?" Drew said. Again, with his typical optimism.

"I guess that's true, but—"

"Mae. We have to go." Drew's tone was a little firmer this time. "He's my boss. I'm the new guy. I need to get in good with him."

Mae frowned into the phone. "Fine."

"Okay, I should go. I've got a meeting in a few minutes," Drew said. "I'll see you when I get home?"

"Sure."

"And hey, try to enjoy this. Remember when we used to wish for everything we have right now?"

Mae nodded into the empty room. She swallowed a lump that formed in her throat. "Love you. See you tonight." She clicked the off button on the side of her phone and placed it on the counter.

He was right. What was Mae thinking? How selfish of her to entertain a negative thought about her life. She was so fortunate, so privileged, and yet—she worried about meeting new people and how well she fit in.

Nobody would know by looking at her that she had grown up poor. So poor that she had to work at doing and saying the right thing in every situation. By now, she had overcome most of the social cues that had been a mystery to her before. Like the first time she had gone for lunch with coworkers at a chic restaurant downtown.

When Mae had scanned the menu that afternoon, her eyes stopped on the description of the hamburger. A burger was safe, and she knew exactly what to expect. She hadn't predicted the waiter would ask her how she liked it cooked. Mae stared up at him for a moment.

"Does it matter how it's cooked?" Mae asked eventually.

"Not to me, but it probably should to you." The waiter smiled warmly at her when he'd said it.

Mae had never been asked this at a restaurant before. They don't ask you how you like your meat done at McDonald's. She waited, unsure what to say. The waiter eventually saved her, thank goodness.

"Would you like a touch of pink in it? Most people do."

"Oh, sure. Yes, thanks."

"Great. That's medium-well," the waiter said. "We can do that." He smiled at Mae again before snapping the menu closed and leaving the table.

Mae filed the information away, something to keep track of to ensure she didn't stand out. These tiny markers had the potential to reveal Mae's past, but it was so embarrassing. She wanted to keep it hidden, to blend in.

When Alice had befriended Mae, Mae was certain part of the reason was that she was doing a good job of appearing to be like everyone else here. There was no concrete reason to think tonight would be any different at the dinner party with Drew's boss. Of course they should go. Drew was right. They had everything they ever wanted. She had come a long way, and she belonged here.

Mae glanced down at the counter and picked her phone back up again. She searched for Drew's boss's wife on Instagram until she found a profile matching the same name in Burlington, Vermont. Evelyn McGrath. Mae clicked on the photo. A woman in a plain white t-shirt with thinly arched eyebrows and bright red lips stared back at Mae. Everything about her gave off the vibe of wealth and status. Her blue, shiny eyes were large and round, deep-set on Evelyn's smooth face. There was something so symmetrical and pleasing about Evelyn. The shape of her high cheekbones, the way her perfectly blown out hair fell onto her shoulders. Most noticeable, however, were her eyes. Mae found them so mesmerizing she could have sworn they were staring directly at her through the screen.

Chapter Four

EVAN AND EVELYN lived on a street where the homes were identical in their impressiveness. The houses, all Victorian-style and opulent, appeared to be newly painted with warm lighting, clean welcome mats, and little chairs on the front porch. Luxury SUVs sat in each of the driveways. Evan and Evelyn's house had a neat cobblestone pathway in the garden leading up to the front door. It was painted in whites and blues and was understated and elegant at the same time. Mae turned to look at Drew as they stood in front of the door, Drew's hand poised to knock. He smiled at her as the door flung open.

The woman from the Instagram photo stood in front of them, looking both stylish and casual as if she hadn't had to try very hard when she put on her tight leggings and long black turtleneck. Mae instantly wished she hadn't worn jeans but was thankful she had at least left the running shoes and hoodie at home.

"Hi! You must be Drew and Mae. Welcome!" Evelyn

opened her arms and stood to one side, gesturing for Mae and Drew to come in. "I'm Evelyn. So nice to meet you."

"Thank you," Drew said. He gave Mae's hand a quick squeeze.

"So nice to meet you too." Mae tried to match Evelyn's enthusiasm. They followed her into the kitchen where Mae could see, despite the dying light, a giant wall of windows in front of her with Lake Champlain and the Green and Adirondack Mountains in the distance.

"Wow," Mae said. "Beautiful." It was one of the most stunning things she had ever seen in someone's kitchen before.

"Oh, I know. Never gets old looking out at that. It was one of the main reasons I had to have this house."

"I love it." Mae nodded and took in the sleek room. In Mae's opinion, it was an admirable quality when your house could look as sparkling as this while also having little kids. No smudged fingerprints on the stainless-steel fridge. No drips of milk drying into crusty, flaking spots on the floor. She wondered if Evelyn had a housekeeper and how often they came. When Mae and Drew moved here, with Mae not working, it hadn't even been a consideration to pay someone to come to clean their home. Mae would do it with all the time she had. The only problem was there was always something for Mae to do—grocery shopping or errands to run—so the cleaning happened only in little bits. Sparkling tubs one day, but no time for the sinks and toilets, or dusting another day, floors the next. Her entire house didn't gleam all at once the way Evelyn's did.

"Thank you," Evelyn said. She took a wine glass off a table where there were bottles of wine, beer in a silver tub filled with ice, and an array of glasses set out. She held it up to Mae. "Can I get you a glass of wine? Red? White?" She grinned like she was saying something mischievous. "Or maybe a beer?"

"Red would be great, thank you." Mae smiled back. She knew not to have the beer, even though she would have preferred it. Too fizzy and burpy.

A tall man with well-styled hair appeared in front of Mae and Drew, extending his hand.

"Hey, Drew. Great to see you again." He turned to Mae and smiled. "I'm Evan, Evelyn's husband."

"Nice to meet you," Mae said. *Evan and Evelyn.* She already knew their names, but when he said it like that, paired together in one breath, Mae couldn't help but shoot a look at Drew. She hoped he'd notice her subtly arched eyebrow. They thought it was funny when couples matched. Mae's cousin and his wife showed up at every holiday dinner wearing matching outfits, and while it was kind of cute, it took everything Mae and Drew had not to share a small laugh over it until they were alone. Drew was distracted, though, already chatting with Evelyn.

"How are you settling in? I guess you've been in town a few months now?" Evan said. He was handsome, and he must have known it. There was an ease about how he stood, his arms crossed over his broad chest, his defined torso tapered to his waist resting against the edge of the counter. Yet, there was something so genuine about him, too. His smile. The way his whole mouth widened, showing off his perfect teeth. It felt like sunshine. A little wisp of something stirred in Mae's chest.

"We're pretty settled. Still have a few boxes to unpack in the basement, though," Mae said.

Evan nodded. He turned to Evelyn and pointed a finger with the hand holding his bottle of beer. "I'm surprised you two haven't met at the school yet."

"Me too." Evelyn leaned across Evan and looked Mae in the eyes as she handed her a glass of wine. Her smile was so dazzling it sent another warm buzz through Mae.

"Have you met any of the ladies yet?" Evelyn gestured to a group of women standing in the living room together.

"I'm not sure." Mae paused and added, "I've only gotten to know Alice so far. I think you know her, too?"

"Oh, yes. I do." Evelyn's voice was curt. She turned to look at Evan. "Should we all move into the living room?"

"Sure. Come with us." Evan stood upright and gestured over his shoulder. "Anyway, I'm glad you guys made it tonight. Always great to get to know the people I work with." He nodded at Drew as he handed him a beer.

They followed Evan into a room with high ceilings decorated with a plush sectional couch, a large, rustic wood coffee table, and unique, modern light fixtures. The walls were painted the color of sand and covered with bright art pieces. A mirror with a shiny gold frame hung on the far wall. Everything was effortless, like a scene from an interior decorating magazine, but warm and homey. Mae loved it and was also envious. She could never make her house look like this.

"Everyone, this is Mae and Drew," Evelyn said. "They're sort of new to the neighborhood—their kids go to Riverpark."

The women turned their heads when Evelyn spoke,

their bodies moving slightly in Mae's direction. One or two of them smiled; the rest appeared disinterested. The men had a similar reaction: partial awareness, but mostly they were doing the least they had to do to still be considered polite.

"Excuse me a sec," Evelyn said. "I have to check on the appetizers. Make yourself comfortable."

Mae took a seat on one of the couches. Drew followed and placed a hand on her thigh. They sat shoulder to shoulder in silence and took in the room around them like it was a movie they were watching, trying to understand the ending before they even got to the middle of it.

THE NEXT HOUR PASSED SLOWLY, with only one or two couples stopping to talk to Mae and Drew. The rest of the guests all knew one another and appeared to be close. They laughed easily at each other's jokes and stood huddled closely together when they spoke. Evelyn was gracious, making small talk with Mae and asking questions when Drew was pulled away to chat with Evan. When Evelyn pointed out similarities between Mae and another mother as a way to introduce them, the woman looked mildly irritated. She glanced at Mae briefly before nodding and then turning back to her other conversation. The night was painful, but Mae was stuck until after dinner.

A dog trotted up to Mae, a regal-looking cocker spaniel with fur the color of honey. Mae leaned forward to scratch him behind the ears.

"You're adorable. What's your name?" Mae said. "You're very sweet; yes, you are." She stopped scratching and leaned back in her seat. The dog jumped up on the couch and nestled next to Mae's thigh. Mae smiled. This was her kind of company.

"This is day five for me," a woman to the left of Mae said. Mae looked up from the dog. "But I can go seven days without washing my hair." She ran her hands down the hair on both sides of her head simultaneously, like she was petting an animal.

"Seven days. That's great," another woman said, her eyes round with admiration. "I only wash my hair twice a week. I'm getting closer to once, though." She twirled her hair around her finger into a curl and then let it fall on her shoulder.

The pride in their voices was baffling. Mae shifted in her seat. She had heard about this—the thing to do was to go as long as you could without washing your hair, not because it was thick or curly and didn't need it, but because it was almost as if the less you washed, the better. Mae had no idea why the women bragged about it, wearing their greasy hair like a badge of honor.

"What about when you work out?" Mae asked. Her hair was always more than a little damp with sweat after a run. There was no way she could not wash it. The women all turned their heads at the same time, arms folded across their chests, hands gripping their drinks.

"I don't sweat when I work out," one of them said. They turned back around to face one another.

"I'm getting my scalp steamed next week," the first one, the one who didn't wash her hair for seven days straight, said. The other women cooed at her, asking for details.

"If they washed their hair a little more, would they really need their scalps steamed?" A low voice next to Mae caused her to startle. She jerked in her seat. A woman sat beside her on the couch, leaning back and shielding her mouth with her hand. Her eyes were framed by thick, full lashes that couldn't be real.

"Corinne," she said. She shot her hand out toward Mae.

"Mae. Nice to meet you."

"You're new? I don't think I've seen you here before." Corinne shifted in her seat and took a sip of beer from a tall glass.

"We moved a few months ago. My husband works with Evelyn's husband. Our kids go to Riverpark."

"So do mine. How old?"

"Ruby's nine and Isla's seven."

"Oh, nice. Mine are twelve, ten, and seven, so I'll probably see you around the schoolyard. It would be nice to chat with someone a little—different—sometime." She gestured discreetly with her head toward the group of women.

Mae glanced from the group back to Corinne. As far as she could tell, there was no difference between them. Corinne had straight blonde hair and wore casual clothes that still gave off an air of money. She smelled floral and spicy, like the expensive perfumes Mae's coworkers in the city used. She fit the Riverpark Mom mold perfectly.

"I guess I am pretty different," Mae said. She laughed

to appear breezy. Self-deprecation was Mae's favorite cover-up tactic when something made her uncomfortable.

"Oh, I didn't mean it *that* way. I meant the bright red lips, the $300 pants." She nodded at a woman nearby in expensive-looking slim black slacks with a silk tank top. Corinne raised her eyebrows at Mae again. "It would be nice if we all agreed to wear the cheap joggers and ten-dollar t-shirts for once. It won't hurt anyone."

Mae laughed. She leaned forward in her seat and felt the tension in her neck dissolve.

"Anyway, sorry to cut this short, but I need to run," Corinne said. "I had to make an appearance, but now I'm going to duck out before dinner. Fridays are big family nights at my house." She stood and placed her empty glass on the table, then adjusted her shirt and smiled at Mae. "Good luck. Hope to see you around!"

Before Mae could ask what Corinne meant by good luck, Evelyn stood at one edge of the room and announced that dinner was ready, and by the time Mae looked back in Corinne's direction, she was gone. Mae's shoulders dropped. Corinne had been the only one here who seemed somewhat like Mae, and she was leaving already.

"I suppose now I have to leave you," Mae said to the cocker spaniel as she stood. He looked up at her and tilted his head.

The women congregated on one side of the room, close to Evelyn, and the men slowly made their way through a doorway into another location. Drew glanced at Mae and then followed the rest of the men. Mae brushed shoulders with him and clasped her hand onto his wrist as he went by her but stopped when another hand reached out and gently tapped her shoulder.

"Mae, don't go with them." Evelyn gave Mae's arm another tap. "We've got the moms' table over here." She gestured to the kitchen.

Mae tilted her head and opened her mouth, but Evelyn spoke again before Mae knew what to say. "The husbands go have dinner in the dining room, and we eat over here." She said it like it was the most normal, natural thing to happen at a dinner party. The other women stared at Mae, their faces blank.

"You ... don't eat together?" Mae looked around. Were they suddenly back in the 1950s?

Drew had already gone into the other room and was probably as confused as she was when he saw the men-only table.

"It's more enjoyable this way." Evelyn shrugged. "They talk about their stuff. We talk about ours. Besides, do I really want to spend my evening listening to Kelly's husband—no offense, Kelly—or have a good chat with my girlfriends?"

Mae put a hand up to her head and swept her hair over her shoulder to buy some time before she answered. This was ... new. She wanted to tread carefully, but it would be hard not to show her surprise.

"Oh. Right. Of course." She stumbled over her words.

Another woman, wearing high-waisted jeans and a cropped shirt, let out a sharp laugh. She held her hand up to her mouth for a second, trying to pretend she was hiding her smile, but then let it drop by her side. She had a square jaw that Mae could see she tried to soften with the beachy waves framing her face. Mae's stomach tightened; a familiar fluttering moved upwards into the middle of her chest. Being laughed at had always made Mae's mouth go dry and her pulse quicken. It was easy to laugh at the girl with no money, the one with awful clothes and a bad haircut. The one who was so different and wrong. She had mostly tried to let go of the way being brought up poor shaped her childhood, but it blindsided her from time to time, immediate and fierce. It didn't help that the woman in front of Mae wasn't trying to hide her enjoyment at Mae's expense.

"Husbands can be annoying, I suppose," Mae said. And then, in a lower voice, "Unless you've got a good one." It was meant to be a joke, but it didn't come out that way. It was laced with bitterness even Mae could easily detect.

The woman flinched like she had never been challenged before, and she gave her beachy waves a tiny shake.

"Didn't you hear Evelyn? I mean, of course, we love our husbands, but do we really want to listen to them monopolize the whole conversation with each other? This way, we can chat about what we want. How many men and women do you know like to chat about the same things when they get together in groups like this?"

Evelyn stood between them and extended her arms, placing one hand on the woman's shoulder and the other on Mae's. She was the peacekeeper, Mae supposed.

"You both have valid points." She turned to Mae. "We definitely enjoy their company, but we decided to try this out almost by accident one night, and ever since then, we've found we like it this way. No harm done, right, Jen?" She smiled at the other woman.

Jen mumbled, "That's what I was saying."

Mae breathed out and tried to smile too. Evelyn nodded back, satisfied. When she turned around, they all followed and made their way slowly into the kitchen, single file and shuffling quietly. Evelyn looked over her shoulder at Mae.

"Don't worry about them," she murmured in a low voice. She rolled her eyes and grinned, letting Mae into her circle.

———

DURING DINNER, more wine was passed around, and the Riverpark Moms loosened up. The conversation revealed to Mae what she had begun to suspect: these women ran Riverpark Elementary School. They were close with several teachers and were friends with the principal. Mae had never heard of that before: parents who were friends with the principal. Wasn't that off-limits? The Riverpark Moms volunteered for and ran the parent council, which meant they were highly involved in every school decision, activity, and event. They boasted about their ability to get their kids into the class with the teacher they wanted each year. If you weren't one of them, it was all left to luck where your kid ended up, if they made the team, or if they had the teacher that was right for them; you could only cross your fingers and hope for the best.

Evelyn, on the other hand, seemed different from the rest of them. She was easy-going and warm, and she looked directly at Mae when she spoke to her, like Mae had all her attention. Mae wondered what it was that

Evelyn liked about most of these women. A person like Evelyn could probably make friends anywhere. She had that generous quality about her, like she would spot you money if you were short and never ask for it back, or she would offer to take your kids for an evening and expect nothing in return.

For the rest of the night, Mae tried to remember to smile and nod and not make more waves, but she couldn't wait to get out of there and tell Drew all about it. She wanted to know if it was as strange a dinner on his side.

Evelyn leaned her head toward Mae. "I know it can be a lot to meet all of us at once." She nudged Mae with the edge of her elbow. "But we're great once you give us a chance and get to know us."

Mae wanted to say something back but was stopped by the sensation of someone staring at her. The woman across the table had locked her brown eyes on Mae like she was seriously considering her.

"I don't think we've met. I'm Leah." Her gaze was unflinching. She had a long, pointed nose and a tiny scar at the tip of it. She brushed a piece of her sandy brown hair over one shoulder. Mae wondered what day of non-washing she was on.

"Mae."

"So, this is your first time at one of our dinners." Leah focused her gaze on Evelyn. "Evelyn is so inclusive."

Mae only nodded. What kind of a response was expected?

"It's like you're one of the gang already." Leah's voice was flat.

"Leah—" Evelyn warned.

"What? I think it's better when we keep things smaller. Close-knit," Leah said. She watched Evelyn for another beat and then turned her head and reached for the bottle of wine.

Mae couldn't make sense of the back and forth. She looked between the women, wishing even more that Drew was seated beside her and not in another room. She would have *really* liked to be at Alice's house, having a glass of wine. Or, even better, at home in her pajamas with her feet up on the couch, Isla snuggled up on one side of her and Ruby on the other, while they watched a movie and ate take out.

"It's fine," Evelyn said, her tone firm. She turned to Mae. "There's a small group of us who get together all the time."

Mae waited, unsure of the direction of this conversation.

"We look out for one another. Help each other out," Evelyn continued. "It's a great little dynamic we've got going."

"That sounds nice," Mae said. What did it have to do with her?

"Anyway, we have a few events coming up that we could use help planning. You should join us sometime."

Leah tapped her fingers on top of the table. "Evelyn wants to let you in," she said. "Like I said, she's so inclusive." Her voice went down at the end of the word, like inclusivity was a negative.

"Let me in?"

"Your husband works with mine, and Evan likes him.

Besides, you seem great, so—" Evelyn shrugged and smiled.

"Oh." Mae's underarms went warm and damp as a tiny thrill shot through her stomach. "Sure. Yes." This is what all those years of feeling wrong could do to a person. The loneliness, the ache in her chest. It could dissipate quite easily, even in adulthood, if someone said they wanted you. Mae struggled to keep herself cool, but she could feel the blush spreading from her face down to her neck.

"Great. It'll be good to have more help, and it'll be nice to get to know you better," Evelyn said. "I'll text you when we start planning."

Mae looked down at her plate as her ears burned.

After a while, everyone went back to eating. Leah pushed her grilled chicken around on her plate, but Evelyn dug in, stabbing a piece of asparagus with her fork and biting the tip of it. Mae took a piece of bread from the basket in front of her and pulled small pieces off before she chewed them. She didn't have to turn her head to sense eyes on her. Leah kept her gaze on Mae as she moved her fork from her plate to her mouth, then reached for her wine. Her eyes flashed with tiny, silent warnings.

Evelyn picked up her glass, raising it at Mae before she took a sip. At the beginning of the night, Mae was so sure this wasn't going to work. She was too different from these women, but now, after getting to know Evelyn better, Mae didn't know what she felt, so instead, she allowed the thrill sitting low in her belly to warm her body from the inside out.

Chapter Five

ON MONDAY, Drew came home from work with a skip in his step.

"My boss thinks we're great," he said, his voice light. He placed his cooler on the granite counter and made his way directly to Mae's side. Drew made himself lunch every day along with a thermos of coffee. Mae loved how conscientious he was about their finances, but she wondered if anyone else at the office packed a lunch every single day or if they noticed the way Drew did. They didn't have to skimp anymore.

"That's good," Mae said. She leaned into his kiss, enjoying the warmth of his body through his shirt.

After the dinner party the other night, they dissected the evening on the drive home. Once they said their good-byes and were in the car, Drew shot a quick sideways look at Mae.

"Was that a really odd dinner party, or was it just me?"

"It's definitely not like any other we've been to," Mae

said. "What did the men talk about?"

"The usual. Our kids, sports, business stuff. Why? What did you guys talk about?"

"They asked me to help them with planning some events," Mae said.

"That's nice." Drew's gaze remained on the road ahead of him this time. "What do you think?"

"Well, they seem like they're a little clique or something. Evelyn said they all help one another out. Whatever that means. I don't know. Something about some of them feels a little off."

"It could be a good thing," Drew said. "Maybe it feels odd to you because it's your first time meeting them?"

"I don't know ..."

"What?" Drew's eyes flicked to Mae and then back to the road in front of them again. "You were worried about meeting new people, but they already want you to hang out with them more. That's great, isn't it?"

"Yeah, but I'm not so sure about them."

"Sounds like it could be alright," Drew said, shrugging one of his shoulders.

Now, Mae made her way to the bedroom where Drew had already gone to change out of his work clothes. He couldn't get out of them fast enough. Straight into jeans and a loose, thinning t-shirt. His at-home uniform.

"What did Evan say?" Mae asked.

"That it was great to get to know us better. He told me Evelyn couldn't stop talking about you." Drew pulled his t-shirt over his head and shrugged his shoulders to adjust it. He smiled at Mae. "I'm sure it'll make my life at work much easier."

"What do you mean?"

Drew sat on the edge of their bed. "Since Evan's my boss, it works out well if you and his wife are friends, doesn't it? That can only be helpful for me—I mean, for us."

"I said I wasn't sure how I felt about those women, though," Mae started. Evelyn seemed great, but Leah—the way she looked at Mae—still made the back of her neck prickle.

Drew frowned. "I know. I get it. I'm not eager to go to another one of those segregated dinner parties either."

"But?" Mae said.

"But this is where we are. Evan's my boss. Evelyn seems to like you, and you already told her you'd help with that event or whatever it was. Maybe we should roll with it."

Mae sat on the edge of their bed. Drew knew "rolling with it" wasn't her strong suit.

Ruby and Isla came into the bedroom, and Ruby stood in front of Mae, placing her palm on Mae's arm. "I'm hungry."

Mae was struck by the warmth of her daughter's small hand. She looked down at Ruby's thin fingers and made a mental note to trim Ruby's fingernails.

"I guess we better feed you then." She stood up and rested her hand on Ruby's shoulder as they went for the bedroom door.

"Mae?" Drew called after her. His voice rose at the end like he was asking her a question, looking for confirmation that she would try with Evelyn and the other Riverpark Moms. Mae pretended she didn't hear.

THE FOLLOWING MORNING, Mae was leaving a coffee shop a few blocks away from the school, pushing the door open with her elbow, a large coffee in one hand and her phone in the other. On the way out, Alice stopped her.

"Hey! Mae. How are you?" She held the door for Mae, and they moved to one side to make room for other people coming and going.

"I'm good, thanks," Mae said. She stood in front of Alice and held her forearm over her eyes, shielding herself from the morning sun. "I think I survived my first River-park dinner party, but it was ... interesting." She only had a chance to talk to Drew about it so far, and Mae felt a sudden need to make sense of it with someone else.

"Oh yeah?" Alice's attention slid behind Mae. Mae turned, but there was nothing of particular interest there. When Mae swiveled back around, Alice's eyes focused on her again.

"Sorry," Alice said. "You were saying?"

"Did you know the women and men eat separately?"

Alice nodded as she brushed a piece of hair away from her face. "I probably should have warned you. Evelyn is unique."

"A lot of them seem *unique*," Mae said. She put emphasis on the word and spoke it slowly, drawn out like it was an inside joke. She waited for Alice to react. Mae hoped Alice would jump in and elaborate, but when she didn't, Mae brought up Leah instead.

"Do you know Leah? Long sandy-brown hair. Really pretty."

"I do." Alice's voice was dull, like she wasn't a big fan of Leah's.

"I got a weird vibe from her," Mae said.

Alice shrugged and glanced behind Mae again. "I wouldn't worry too much about her. Leah doesn't like new people."

It was an odd thing to not like new people before you knew them. "How come you weren't there again?" Mae asked. "Evelyn said she knows you."

"It's complicated."

Again, Mae waited for Alice to continue, but it was clear she wasn't going to. The entire conversation was like pulling teeth, something she hadn't experienced with Alice before. "Do you have time to sit?" Mae gestured inside the coffee shop.

Alice gave her head a quick little shake, and then her face brightened again. "I'd love to, but I can't right now. I need to get some things done. I'm picking Hailey up early from school today for a little mom-and-daughter time."

"Oh, that's nice. A special occasion?"

"No. Just trying to keep her close. Time goes so fast; I don't want to miss anything."

Mae was about to agree when her phone buzzed. She flipped the screen up toward her.

"It's Evelyn." When did she get Mae's number?

"I'll let you take that," Alice said. Mae wanted to say something else, to ask if Alice was okay, but her phone kept ringing, and it rarely rang these days.

"Talk soon?" Mae said.

Alice gave a quick nod. She turned and left before Mae could say anything else.

Mae clicked her phone on and held it up to her ear. "Hello?"

"Hey, it's Evelyn. Is now a good time? I hope I didn't interrupt you."

"Hi, yes! Now's fine. I'm at a coffee shop with Alice, but she had to run."

"Alice?" Evelyn seemed surprised. "I didn't realize you were that close."

"We're friends," Mae said.

"Huh."

"What?

"I don't know," Evelyn said. "I think Alice is a bit of an odd duck. Between you and I, she can be a little judgemental. I'd watch what I say around her if I were you."

Mae shifted on her feet and folded one arm under the other. "Oh."

"Anyway, I was calling to see if you had a good time at dinner. Everyone loved you."

That wasn't true, but Mae wasn't going to say it out loud.

"I did, thank you." Also not entirely true.

"Oh, good. I feel like we didn't get much of a chance to chat. I want to hear more about you. Where did you say you moved from again?" Evelyn's voice was smooth, a little low and throaty, and it gave her an air of confidence. Like the things she asked about were very important.

"Montréal. We've moved around a little for Drew's work, and now I'd like the girls to be settled."

"You don't work, do you?" There was no judgment in Evelyn's tone, although it was an odd question. Most women Mae knew *did* work. It was only here that the majority of the mothers seemed to stay home. Before, she would envy the women who seemed to have it so good. Now, she supposed she was one of them, except for the fact that she and Drew didn't have gobs of money or high-end cars.

"I quit my job when we moved here," Mae said.

"That means you've got time to join us at FlyWheel! We go work out together a few times a week after school drop-off in the morning. We're freaks for FlyWheel." She laughed at her own words. "It's the cycling gym in town. Can you come?"

"Sure. That'd be great." The words dropped out of Mae's mouth before she knew what she was saying. Mae hated indoor cycling while being yelled at, but the thought of getting to know Evelyn was tempting. There was something undeniably likeable about her.

Besides, Drew said it would be good for him at work. This was her chance, wasn't it? It also might make it easier on Ruby and Isla at school if Mae tried a little more. There was nothing wrong with improving herself. Maybe then her daughters would be invited to birthday parties and play dates and get asked to be on soccer teams and to join clubs. Maybe they wouldn't be on the periphery the way she always was.

They ended the call, and Mae made her way to her car. She opened the door and got inside when her phone buzzed again. This time it was a text message. Alice's name flashed across the small screen.

Let's have that glass of wine soon. We should chat.

Chapter Six

SEVERAL DAYS LATER, Mae still had every intention of making plans with Alice. But first, she drove for an hour and a half back to Montréal. She stood in front of a familiar house and knocked on the door. The sound of little feet came thundering through the other side.

"Hi, Lily!" Mae called.

Lily was Grace's daughter, and like most two-year-olds, she never did anything quietly. Mae smiled when the door opened, revealing Lily. Grace, Mae's closest and oldest friend, stood a few feet behind her.

"Hi!" Mae said again. Lily tilted her head of frizzy curls to one side in response and stared up at Mae, silent. She had on a pair of polka-dotted pajamas that accentuated her small, round belly.

"I'll say hi on her behalf." Grace laughed and leaned in over Lily's head to kiss Mae on the cheek.

Mae couldn't blame Lily for being shy—when was the last time she had seen her? It must have been at least a few months. Grace led a busy life, and since Mae moved, more and more time stretched out between their visits. Mae missed the familiarity of Grace, but she knew that even when it had been a long time without seeing one another, it would be like old times in college as soon as they met up again. When Grace called and asked if Mae could come for a last-minute visit, Mae didn't even have to think about it.

"Keep your shoes on—I'll be ready in a second," Grace said.

"Why did we decide to run again?" Mae asked.

"You'll be fine. We've got this." Grace crouched down to lace up her bright blue shoes. They had hints of pink on them that didn't match her leggings which also didn't match the light jacket she had on. Grace loved to run and went five out of seven days a week, but she didn't care at all about how she looked while doing it. Her running clothes were practical and a far cry from the workout clothes Mae saw around her neighborhood. It was refreshing.

When Grace stood, she let out a short, loud breath of air. "Okay. Let's go."

Lily looked up at Grace and grabbed onto her hand. A clear sign: mom was not allowed to leave. Grace pointed her face down and ran a hand over the side of her daughter's head. "Where's Daddy? He's making you pancakes, remember? I bet they're ready."

Distraction at its finest. Grace's husband, Rob, appeared at the doorway, a tea towel slung over his shoulder and a hot pink spatula in his hand.

"Hey, Mae." He waved before scooping Lily up into

his arms. "Sorry I can't visit with you, but Lily and I have some cooking to do." He looked down at Lily in his arms. "The pancakes are almost ready."

"With choco-chips?" Lily asked.

"Sure," Rob said. He went to leave and turned his head toward Grace, away from Lily. "Don't worry—I also added chia and hemp seeds."

Grace laughed and shook her head. "Who have I become? Hemp and chia. Remember when we were kids? I used to eat PacMan cereal with marshmallows in it, and the best part was when the milk would turn pink."

Mae laughed with her. "Oh, those days are long over, my friend. Wait until you start making school lunches. There's fierce competition to not only make the healthiest but the prettiest lunch for your kids. You have to be creative."

"Lunches have to be *pretty*?"

Mae only smiled. "Where are we going today?"

"Let's do the loop around the pond. It's nice and short. Then we can walk to the coffee shop for the best part of the run: the part where you're done."

Running for Grace and Mae had always been part exercise, part therapy. When Mae started jogging back in college, she did it alone, sometimes with music, and sometimes with silence so she could get lost in her thoughts. She had never thought she would be the type to run and talk. Though when she began to go with Grace, her friend always wanted to chat. It didn't take long for Mae to like it. Grace had that effect on people; she could talk to anyone and make them feel comfortable.

They set a slow pace at first, and Mae's thighs tensed

with the effort. It usually took a good ten minutes before her breath steadied and her legs got lighter. She glanced over at Grace, who was bouncing with each step, her arms swinging lightly at her sides.

"Did you get a good sleep last night?" Mae asked.

"Yeah, I went to bed early. Doesn't everything in life seem so much more possible when you get enough sleep?"

"I didn't think you'd be getting all that much yet. My kids weren't great sleepers as toddlers."

"Lily's a rock star. Sleeps in regularly."

"Oh, come on. That's not fair." Mae was only half-joking. Grace let out a light laugh in between heavy puffs of air.

Their experience of motherhood wasn't the only difference between them. Grace had always been a thrifty person, but not out of necessity. It was the way she viewed the world: you save most of your money. Mae was okay with spending a little now that she had some of it. When they were younger, the summer after college had ended, Grace and Mae went backpacking in Ireland, staying in hostels and eating on the cheap—dry bread and a hunk of cheese from a local grocery store for breakfast, rice and sauce from a jar at lunch. They only splurged when it came to things to do, like taking a boat to the Aran Islands or touring the Guinness brewery. It was natural for Mae to be creative with very little, but the more she had, the more she grew out of that easy-going phase, while Grace hadn't.

At the end of the jog, Mae slowed to a walk and then bent over at the waist to stretch her tight hamstrings. At least Grace was okay with shelling out money to get herself an expensive coffee at a cute shop nearby.

They took their seats after grabbing their mugs of coffee, and Mae stretched her legs out in front of her.

Grace sat back, her face flush with the exertion and the fresh air. "That was good. Now I can get on with the day."

"What do you have to do today?" Mae asked. After coffee, Mae was going to do some shopping before returning home. She wanted to stop by a few of her favorite shops, and she had yet to find bagels as good as Montréal's.

Grace took a sip of her coffee and then placed it in front of her, one hand wrapped around the mug for warmth.

"Oh, you know—groceries, laundry, take Lily to mom-and-tot gymnastics. All the things I can't get done during the week when I'm working." Her eyes flicked to Mae's face as if something had just occurred to her. "What do *you* do all day now?"

"Same kind of stuff, but it's stretched out. Slower pace, you know."

"Mmm," Grace hummed as she sipped her coffee again. "It does sound nice, but I've got to admit, I don't think I could do it. Staying home alone all day? I don't know. I like my life busy."

Mae considered Grace's face when she said it. There was no maliciousness she could detect.

"It's working for me right now," Mae said. "Anyway, how's your job?"

Grace was an editor at a small online magazine called *Blaze*. It was growing steadily, mainly because Grace cared about putting out articles that mattered to a lot of women—health, motherhood, women's bodies, and mental wellness.

"It's good. Same old. We're focusing on weighted blankets this week. Can they make you sleep better? Do they actually help with anxiety? I'll let you know when we get a conclusive answer." She smiled at Mae. "But seriously, what's going on with you? How's the new place? Make any new friends?"

Mae looked up from her coffee. "I met a bunch of women in the neighborhood. A few of them are nice."

A wave of guilt washed over Mae when she remembered Alice's unanswered text. Alice was the only real friend she had so far; Mae needed to get back to her this week. Of course, maybe there was something starting with Evelyn, too. Not quite a friendship yet, but perhaps it could be.

"We went to a dinner party," Mae said. "It was a little strange, though."

Grace tilted her head to one side and raised her eyebrows as she sipped her coffee. She swallowed. "Strange?"

"For starters, apparently, it's really great *not* to wash your hair. The longer you can go between washes, the better?" Mae shook her head.

"I might need to write a piece for the magazine on that," Grace said. One of her arms rested over the back of her chair while her body slumped into the seat, worn out after the exertion of the run. Mae leaned back into hers and crossed her legs at the ankles.

"Also, the women and men don't eat dinner together."

Grace's eyes widened. "What? At a dinner party you

eat separately? At different times? Please don't tell me the men go first."

"No, at the same time. But the women go into one room and the men into another. I sat around a big table with all the moms."

Grace let out a low sigh. "Wow. That is weird." She shook her head. "What else happened?"

"Nothing much." Mae shrugged. "Well, there was one thing. They invited me into their group to help plan fundraisers and go workout and stuff." She tried to sound airy and casual like it wasn't a big deal.

"What are you going to do? Are you going to sell your soul to join them?" Grace's eyes flashed. She was teasing, but Mae's shoulders tightened around her ears. She didn't laugh.

"Grace, they don't seem that bad."

"You sat here and told me how weird their dinner parties are and then said they want you to be a part of an exclusive rich women's club. You don't think that seems bad?"

"Okay, when you put it that way, it sounds ridiculous, but it's better than having no friends at all, isn't it?"

"Is it?"

"I don't know." Mae wanted to change the subject. "This is my life now, and it feels better when you belong. I want to assimilate, make friends. All the things everybody wants. And they seem to want to be friends with me."

Mae wouldn't admit it out loud to Grace, but the idea of being in the rich women's club was kind of enticing. Sure, they might seem a bit shallow on the outside, but Evelyn was friendly. Corinne was interesting, too. So maybe there was more to most of these women. It was strange, though, that Alice wasn't right in the middle. It didn't make sense to Mae that Alice apparently didn't feel the same way she did about Evelyn.

"Hey, I just thought of something," Grace said. "We're talking about doing a big piece for *Blaze* in a month or so about women in their 40s. Like a profile. Everything about their lives—sex, health, work, kids, partners. We're trying to get a variety of women from every background."

"Sounds interesting," Mae said. She sipped her coffee and glanced at her mug as she placed it in front of her.

"Maybe you can tell me about your new life. You know, in your neighborhood."

"I don't know ..." Mae wasn't sure what exactly Grace was asking, but she didn't immediately warm to the sound of it. Social media was one thing; Mae shared pictures of her children for friends and family to see, she updated her status, and she tweeted now and again. But she rarely ever revealed too much. The idea of people she wasn't very close with knowing everything about her made her neck itch.

"Why? We're the target audience—women in their 40s, some with partners, some with kids, but I can't profile myself. And anyway, the twist is, you live in a way that I don't think gets talked about openly all that much."

"And what way is that?"

"You don't work, live in an affluent area, and hang out with rich women who seem to live very different types of lives. I want to know how they live, and I'm sure others will, too."

"That sounds like I'd be bragging."

"That's not what I mean. I think the life you're leading now and the lives of those women sound fascinating. I mean—dinner parties where you don't sit together? You mentioned their monstrous homes. I wonder what they do at their ladies' nights." Grace's face lit up with excitement.

"Can I let you know?" Mae asked.

"Of course. In the meantime, try to silently file everything in the back of your brain when you hang out with them."

"Okay." Mae agreed, but she wasn't committed to the idea yet.

"Watch yourself, though. All that time together, and you might end up like them. The next time I see you, you'll have dirty hair you're proud of," Grace teased.

"I'm still me, Grace. I'm not going to change radically."

"Okay, good. But if you start telling me richer means better, I'm coming to kidnap you."

Mae laughed, but her heart wasn't in it. Something nagged at her. There was so much still to uncover about Burlington.

Chapter Seven

Evelyn was already at the schoolyard on Monday morning when Mae got there. Her mouth was set straight and thin across her face, her chin pointing up, and a deep line had carved a trench between her eyebrows. She glanced sideways at Mae, then looked away again before Mae could react. She was so friendly when they spoke on the phone, but now everything about Evelyn's body language was closed off, and Mae wondered if she had read into their last exchange incorrectly.

Shortly after, Leah appeared, moving across the blacktop in a brisk manner. She stopped and adjusted her son's backpack and then leaned over to kiss his forehead. After he found his friends and moved on, Leah stayed in place, frowning as she fidgeted with her purse, placing her hands inside her pockets, then pulling them out again to examine her fingernails up close. She looked around, her serious eyes squinting as if she couldn't see past a few feet in front of her.

Mae couldn't help but notice how Leah's eyes rested on Evelyn for a moment, then looked away, then looked back. She kept waiting for Evelyn and Leah to call out to one another, to reach out for a hug as they got closer, but Leah only gave Evelyn another sidelong glance and turned to walk away.

Mae touched the base of her neck the way she always did when she was uneasy. It gave her a minute to process. What was up with Evelyn today? What was Leah's story?

"Hey."

Mae's head jerked to the side. Evelyn was suddenly next to her.

"Oh, uh. Morning," Mae fumbled. "How are you?"

Evelyn shrugged. "You know. Living the dream." She turned to face the kids in front of her, watching over them with the poise of a mother lion as they ran shouting and laughing.

"Thanks again for dinner the other night," Mae said. "It was great."

Evelyn glanced sideways, allowing a small smile, then turned her head back to the kids in front of her, her forehead creasing as her eyebrows scrunched together.

"Lisa told me something upsetting," Evelyn said, as if Mae knew who Lisa was. "You'll probably hear it through the rumor mill, so I thought I should tell you."

"What's that?"

"Alice is missing."

Mae turned her head so sharply her neck cracked. "What?" She had that text from Alice, though. They were going to meet up for a drink. "What do you mean missing?"

"Maybe she left." Evelyn pushed a stray piece of hair away from her face. "Nobody really knows." Her voice was distant.

Mae's skin tingled. She took a step back to steady herself while her mind worked it over. *Missing or left?* Which was it? The two words had vastly different meanings.

"Apparently," Evelyn continued, "her husband said she got up and made breakfast and went through the morning routine as usual, but then, near the end of the day, the school called him to come to get the kids. She never showed up. When he got home, the house was silent, and she was gone. Still. Some people think she left. They think she couldn't cope."

In her nine years of being a mother, Mae couldn't imagine up and leaving one day. The thought was unfathomable. There had to be some explanation. Her muscles were numb, and her entire body was heavy. Somehow, she managed to move closer to Evelyn.

"How could no one know where she went?" she croaked. Her eyes scanned the groups of women around her. If Alice was missing, why wasn't anyone alarmed? Why weren't people around them talking about this?

"She didn't leave a note or anything. She just ... vanished." Evelyn turned to face Mae, her big eyes even more pronounced than usual and she shook her head. "Isn't that awful? I can't imagine she would abandon her kids. Leaving all this?"

Mae didn't answer. Instead, she continued scanning the yard until she spotted Ruby and Isla. She let out a heavy breath while her mind worked it over. What did it take to push a mother far enough to leave her kids behind? Mae understood how sadness could find you. She hadn't experienced it herself, but she knew of a few friends and acquaintances who had, people who had been nearly broken open by it. Depression wasn't choosy; it came for you whether you were rich or poor, whether you had a circle of support or not.

That kind of depression didn't fit with the Alice Mae knew, though. Unless she was an expert at hiding it. Mac watched Isla talking to another little girl. Their heads were bent together, almost touching, examining something in the palm of Isla's hand. They were smiling and relaxed, as if nothing was wrong. Nothing in their little world was. Yet, for Mae, she couldn't comprehend what had just happened in hers. What did it mean if Alice didn't leave? Did someone hurt her? Or maybe she was in the wrong place at the wrong time. It would be better to think she ran away. The other answer was so much more sinister. Mae's body swayed slightly.

"Should we call the police?"

Evelyn stood still, her stare blank as she watched the vast sea of kids in front of her. "I'm sure her husband will take care of that."

"I hope she's okay."

"Me too." Evelyn put her hands into her pockets.

When the bell rang, the kids scattered like ants, squealing and rushing to line up, as if they were surprised by the sound. It rang every day at the same time, and yet they always seemed shocked by it.

A woman a few feet in front of Mae threw her head back, laughing at something her friend had said. Mae was struck by how casual she appeared. In fact, most parents were standing on the blacktop in the early morning, sipping coffee, having relaxed conversations, and acting as if everything were perfectly normal. Mae envied the way their lives hadn't been changed in an instant by this news. But didn't some of them know Alice? Weren't they worried about her? Mae had never thought she would know someone who had gone missing; it was a surreal feeling, but it didn't appear to strike anyone else as shocking. She couldn't stand around like the rest of them.

"We should do something." Mae turned her head to face Evelyn, but she mustn't have heard over the noise. She had already started to walk away.

Chapter Eight

Back at home, Mae picked up her phone and scrolled through her old text messages with a shaking hand until she found Alice's name.

Let's have that glass of wine soon. We should chat.

Mae pressed the call button and waited. No answer. She listened to the beep and then spoke.

"Hey Alice, it's me, Mae. Give me a ring when you get this, okay? Didn't see you this morning and was wondering how you are."

Next, she called Drew.

"Alice is gone."

"Mae?" The confusion in Drew's voice was thick.

"My friend, Alice. She's missing. Evelyn told me. Alice's husband got a call from the school to pick up the kids yesterday. When they got back to their house, she was nowhere."

"Were her things there?"

Mae hadn't thought to ask such a logical question in the moment.

"I don't know."

What did she know? Not a lot. She searched her memory for when she last spent time with Alice aside from dropping off and picking up the kids at school. It was a few weeks ago, the evening they met up at the local bookstore for an event. There was a book launch, and because Alice liked the author, she was thrilled the woman was coming to Burlington to talk about it.

"Do you want to come with me?" Alice had asked.

"Sure." Mae didn't need to be convinced. She used to go to events like this in Montréal all the time. She showed up wearing one of her old work outfits—all black and chic, the kind of thing that never goes out of style. It was nice to put on something dressy again.

"You look great." Alice had handed her a glass of wine. The bookstore was small and cozy, set up inside an old house with vaulted ceilings and creaky floorboards, and the entire night had been fun and relaxed. It felt like the kind of night you had with friends you'd known forever. They mingled, ate appetizers, and had another glass of wine. Being with Alice was easy, like it was with Grace.

Now, Drew's voice broke through Mae's memory. "It's definitely odd, but you don't know what's going on with her. Maybe she needs a little break. Like a getaway or something. Maybe she went somewhere."

"To up and leave her family and not tell anyone? I don't know. That doesn't seem likely." Mae hesitated. "What if she didn't leave by choice?"

"You don't know what's going on with someone until you're in their shoes," Drew said. "There could be a million rational explanations. You never know. Anyway, I'm sure her family is checking into it."

Mae supposed it was true but still couldn't shake the feeling that something wasn't right. Her head hurt, and the back of her throat ached. She slipped off her shoes and curled into a ball on the couch. If this ever happened to her, she hoped someone would be more concerned, that they would do more than gossip about it over coffee at the schoolyard or explain it away. Mae wasn't sure she could wait around to see what happened.

"Maybe," Mae said. "I don't know. I think I should probably call Evelyn to find out more about it. She seems to know everything around here."

"You said she already told you. I wouldn't go stirring stuff up that's not your business."

"How can I do nothing?" Mae's eyes began to well up. Why was Drew being so nonchalant?

"Very easily. You do nothing because you don't know what happened. Wait to hear what's going on. Trust me on this."

Maybe he was concerned for Mae's safety, or maybe it was simply that he didn't want to stir the pot; still, Drew knew this wasn't her way. She had to know what had happened to Alice.

"Fine," Mae said eventually, even though it wasn't.

After she hung up, Mae stood in her kitchen looking out the large front window with her arms clasped behind her back. The bare trees on the front lawn stood on top of patchy grass, worn down from a long summer. She thought about Alice, Evelyn, and even Leah, and wondered what they were doing right now. She wondered what else could be happening in Burlington that nobody was talking about.

Chapter Nine

A FEW DAYS after Alice's disappearance, Riverpark Elementary hosted its annual book fair. Ruby and Isla ran straight for Mae after school the day the order forms were handed out, shaking the papers at Mae with mouths stretched in giant grins. They wanted to show her everything they had already circled on the forms as soon as they got home, and they hadn't stopped talking about it since.

Mae tried to match their enthusiasm, but most of her thoughts were taken up by Alice. Every time Mae texted and called, there was no answer. If she knew Alice's husband better, Mae could have tried him, but they hadn't even properly met yet. The police must have been involved by now. Mae wondered if they would contact her. In the meantime, all she could do was wait.

"I'm not giving you money to buy a necklace," Mae said to Isla. She was sitting at the kitchen table, hunched over and flipping through the order form, okaying or vetoing the things Isla had circled as part of her wish list. "This is called a *book* fair, remember?"

Isla's small mouth formed a straight line across her face as her eyes darted to the side of the room. Mae could tell her mind was working on what ·exactly to say to increase her chances of getting that cheap locket.

Ruby came into the room and took the seat next to Mae.

"Mommy, how much money can I get for the book fair?"

"I thought I'd give you each $20. I'll make sure it's in smaller bills, though. Easier to make change."

"That won't be enough."

Mae's head jerked back, her eyebrows bunched into a knot. "Excuse me?"

Ruby sighed. "Everyone gets more than that. Jackson said he always gets $100."

Mae tried to imagine in what world they were living in now, where it was perfectly normal for a nine-year-old kid to be given $100 to spend at a book fair. She tried to picture which one of the perfect Riverpark Moms was Jackson's mother and what on earth she was thinking, but Jackson's mom could have been anyone.

"We don't have $100 for book fairs, Ruby. That's way too much."

"You could go to the bank. Use your debit card."

Mae stood and went to the cupboard to grab a glass. She turned her back so Ruby wouldn't see the expression on her face. Sometimes it felt better to look up at the ceiling and quietly sigh in irritation than to stop what you were doing, patiently place a hand on your child's arm and teach them a life lesson.

"Mommy." Ruby's tone was edging on annoyed. "Can I get more money?"

"No, you can't. $20 is plenty to spend at a book fair. You don't need any more than that."

Ruby shoved her head into her hands. "Emily said our family doesn't have money like the rest of the families in our class."

Mae turned around at the sink where she had been filling her glass with water. Her back stiffened at the words coming out of her daughter's mouth. She took a deep breath before speaking. "Who is Emily?"

"A girl in my class."

"And how would she know how much money we have?"

Ruby shrugged. "She said that's what her mom said."

Mae's mouth went small and tight. Her eyelids felt heavy then, weighed down with disappointment in humans. When you got older, you were supposed to get smarter. You were supposed to grow out of that petty, mean streak.

"Emily and her mom are wrong to talk about us like that. They have no idea what we have and don't have. And what have I always told you about talking about people behind their backs?"

Ruby lowered her head onto the table in front of her, pressing her face into her forearms like she regretted bringing any of this up. "That it's not nice," came her muffled voice.

"That's right."

"But I'll be the only one. Everyone else will have all this really great stuff from the fair, and I won't. Emily and Lucy and a bunch of us were going to get these gel pens and have a special club. I'll be the only one left out." Ruby's voice was getting higher now.

"You can still be friends with them even if you're not in the club," Mae said.

"No, I can't. They won't like me if I'm not like everyone else."

A sharp slice went through Mae's chest. Where had Ruby picked up that idea from? Mae looked down at the sink in front of her. There was a tiny piece of lettuce that refused to go down the drain even though Mae tried to wash it away. She picked it up and flicked it into the garbage bin beside the sink.

"Of course, they will," Mae said. "You're a good friend, Ruby. You're smart and funny, and they should love you for who you are. And so should you. You're perfect."

"You don't understand," Ruby mumbled. She stood up and stormed out of the room.

THE INSIDE of Riverpark Elementary School looked like any other school Mae had seen. It was fairly old, in fact, with yellow hallway floors speckled with grey dots, brown carpeting in the school office, cold, painted concrete walls and a dusty old gymnasium. She wasn't quite sure what the hype was—but there had been hype. When the Riverpark Moms spoke about the school at

Evelyn's dinner party, they glowed with pride. It was a bonus that many of them had attended that school themselves as kids. Mae watched them as they spoke, deeply confused by these women made up of contradictions. They wore expensive clothes, drove high-end cars, and spent tons of money on their hair, but they were proud of this old, shabby school because they had gone there when they were kids. Mae didn't see how attending a regular old elementary school could be connected to status.

She followed one of the other volunteer parents who had come to set up for the book fair down the hallway into the school's library. Metal bookshelves lined the room, filled with brightly colored books. Banners sat over them, designating topics—science, adventure, animals. There were boxes and boxes of glittery things: erasers and bookmarks, posters, rocks and gems, and diaries with sequinned covers.

"Remember when book fairs used to be about the books?"

Mae turned toward a tall man, handsome in a casual way, standing next to her. He smiled as he pulled a hand out of his pocket and held it to her. "I'm Jeff."

"Mae."

"Mae." His eyes flickered with recognition. "You were at Evelyn's for the dinner party?"

Mae tipped her head to one side. "Oh—yes. I was. Were you?" How had she missed him? Her mind blanked with anxiety. How rude of her not to notice him.

"I was only there for a little bit." He held up his hands like he was surrendering and smiled warmly. "I'm Leah's husband. Ellie and Jasper's dad. I'm here for the book fair every year because I work with the publishing company."

Leah's husband. Mae didn't know what she expected of the man who was married to Leah, but he wasn't it at all. To begin with, he was welcoming. The very opposite of Leah. And he worked in children's books? She assumed most of the Riverpark husbands were money managers, doctors, or CEOs.

Jeff was on the stocky side. He had a wide face and a thick body that suggested he might have been an athlete back in his day. Probably football or rugby. The hair at his temples was greying, as was the stubble on his chin, and it gave him a distinguished look. Mae had yet to see uncolored grey hair sprouting from any women's heads, but it didn't look out of place on Jeff. She wondered if all the husbands were handsome around here.

"Nice to meet you."

"I think I'm here to help you," Jeff said, gesturing to the piles of unsorted books.

"I have no idea what I'm doing."

Jeff held Mae's eye for a minute and then grinned. "Do any of us?"

Afterward, when another parent volunteer showed Mae and Jeff what to do, Mae settled into her spot on one of the small, hard plastic chairs and emptied box after box of kids books, sorting them by genre and handing them to Jeff. She was certain he didn't have to do this—the boring job of volunteering—he was from the publishing company, after all, but he didn't seem to mind. He looked like he was enjoying himself as he lined books up, talking to Mae about his job, his kids, and the school.

"How was your dinner at Evelyn's?" Jeff studied the back of a book before he lined it up along the others, slim and perfectly in place.

"It was nice," Mae said, though 'odd' would have been the better word; she decided not to get into it.

Jeff nodded, silent for a while, and then he spoke again, still directing his face down at the pile of books on the table. "It's great that you ladies do that. You know, just the women. Time to yourselves to talk. Did you and Leah get a chance to chat?"

"Not really," Mae said.

Jeff's neck stiffened. "That's too bad."

"It is?"

"I think it's good for Leah to meet new people."

Mae eyed him. *What exactly are we talking about here?*

"She has a lot on her plate with the school, the kids, and the house. I know she can use good friends."

Mae nodded as if she understood anything about Leah. It struck her as odd that Leah could need friends; Leah with her confidence that appeared as all-encompassing as her personality. Jeff gave his head a small shake like he realized he was saying too much.

"It can definitely be hard being alone all day," Mae said. "Friends are important." She thought of Alice then and sat up straighter. "Actually, it was my friend who ... disappeared. Alice. The mom from the school here who's gone missing. Did you hear about that?"

Jeff cocked his head and peered at her. "I did hear, yeah. It's awful. And strange."

"I know," Mae agreed. "Do you know anything about what happened?"

He shook his head. "No. I feel bad for her husband, though."

"Do you know if the police are involved? I haven't heard much." She was pushing, maybe a little too much, but Mae wanted to know.

Jeff twisted the watch on his wrist a few times. "I think they're looking for her." He rubbed at the back of his neck. "I've heard they're asking questions. It's mostly all speculation so far."

She wanted to ask him more, if he knew if Alice was in touch with anyone or why it seemed like nobody was worried much about her, but a handful of people came through the doorway, and Jeff turned his attention to them. Leah was in front, gliding into the room like this was her house. She laughed at something someone said and pushed her hair over one shoulder before scanning the room. She connected her eyes with Mae's and then made a beeline for Jeff.

"Hey, babe." She put an arm around his waist and leaned in to kiss his cheek. The scent of her shampoo drifted down to Mae—lemony and sharp. She looked down at Mae, crouched into the child-sized chair, and gave a half-hearted smile.

Mae pressed her closed lips into a smile and held her hand in a wave.

"What are you two talking about?" Leah asked. She turned to Jeff and flashed a grin, with the bottom row of her teeth exposed, like she was trying too hard to be nice.

"Nothing much." Jeff shrugged.

Mae studied him. She tried to read his body language, but she had just met him. She didn't know enough about him or Leah to interpret what was happening between them with any certainty.

"I was asking about Alice," Mae said. "I'm worried about her."

Leah leaned in to murmur something to Jeff and then glanced down at Mae through partially closed eyelids.

"I didn't realize you were friends," she said. "We don't have any details, but we're fairly certain she left on her own. Probably had a breakdown or something. That can happen around here."

"Oh." Mae's head remained angled up, pointing toward Jeff and Leah, but her eyes shifted to over their shoulders. She stared into the distance at nothing, trying to determine what kind of a question she could ask that would get them to give her an answer she could make sense of. "You don't think something might have happened to her?"

"Why would you think that?"

Mae shifted in her seat. "I don't know. I didn't mean—"

"Be careful about making assumptions," Leah said. "It can be taken the wrong way." She leaned into Jeff and brushed her lips across his stubbled cheek. "I better go."

Mae turned Leah's words over in her mind. It sounded like a thinly veiled threat. It escaped her why Jeff would think there was any possible way she and Leah could be friends. Instead of leaving, Leah walked over to the group of women who had come into the library and settled herself beside them.

"I should go too," Jeff said, checking his watch. "I've got to get back to work. It was nice meeting you, Mae."

Mae nodded, glad he was leaving. An aching sensation from being around people for too long when you're as introverted as Mae was filtered through her limbs. She went back to the shelves and began lining up books and sorting piles of erasers. She was deep in her thoughts when a voice interrupted her.

"I see you've already been roped into volunteering your time."

Mae turned to find Corinne standing over her with a hint of a smile and one eyebrow arched. Her shoulders softened. Corinne had put her at ease at Evelyn's dinner party, and now she did the same again. Mae laughed. "I didn't know you were here."

"We all have to put in our time." Corinne gestured around her and then settled into a seat. "What do you think of it here so far?"

"The school?"

"Yeah, and the neighborhood."

"It's nice," Mae said. "How long have you been here?"

"I guess it's been about ten years now." Corinne looked up at the ceiling. "Wow, yeah. It's been a long time."

"And you're happy?" Mae posed it as a question, but she assumed the answer was yes. Of course you were happy when you had a quiet life in a beautiful little suburb.

"Sure." Corinne shrugged. "The kids are settled and have some good friends. My husband and I love our house." She stopped short, and Mae's head dipped, her neck extended as she hung onto Corinne's last words, waiting for her to continue.

"But?"

"What? No. Nothing," Corinne said. She lowered her voice a touch. "It's just—I'm guessing you've noticed the lack of diversity. Almost everyone is blonde with blue eyes. I realize that's exactly what I look like ..." her voice trailed off. She was quiet for a moment and then spoke again. "But since I didn't grow up here, I find it kind of weird, especially in this day and age. It's so ... homogeneous."

Mae had noticed, but nobody aside from Drew had mentioned it before. It *was* weird. This bubble certainly wasn't representative of real life. Mae loved that part about working in a bigger city—people with different stories and experiences. Drew brought up the sameness here late at night once when little ears weren't listening, but Mae didn't want to uproot the kids and make them change schools. She had enough of that growing up. Forcing them to make new friends halfway through a school year wasn't fair, but maybe raising them here would be as bad. Mae hoped the neighborhood would change with time as more families moved in and out.

"I noticed," Mae said. "I find it odd, too."

"I could sense that," Corinne said.

They went back to the sorting and shelving, organizing piles of books while they talked about their kids, what activities they were in, and the best places to get a coffee around town. Corinne listened when Mae spoke, looking right at her, giving Mae her full attention. In a lot of ways, she reminded Mae of Alice.

"I'm guessing you heard," Mae said. She was focused on the books in front of her, but she stopped and glanced at Corinne.

"Heard what?"

"About Alice. What do you think happened?" Mae asked. She didn't care about Leah's warning. Maybe Corinne would know more than Jeff did.

Corinne shifted in her seat, uncrossing and then re-crossing her legs. She studied the pile of erasers and pens in front of her as she sorted them. "I'm not sure. I don't like all the gossip, and I really didn't know her well."

"I wonder what made her leave. Or, what if she didn't leave?" Mae lowered her voice. "I can't get a hold of her. What if something happened?"

Corinne reached out to touch Mae's arm. "I've kind of learned the hard way that it's not to your advantage to ask too many questions or be too nosey around here."

Mae's scalp prickled.

"I hope she's okay," Corinne continued quickly. "She probably is. Anyway, I should get going." She stood up as another group of women entered the library. The next shift of volunteers, only this group was made up of all Riverpark Moms. Mae recognized most of them from Evelyn's dinner party. She watched them make their way to a table and sit down. The way they talked, the easy smiles on their faces, they always looked like they were just so pleased with each other.

Corinne turned to go, then she stopped and nodded at the group of women. "They're pretty tight-knit," she said. "They don't let new people in easily. It's not personal."

"Aren't they your friends?" Mae asked.

Corinne paused. She scratched at her cheek. It felt like ages before she spoke again. "Sorry, you caught me off guard." Her voice was quiet. "I've got to run." Then she turned and left, moving through the doorway quickly, ignoring the group of women as she went.

Chapter Ten

THE DISAPPEARANCE WAS on the local news now. Mae watched the reporter talk about Alice in a detached manner.

"Alice Christie, who left her home in Burlington under mysterious circumstances several days ago, hasn't been seen since. Police have been searching, but there has not yet been any trace of her."

Mae watched to the end and then flicked off the screen. The steady tone of the reporter disturbed her. Mae knew they spoke without emotion when reporting the news, it was their job, but Alice was her friend. It was too surreal. She went from room to room in her house, picking up things that didn't belong, placing them back where they should be; a pair of Isla's socks on the living room floor, modelling clay on the kitchen counter, Drew's ballcap hanging on a chair at the table. It kept her busy, at least. Mae wiped one hand on the side of her sweater. Her palms were damp, slick with anxiety. This had never happened before, and Mae had no idea what to do or how to react. Was it appropriate to have lunch with someone when your town was in the news, and your friend missing? Because that was what she was about to do.

The other day, Evelyn invited Mae over, and Mae said yes. She liked the idea of having something to fill the afternoon. When Ruby and Isla were babies, Mae always tried to plan at least one activity to get them out of the house—a play date, a trip to the park, even if it was only to go grocery shopping—otherwise, the hours dragged by until Drew came home each evening.

When she got to Evelyn's, Mae was given a tour of the upstairs. It felt like one minute Mae was meeting Evelyn, and the next she was inside her closet. They were standing in the middle of Evelyn's walk-in, and Mae had never seen so many clothes and shoes lined up before. She thought that was for celebrities—loads and loads of bags and shoes that were meant to be accessories instead of one pair of shoes or one purse for each season, like Mae had always done. She couldn't deny it would be nice to live like this.

"I need to clear some of those things out," Evelyn said with a shake of her head. "I have too much."

Mae could tell Evelyn didn't really mean it. In her head, she silently made a note of the details that went into the design of Evelyn's house: the colors she used in the bedroom, the mirror she had chosen for the bathroom. These were things Mae would like to remember when trying to make changes to spruce up her own house. It was easier for Mae to imitate something she saw in front of her rather than try and put it together herself. She wasn't skilled in décor and style the way Evelyn was.

Downstairs in the kitchen, Mae sat on a stool at the breakfast bar while Evelyn grabbed things from the fridge. She chatted about herself and asked Mae questions at the same time as she set out the food: a plate with three different kinds of cheese surrounded by grapes, another one with fresh bagels, little pots of jams and jelly, and a platter of fruit. Mae noticed a soft pull in her shoulders as her entire upper body relaxed. Being here now was different from the dinner party. She could picture herself spending more and more time with Evelyn.

When Mae first met Grace, it was easy like this. Grace was so comfortable around new people that she did most of the talking, but Mae didn't mind. It gave her a chance to see first-hand how genuine Grace was. Grace talked and talked, and Mae felt she knew her better than any friend she'd ever had after only one afternoon.

"I heard you helped out at the book fair?" Evelyn asked. She pulled two plates from the cupboard and motioned for Mae to place them on the table next to her. "That's nice of you to get involved already. Some people never give back to the school. Can you imagine?"

Mae shook her head, mostly because she could sense that was what Evelyn was expecting. In truth, it didn't really bother Mae one way or the other if someone volunteered their time at the school or not.

"I also heard you were asking about Alice." Evelyn's head was down, focused on slicing the tomato in front of her.

She heard? Mae scanned her memory for anything odd about that afternoon at the book fair when she met Jeff and sat with Corinne for a while, but nothing stood out.

"I'm worried about her," Mae said. "Wait. Who did you hear from?"

Evelyn looked up. "Leah."

Mae raised her eyebrows before she could stop herself.

"Oh, it's no big deal. It's not like we were sitting around talking about you." Evelyn laughed. "She mentioned you were wondering about Alice."

"Have you heard from her?"

Evelyn shook her head and picked up the plate of sliced tomato and placed it on the table. She gestured for Mae to sit. "Sorry, I haven't heard anything," she said. "Food's ready. Let's eat."

In between dining on fruit and cheese, toasted bagels topped with salted tomato, Evelyn told Mae more about herself. She grew up in Burlington, and her parents still lived here. They were both retired teachers who taught at the high school Evelyn went to as a teen. Mae couldn't imagine that much closeness, but Evelyn didn't seem to mind it. Evelyn said most of the people she went to school with stayed here, too. Only a handful had moved away.

Afterward, they sat on the couch in the living room with their legs folded underneath them. The longer they stayed there and talked, the more comfortable Mae found herself. Maybe it would work out—living here, having lunches, a whole world unfolding for her that she could be a part of. It was undeniable that it was nice to be on the inside.

"Thank you," Mae said. "This was great." She gestured around her.

"Of course." Evelyn smiled. "But I've been doing all the talking; I want to hear about you now."

What was there to say? Mae didn't usually offer up details of how she grew up—with very little money, and not many friends.

"I'm kind of dull. Stuff with the kids, day in and day out."

"What about your friends from Montréal? I bet you had a great time in that city."

"The city was nice." Mae wrapped her arms around her body. "But I've only got one close girlfriend I met in college, and aside from her, I never really had a core group. I was a bit of an outsider growing up."

"Really?" Evelyn said. "How come?"

"We didn't have as much of—all this." Mae looked around her. "I guess I always felt a bit wrong because of it. I was made fun of a lot, and I never really connected with anyone." Heat crept into Mae's face. That might have been too much to admit. She shrugged and tried to smile to show it was okay, but the pain of being brushed aside most of her childhood was still there. Being isolated was something Mae would always carry with her.

"That's too bad, Em. Kids can be so mean." It was foreign to be called a nickname that nobody else had ever called Mae. You really couldn't shorten a name like Mae, but Evelyn had done it. Mae was "Em." She liked it.

Evelyn turned her body on the couch so she was facing Mae, unfolding her legs from underneath her. "Anyway, it's different now, though. You live here. And you met me."

Having Evelyn listen to her made Mae's body feel light and sharp, like air.

"Hey, why don't you come to Leah's house Friday

night? We meet every month to talk about events, and now that it's getting closer, we've got to work on the planning for that Fall Harvest Social I mentioned." She sat up straighter.

"That would be great," Mae said, although she wasn't sure how she felt about going to Leah's house.

"Good!" Evelyn clapped her hands together. "Anyway, I guess we should get the kids soon."

Mae's shoulders slumped. She didn't want this to be over yet. They were only scratching the surface. Still, she followed Evelyn as she stood and made her way to the door.

"I'm sorry about all the jerks at your school when you were growing up. That's not right," Evelyn said. "But now you've got me and Leah and the rest of the ladies. We're great people."

"For sure," Mae said. She shoved her feet into her shoes and hesitated before putting her hand on the doorknob.

"Let's do this again." Evelyn winked at Mae. "Just you and me."

Chapter Eleven

THE GROCERY STORE was busy and loud, but Mae enjoyed the solitary act of shopping for food. Wandering up and down the aisles slowly, studying the shape and texture of the produce—the dimpled skin of a lemon rind, the sharp points of a pineapple. While she did it, she had time to let her mind wander.

Today she was thinking about the nervous buzz around the school that morning. It was because the police were now involved. Mae overheard a group of parents talking about it, so she edged herself close enough to listen. The police had talked to Alice's husband. The officers also said that in most cases, with no sign of forced entry or a struggle, people usually came back on their own. Mae wasn't convinced.

Yesterday, Alice's son and daughter had come back to school for the first time since their mother disappeared and walked past Mae, holding onto the hands of Alice's husband. She watched them from afar. They refused to let go of their dad even as he bent over and put his face near the side of their heads as he spoke to them, an encouraging but tired smile on his face. Mae studied him for signs of—something. What did you look like when you were going through something like this?

She wondered how they were all managing to make it work. Were the kids eating hastily thrown-together butter sandwiches at school each day, or did Alice's husband already know who liked what in their lunches? Were their clothes folded and put back into their drawers the same way, or was everything a little out of place, a little different now that Alice wasn't there? How did a family cope when someone heavily involved in raising the kids was missing?

Mae looked away momentarily as Alice's husband struggled to get his children to detach themselves from him. She glanced around the yard and spotted Leah. She was standing in the middle of a group of women, her hands on her hips and her neck extended, her chin pointing slightly upwards like she was holding court. None of them appeared to notice Alice's husband; their faces showed no concern when he walked by, and there was no change in their body language.

Mae was compelled to get closer to him. Maybe then she could find out more. If she distracted the kids so he could pull away from them, she could introduce herself and ask him how he was.

"Hi guys," Mae called out to the kids as she moved closer. They all turned their heads and glanced around for the source of the voice. "I'm Ruby and Isla's mom," she said, mostly for Alice's husband's benefit.

"Hi," he said dimly.

Hailey had the same facial shape as Alice. She was a tiny version of her mother—the same color of hair, the same small mouth. A heaviness settled into Mae's limbs, and she wondered if it pained Alice's husband to look at his daughter and be reminded of his wife.

Mae turned to the kids, "Hey, I heard there's a Spirit Day coming up. Is that true?"

Alice's son nodded. "Pajama Day," he said with a small voice.

"I love Pajama Day. You guys are so lucky. Do you know what day? I don't want my girls to miss out."

"Friday," he offered. "I have new dinosaur pajamas. Hailey has a unicorn onesie." He pointed toward his sister.

"It's so soft." Hailey smiled a little.

Mae smiled back, relieved but not drawing attention to it, when Hailey slowly shifted her body an inch away from her father. "What color is it?" Mae asked.

"Teal and white." Another girl ran up to Hailey then. They turned their bodies away and started talking, engrossed in a conversation about animals.

"Okay, love you guys, have a good day at school," Alice's husband said as he handed his son a backpack and kissed the top of his head. He glanced at Mae with appreciation as his kids waved and wandered away, both distracted now.

"Thanks for that," he said.

"No problem," Mae said. "I don't think we've properly met. You're Alice's husband, right?"

He studied Mae for a moment before nodding briskly. "Sorry, I have to go. Thanks again."

"Oh, but I was—" Mae was surprised by the urgency

in her voice as she called out after him. She was hoping she could hold him in place, but he walked even faster, his body getting smaller and smaller. Damn it. She should have been gentler. Now he was gone, and she didn't learn anything new about Alice.

After a minute, Mae made her way around the group of women nearby, trying to avoid eye contact, but she couldn't help but notice Leah watching her.

Back in the cold grocery store aisle, Mae rubbed at the goosebumps on one of her arms as she focused on the plain yogurt in her hand. Sensible, plain yogurt. The girls hated it unless Mae added a splash of maple syrup, but Mae insisted on buying it. It made her feel good to buy the healthy foods and make responsible choices regarding her family. She put it in the cart and kept moving up and down the aisles on autopilot.

When Mae glanced down to scan the list in her hand, she felt an overwhelming sense of satisfaction. Everything had been picked up, put in the cart, and neatly crossed out. Since quitting work, she found a lot of enjoyment in ticking things off her to-do list. It had given her a sense of achievement.

Mae made her way toward the end of the aisle and around the next corner. Leah was there, in the middle of the row, studying the cereal boxes in front of her. Mae stopped her cart. What were the chances she could turn around quietly, slink away into the next aisle, and even get out of the store without being seen? Her stomach opened into a pit when Leah turned and looked directly at her.

Mae reluctantly pushed her cart forward. "Hi."

Leah nodded. "I heard Evelyn invited you over tomorrow night."

"Yeah. Hope that's okay."

Leah shrugged. "Sure. Evelyn says you're great."

Mae was suddenly aware that Leah was speaking to her with a small smile on her face as if she were offering a tiny olive branch, and Mae didn't know what to do.

"She says you're joining our MOB meetings?" Leah asked.

"I'm sorry?"

Leah laughed. "Oh. Right. I keep forgetting you don't know some things yet. We call ourselves the Moms of Burlington sometimes. The MOB." Her eyes darted over Mae's face intently as she spoke, as if she were looking for a reaction. "Anyway, you told Evelyn you're game to help out, yes?"

"Yeah, sure. Sounds good."

"That's great because we need you to do something for us already."

"What's that?" Mae asked. If it was for the upcoming harvest social, she hoped it wasn't something she wouldn't know how to do. Mae could pick up supplies or place an order for food, but outside of little tasks, she didn't have much experience with planning fundraisers. This was her first rodeo, and Mae already could tell the expectations would be high.

"You're friends with Corinne Richmond, right?"

Oh. That wasn't what Mae was expecting.

"I'm still getting to know her, but yeah. I think so," Mae said.

Leah moved a little closer. "She's been a little off lately. A little unbecoming, I guess you could say."

Mae's face contorted into surprise. Who used that term? Besides, Corinne had only ever seemed nice to her.

Leah was quick to keep talking. "It's not a big deal. We thought someone should check up on her, and make sure she's okay. That's all."

"Check up on her? Why me?"

"I saw you two at the book fair." Leah shrugged. "You seemed like two peas in a pod."

"I don't even have her phone number," Mae said. It would be weird for Mae to call Corinne out of the blue.

"Give me your phone." Leah held her hand out. When Mae hesitated, Leah sighed. "I'll put Corinne's number into it. It's fine. You guys are friends, aren't you?"

Mae slowly handed it over and watched as Leah typed something in.

"There. Now make sure you ask her what's wrong, okay? It's very important that we know what's going on." Leah handed Mae her phone.

"Why don't you ask her yourself?"

Leah had a pinched look on her face. Mae must have said something wrong. "If you don't want to, I can ask Evelyn instead."

"No, it's okay. I'll talk to her." Mae eyed the end of the aisle. She wanted to leave now. Part of her thought she had the energy for Leah, but another part was suddenly tired. Could she really hang out with someone who used the word 'unbecoming' seriously?

"Good. Thanks." Leah turned and gestured at the

checkout. "I should go. Let us know what you hear from Corinne as soon as you talk to her. We're all concerned."

Mae nodded. Then she went down another aisle, scanning the boxes of crackers without really seeing them, trying to decide if she should be concerned, too.

Chapter Twelve

In her kitchen, Mae moved from the sink to the refrigerator to the counter as she prepped food for dinner. Ruby and Isla were home from school, worn out from all the learning and activities, and slumped together on the couch watching TV. Drew was grabbing a quick drink with Evan and a couple of co-workers and would be home a little later tonight, so Mae poured herself a small glass of wine and put on a podcast as she worked.

When the podcast ended, she put her knife down on the cutting board and picked up her phone. She had a missed text from Evelyn.

Heard you ran into Leah? She said you guys chatted.

Mae smiled to herself. She tapped a message back. *Yes! It was—* Mae paused. Then she tapped back, *nice!* A little white lie, but Evelyn didn't need to know that.

See you Friday night! Evelyn wrote. *Bring a bottle of red.*

Mae sent Evelyn a smiley face and then opened a new

message. She had been procrastinating, but Mae figured she should try to arrange a time to chat with Corinne now, so she could tell Leah she had done it.

Hey Corinne, she texted. *It's Mae. I got your number from Leah. How are you?*

She waited for a response. Before long, the bubble appeared to show Corinne was typing back.

Hey! Good thx. You?

Mae asked Corinne if she was free for a glass of wine later that night.

Fun! Would love to. Downtown Bistro?

Mae had been to Downtown Bistro before. It was a chic little restaurant with dark walls and black cloth napkins where you could grab a glass of wine or a martini. If she called to make a reservation right now, she could request a table in the corner, right by the window, where they would be secluded. The perfect place for a quiet conversation.

She picked a time after Drew would be home from work, and then, after calling the restaurant, Mae put her phone down. She went to the fridge and pulled out the raw, cold bunches of broccoli and placed them in a colander before putting them in the sink. She turned on the tap and pulled on the hose attachment, spraying cold water over the florets, and turned the broccoli over, ignoring the spray from the water that landed on her shirt, leaving tiny droplets glimmering in the light.

A shiver went through Mae, causing the hairs on her forearms to stand up. Mae told herself it wasn't that she was uneasy with what felt like spying. No, it had to be the cold water from the tap.

AT THE BISTRO, Mae asked for a glass of Cabernet Sauvignon. Corinne arrived a few minutes after Mae and ordered the same.

"Hey," she said when she sat down. "This is nice. Thanks for asking me." Corinne had on a bright pink off-the-shoulder top that highlighted her defined clavicle and her tanned upper arms. Mae wanted to ask her what bra she was wearing. She had yet to find a proper-fitting strapless bra, which meant the entire bare-shoulder trend had been one Mae could never partake in.

"Good to see you," Mae said instead. She kept telling herself that this was innocent. Yes, she was here to find out what was up with Corinne, but she would never tell Leah anything too personal or private. It was an excuse to have a glass of wine with a new friend, with the added bonus of getting on everyone's good side. That was all.

They made small talk about the weather and their kids for a few minutes. Then Mae decided to approach the subject.

"How have you been doing? Are you okay?" She leaned in when she said it and spoke softly.

"I'm fine. What do you mean?"

"I heard through the grapevine that you might be, uh —" Mae fumbled.

"You heard what? And from who?"

"I'm sure it's nothing. Leah was asking about you the other day. It wasn't a big deal, but she was wondering if everything's okay."

Corinne's brow furrowed. Mae was glad she decided

to leave out the part about Leah saying Corinne had been acting 'unbecoming.'

"What did you tell her?"

Mae's foot began to bounce. She folded her arms across her lap and thought about what to say, maybe for too long.

"I said I would ask you for her."

"That's why you asked me to meet you here." Corinne's voice was flat now.

"No, not at all," Mae said. "I wanted to get together." Again with the little white lies. The truth was, she *did* like spending time with Corinne and was happy to go out for a night with her, but it was too embarrassing to admit the other truth. There was a part of her that wanted to be on the inside of things with Evelyn and the other women rather than the outside. Life is easier when everyone likes you; Corinne must have understood that.

"Okay." Corinne released a slow, long breath of air.

"What?" Mae asked. "Hey, I'm sorry. I didn't think—"

Corinne waved a hand at Mae. "It's fine."

It wasn't. Mae could detect it.

"Did she say anything else about me?"

Across the restaurant, the massive window that faced the street revealed darkness outside. It was too hard for Mae to see much of anything but a hint of shadows.

"She said something sort of odd."

"What was it?"

"I don't know if it means anything, but she said you seemed off. Kind of like your behavior was strange." Mae fiddled with the edge of her shirt with one hand. "I'm sure it's nothing, though." She looked up and tried her best reassuring smile on Corinne.

Corinne's tone was subdued when she spoke again. "Yeah. Who knows?" She blinked and then sat up a little straighter, moving her legs to one side of her chair. "I have to run to the washroom. I'll be right back."

Mae watched her go. She would have to tell Leah that Corinne was fine, and that was it. She leaned forward in her seat, adjusting one thigh and then the other.

Corinne left her purse behind, open on the seat next to the one she had been sitting in. Mae's eyes darted from the purse to the hall Corinne had disappeared down and then back to the purse again.

Could she? Hell no, she wouldn't do that. What was Mae expecting to find, anyway? There was nothing going on here. Then again, maybe it wouldn't hurt to try a little harder to find out more. When you asked anyone how they were, the answer was almost always 'fine,' whether they were or not. What if Corinne wasn't okay? She could be depressed. She might need help but not want to say anything. What if she ended up like Alice?

Mae glanced down the hallway. No sign of Corinne yet. She leaned forward, shifting her body weight slightly and reached a hand out, placing her fingers on the very edge of Corinne's small purse, pushing it open. Just a tiny look.

Inside, Mae could see a wallet, a tube of lipstick, and— was that a bottle of pills?

Her fingers gripped the bottle so she could get a better look, but she was sitting a little too far and it was too dim to read the label.

A door swung open, and the sound of people talking caused Mae to jump. She dropped the bottle and put her hands in her lap. Her head snapped around to the entrance of the bistro. It was only a couple coming in, probably to grab a drink.

When Mae turned around again, Corinne was on her way back. Mae looked down and stared at the tops of her knees. What the hell was she thinking? She wasn't a snooper, and anyway, she didn't even know what she was looking for.

"You know what I think this is about?" Corinne said after she sat down, launching back into conversation, "I've been a little concerned about some things, and I don't hide it well. For the most part, I've been friendly with all of them, and I guess they've seemed okay, but now I'm starting to have some doubts."

The waiter came by, and they each ordered a second glass of wine.

"And some water for the table," Corinne said. She spoke with such confidence Mae had a hard time picturing Corinne ever doubting herself.

"Why are you concerned now?" Mae asked.

"The more time I spend with them, the more and more I find myself being so ... not myself. Like, last week, for example. I was at lunch with a few of them, and all of a sudden I was telling them personal things about my life that I would never normally share. They just seemed so ... charming. I let my guard down, and the next thing I knew, words were coming out of my mouth like I had no control."

"But friends tell each other things, right? I'm sure it's fine."

Corinne shook her head. "Once they know something about you, they can hold onto it and use it at a later date."

"No," Mae said. Evelyn wouldn't do that—would she?

Corinne remained quiet for a moment; her mouth set in a thin line. When she spoke, her voice had changed. It was low, almost sad. "I guess I realize now they're hard to trust. Leah was at that lunch. I thought things were fine with her and me." Corinne met Mae's gaze and held it. "But I see she's sent you to grill me."

"That's not what this is," Mae insisted.

Corinne arched an eyebrow. Mae wanted to reply but didn't know what to say.

"Listen, I know you're only doing what Leah asked," Corinne said. "Don't worry about it. I can trust you."

Mae's skin was suddenly itchy. She rubbed at her forearms and ran her fingers through her hair at the temples. As much as she liked Corinne and going for a glass of wine on a weeknight, she was uncomfortable with this. Corinne tilted her head. There was a tiny mole on her right cheek that Mae focused on instead of looking into her eyes. It reminded her of Alice.

"At lunch the other day," Mae said. Her voice was scratchy, as if the back of her throat were sore. "Did anybody talk about Alice?" She wondered at first if Corinne heard her.

"Not really," Corinne said eventually. She glanced around the restaurant, craning her neck. "They've been a while with our wine, haven't they?"

"Not really?" Mae repeated.

Corinne sighed. "I'm worried about her too, but I didn't want to push it."

Before Mae could ask what she meant, Corinne changed the subject and started talking about her kids, telling a funny story about something cute her daughter did. She became so animated when she spoke of her children that Mae didn't know how to bring the conversation back to whatever was being left unsaid about Alice. Instead, Mae listened, she nodded and smiled at the right times, but there was a hum in her ears as if she was underwater.

Chapter Thirteen

For several hours afterward, Mae lay in bed, eyes closed but wide awake, trying to break down how the night had gone with Corinne. By the time the bill arrived, and they air kissed goodnight, Mae wasn't sure where they stood. If she were better at reading body language, maybe she would know what the small, half-smile on Corinne's face meant or if she should read into the fact that Corinne didn't mention they should do it again.

The next morning was slow. Mae fumbled through breakfast and packed lunches in a groggy, silent state. Two glasses of wine on a Wednesday night may have been no issue when she was younger, but there seemed to be repercussions for everything when you were in your forties. After the girls went to school, she grabbed her keys and left the house to run a few errands. On her way back, Mae turned her car down Alice's street. Something about last night, about Corinne's unwillingness to talk about Alice, made Mae feel the need to go there.

She couldn't recall which house number was Alice's, but she did know that it was on the right side of the street when you were heading toward the water. It had gray stone siding and her husband drove a white SUV.

"Shit," Mae said when she saw Alice's husband. He was exiting a front door and walking toward his vehicle. Mae hadn't prepared for this, but now she couldn't drive away. He paused with his hand on the driver's side door and looked in her direction, eyes squinting. He must have been wondering why a car was creeping forward at a snail's pace out front of his house with a woman alone inside it.

"Shit," Mae said again when he started walking in her direction. She stopped her car.

He approached with his head bowed. When he got to the side of her window, he looked up and gazed inside at Mae. There was a pinched expression on his face, kind of like Leah's. Mae should be used to this by now.

"Do I know you?" he asked when Mae reluctantly rolled down her window.

"I'm Mae. A friend of Alice's," she said. "We met at the school the other day."

He took a step back but gave Mae a probing gaze. He wore a pair of dress pants and a crisp shirt like he was heading into an office. Mae wondered if he had to work out a deal on flex hours and if he resented Alice for it.

"I don't know why I came here," Mae said. "I guess I wanted to see if everything was okay."

He frowned and put his hands in his pockets. "She's not back yet. I'm sure she'll call you when she is."

"You've heard from her?"

"Not yet." He shook his head and looked down at his feet.

"But, the police—" What did Mae want to ask? Even she didn't know.

The muscles in his jaw clenched. His Adam's apple bobbed up and down slowly when he swallowed. "I'm late for work."

Then he turned and left.

———

LATER THAT MORNING, a note arrived for Mae.

She returned home and pushed through the front door, grabbing a handful of flyers and envelopes from the mailbox as she went. She peeled her coat off and hung it on the back of a chair. The house was tidy and gleaming in the mid-morning sun because Mae made sure to leave it that way. It was satisfying to come home and see a shining granite countertop with no clutter on top of it, and no dishes left in the sink or on the counter above the dishwasher. Ruby and Isla's crafts and bins of markers and pencil crayons were no longer being stored in the kitchen but put away in their rightful spot.

Mae flung the mail onto the counter and was about to turn the laundry over from the washer to the dryer when something caught her eye. One of the envelopes was small, not the typical letter size, and plain. Nothing was written on the front except for Mae's first name.

She picked it up and turned it over in her hands, examining the crisp stationery. It was clean, smooth, and looked expensive. Mae stuck her finger under one edge and ripped it open. Inside was a folded piece of paper. She opened it and found neat writing, graceful and elegant.

You ask too many questions.

Mae flipped the letter over but found the rest of it blank. A twist of fear wound its way through Mae's chest. She put the letter back down, trying to keep her hands still. She looked around the empty room and was suddenly hot. Too hot. Mae pressed a hand to her sternum and then fumbled in her purse for her phone. Drew's reaction would tell her everything. If he was calm, it wasn't as big a deal as Mae thought it was. If he was concerned, she would have to do something. Call the police? With Alice gone, Corinne's words ringing through her head, she didn't want to take any risks. Drew would know what to do.

He picked up after the first ring.

"I got home and found a note for me in the mailbox," Mae said before Drew could speak. "It said you ask too many questions."

"Wait, what? What's going on?" Drew asked.

"There was a note in the mail for me." She read it out to him slowly, enunciating each word as if that could help him understand the gravity of the situation.

There was a muffled sound in the background on Drew's end. "I'm closing my door," he said in a low voice. "Now, what the hell? Are you sure it's for you?"

"It had my name on it."

"Oh." He paused. "That's so weird. Who would do something like that?"

A few years ago, Mae read an article in the *New York Times* about an executive at an investment bank. He was rich and smart but also psychotic. After each breakup, he threatened three of his ex-wives and girlfriends, one right after the other, systematically. He swore he would burn their homes down, tailed them when they left work, and violated restraining orders they took out against him. He also sent all of them threatening anonymous letters. One of them said *I can see you* made up of letters cut out from magazines. The thing Mae remembered as the most horrifying about the article was that the guy kept his job. His bank managers were told about what he did, but nothing happened to him. He might still work there. Even the police didn't do much. That's the thing about money; if you were rich, you could get away with almost anything.

Mae's head was foggy. There was nobody from her past who would want to scare her, no crazy ex-boyfriend. She used to be a poor girl who everyone ignored or forgot about. It had to be someone here, in Burlington.

"I have no idea who it could be," Mae said. "Should I go to the police?"

Drew was silent for a moment. "Maybe."

"Do you think we're in some kind of danger?" She thought of Ruby and Isla. Her stomach ached with fear. She made her way to the couch on shaking legs to take a seat.

"No," Drew said. "It doesn't actually say much. I think somebody is trying to be a bully, but I have no idea why."

"Neither do I."

"Hold onto it. Let's be cautious for now, and if another one comes, we'll definitely go to the police."

Mae was relieved by Drew's suggestion. She didn't want to go to the police right away. She didn't want this to be a thing—especially now that she felt she was just getting to know everyone better. If it was a big deal, she would have to draw attention to herself. She folded the note and went to her bedroom to slip it into the back of the drawer in her nightstand.

"Do you want me to come home?" Drew asked.

"No. But don't be late tonight, okay?" Mae said into the phone.

Drew promised he wouldn't, so Mae hung up. She glanced down at her nightstand and the back of her neck prickled.

Chapter Fourteen

HAVING a hair appointment on a weekday was a novelty to Mae. Only three months ago, back in Montréal, she would have had to squeeze it in on weekends, usually at an inconvenient time, but now, sitting in a salon she had never been to before, Mae studied herself in the giant mirrors. There were dark circles under her eyes. She tried to cover them with makeup that morning, but in the natural light coming through the windows of the salon, she could see only dry, lined skin.

The stylist, Ricki, had gorgeous dark curls that bounced when she came over to where Mae was sitting. That was a good sign, at least—Mae didn't trust any stylist with hair that was hidden in a ponytail or a messy bun. Ricki ran her hands through the bottom of Mae's hair from the nape of her neck toward the back of her head.

"What are we doing today?" Ricki asked, smiling at Mae's reflection.

"Just a trim, I think."

Mae was glad she had come here. It was a small distraction from Alice and the note. Although, when Evelyn first suggested this salon, Mae was embarrassed by what Evelyn meant.

"You know, I've got a person who can really work wonders with hair," Evelyn had said. She gathered her own hair in her hand. "If you need it?" Her voice went up at the end as if it were a question. It wasn't.

"I think I'm okay," Mae started to say. She hadn't had time to do anything with her hair that morning, just a quick brush. It must have looked disheveled.

"It's no problem. I'll book you an appointment right now. I think you could use it," Evelyn said. She pulled out her phone and made the call, her voice bright and quick. When she was finished, she told Mae about how much she would love Ricki. Mae found herself nodding emphatically, agreeing that she needed a new look and saying that Ricki sounded great, but she couldn't deny the stinging feeling. It was everywhere around her, like air.

"I think you'd look great with a set of hair extensions." Ricki fiddled with Mae's hair; it was still wet after it had been cut. Mae almost laughed. Hair extensions were for people who had someplace to be, people who were seen. They would be wasted on Mae, and besides, they had to be expensive. She was about to protest when Ricki continued talking, telling Mae about how natural they were, how they would add volume and get rid of the limp look to her hair, and how most women needed a little help with volume.

It actually didn't take much work for Mae to buy in. The next thing she knew, she was watching Ricki attach strands of someone else's real hair to her own head with sticky tape. Tape. Imagine that. The things some women did.

"I'm going to blend it in now." Ricki smiled widely at Mae. "You're going to love it!" Mae watched as Ricki worked, cutting, blending, and spritzing with some kind of product and then styling Mae's hair. When she was done, Mae saw that Ricki was right. You couldn't tell she had someone else's hair attached to her head, and she did look better. She blinked at herself in the mirror and told herself she wouldn't let anyone know her gorgeous, thick hair wasn't real. She flicked it over her shoulder, ignoring the dull, itchy sensation on her scalp, and smiled at her reflection.

THAT SAME NIGHT, Mae fiddled with a lock of her new hair on the way to Leah's house. She liked the way it felt between her fingers, glossy and smooth as it weaved in and out of her pointer and middle finger.

When Mae heard the street name Leah lived on, she knew exactly what to expect. The homes in that area were gorgeous, and some were settled right on the water. Leah's house, Evelyn said, had been completely renovated a few years ago, and now that Mae was in front of it, she couldn't wait to see the inside. Outside, it was white with green trim and large windows. Elegant; that was how Mae would describe it. By comparison, Mae's home was much smaller and had more of a cozy and comfortable vibe—a cute home at the top of a sloping hill. Leah's was all big, beautiful, and lavish in the middle of the street. Very fitting, Mae thought.

Mae knocked on the front door and then took a step backward. She would much rather spend time at Evelyn's one-on-one, as they had at lunch, instead of attending a gathering like this. Evelyn was different when nobody else was around. At lunch, she had been so real, like she could let her guard down, but tonight, it would be a big group of women. There would be chatter and appetizers and, after the meeting, probably wine-fuelled gossip. Mae thought of Corinne's warning over wine the other night. She told herself she wouldn't say anything that could be used against her later.

"Come in," Leah said, straight to the point when she opened the door. Mae followed her into the living room, where most of the women were curled up on the couches, legs folded underneath them, notebooks and planners in their laps with a glass of wine beside them.

"So glad you can join us, Mae!" Evelyn was warm as usual. Mae made her way to the empty seat next to Evelyn and accepted the glass of wine Leah offered her.

"Great pants." Evelyn nodded approvingly. Mae stretched her legs out in front of her and admired how her leggings made her calves look slender.

"Thanks."

The women launched into a deep conversation about the school—there was a fundraiser coming up, and they would have to decide who should do what. They talked about the upcoming Fall Harvest Social and how much work it would be. Mae hoped they would tell her flat out what she needed to do. She wasn't the type to volunteer to take something on, especially when she had no idea what their standards were. What if she picked the wrong fabrics for tablecloths or chose the wrong kind of music?

Mae leaned over toward Evelyn while the conversation continued about tickets and vendors. She kept her voice low. "Hey, so Corinne is fine. I had a drink with her, and she said she was good."

Evelyn turned to Mae and arched an eyebrow. "I didn't ask." Then she smiled.

"Oh. I thought Leah would have mentioned—she asked me to check on her."

"Did she?"

Mae stared blankly for a minute, waiting for Evelyn to continue. When she didn't, Mae questioned herself. Was she going mad? Had she made something out of nothing? Maybe she had misread all of this.

"I thought you knew what was going on," Mae said.

Evelyn shrugged. "No, but I can ask Leah what it was about if you want me to?"

"Uh, that's okay."

"Hey, listen," Evelyn dropped her voice into a whisper now so that they wouldn't disrupt the woman speaking to the room. "That reminds me. I've heard you're still asking around about Alice?"

Mae twisted her body to face Evelyn. She didn't feel like she'd asked too often. "Is there any news yet?" She might as well ask while they were on the subject.

Evelyn closed her eyes and shook her head no. "It's so awful." She opened them back up again and reached out to place a hand on Mae's arm. "It's really sweet of you to be concerned, but you're still new here, and you don't know everyone as well yet. We've known Alice for years. Let us handle it, okay?" Evelyn gestured to the women around the room.

Mae wanted to ask what she meant by 'handle it,' but didn't. "Sure. I thought maybe I could help. If anyone knew where she was or what the police had found out—"

"No, I know. And I totally understand why you want to help. I'll keep you in the loop with whatever we find. Promise." She gave Mae's forearm a gentle, reassuring squeeze.

"Okay, thanks," Mae said. "No answers from the police, then?"

"Nothing yet. You can stop asking now." Evelyn took her hand back. Her voice lost some of its warmth, and Mae stiffened. She tried to read Evelyn's face, tried to tell herself that it was nothing.

Evelyn leaned in closer then. "Your hair looks fantastic, by the way." She twisted her body back around to face the room.

"Thanks." Mae pressed her lips into a smile, unsure of what had happened between them.

Eventually, the main conversation turned to personal things. The women started by reminiscing about last year's lunches and trunk shows, things Mae knew nothing about. They laughed about their ladies' nights out and the women-only weekends away. Mae listened silently as the women around her talked about a world Mae had never been a part of. When someone mentioned bonuses, it struck Mae as odd since only a few of them had jobs.

"God, I can't wait for my year-end. I need some new clothes." It was a woman named Kelly, one of the moms from the dinner party. Mae was certain she didn't work; she had seen her around the school so often. The other women nodded in agreement.

"I negotiated my bonus with Patrick the other night," a woman Mae didn't recognize said. "I've got a brain for making deals. Good thing I used my business degree for something. I mean, at least it's not going to waste." She laughed.

Mae sat up and shifted in her seat. What were they talking about?

"Do you have one, Mae?" Leah was staring at her.

Mae's head snapped around. "Uh, have one?"

"A wife bonus," Leah said sharply like Mae was slow.

"I'm not ... I mean ... I don't ..." Mae stuttered. Her brain couldn't work fast enough to process the question and answer in a way that made sense. She had never heard of a wife bonus before. What on earth?

"I'll take that as a no." Leah smirked.

"It's no big deal. Some of us have them." Evelyn stepped in. "It was hammered out in our prenups mostly. We get an annual bonus based on how well our husbands' year is."

"But also on our own performance," Kelly interjected. "How well we manage the home budget, whether the kids got into the class with the good teachers, that kind of stuff. I always get a full performance bonus." She was shining with pride.

Mae's eyes widened until the sockets started to ache. She blinked and looked away, composing herself. Wife bonuses. This was one of the strangest things she had ever heard. It was so archaic, wasn't it? These were obviously smart, accomplished women, some of them with business degrees. They were running the school and hosting fundraisers, but they were also waiting for their allowance from their husbands?

"It gives us some financial independence," Evelyn said. "We can go on our weekends away, plan top-notch events, and shop when we want to without having to explain our purchases, you know?"

"Nobody's checking over our credit card statements," Leah added. "It's like when I had an income. I used to work, and I can, but now I don't need to."

That was a brag. Mae could detect the hint of a challenge in Leah's words: *Try to judge me, to question me.* This was perfectly normal to the Riverpark Moms—to the MOB. Maybe it was normal. Maybe everyone had one.

Afterward, the conversation changed to their upcoming schedules; the pancake breakfast at the school, the next FlyWheel cycling class, but Mae only half-listened. A seed of doubt was making its way into her gut and spreading outwards like ivy. If they ever knew how far she was from being the kind of wife who had a bonus. She thought of her upbringing again. Of how hard her mother had worked to give Mae as much as she could, and it paled in comparison to what these women had.

Her gaze moved around the room as each woman spoke, a half-smile on her face to show that she was interested, that she was listening, but her head was buzzing. She only stopped when her eyes met Leah's. Something passed between them, something uncomfortable that she couldn't put her finger on. Mae smiled, but Leah only gave a barely-there Mona Lisa smile in return.

Chapter Fifteen

JUST BEFORE NINE-THIRTY the next morning, Mae got a text from Corinne. It was a link to an article in the local paper. That was it. Mae clicked on it.

Local Woman's Car Found Abandoned at Edge of Park

Mae set her keys back down on the kitchen countertop, the metal clinking loudly on the granite. She had been about to run a few errands, but the text stopped her in her tracks.

Police were called to Waterfront Park around 8:45 a.m. Wednesday after a witness reported an abandoned white BMW Roadster. A woman was reportedly seen walking away from the vehicle.

There was a police presence in the area until 11 a.m. as they conducted a search for the driver. Police believe they've now identified the female driver as a local woman who lives in the neighborhood and are looking for her.

Police would like to hear from anyone who may have

information and are asking them to call the Division Three staff sergeant.

Mae stopped reading at the end of the article, her mind racing, and clicked over to her text messages. She texted Corinne back, *Alice???* but Corinne didn't respond.

The morning sun had been filling the kitchen as she read, brightening the room and warming the surfaces despite the late October chill. Mae sat on the edge of a chair and stared at the article again, skimming it this time.

A woman was seen walking away.

Alice was okay? A wave of relief washed over Mae, but it was fleeting. Waterfront Park was nearby; the girls had gone there to skip rocks in the lake and gather sticks and pinecones for crafts. They had walked there as a family. Now, it was connected to an abandoned car and a missing person. It was unsettling. And what on earth was Alice going through at that moment? Mae opened up her text messages again and sent another one to Corinne.

What do you think it means?

After a while, the bubble appeared.

I guess Alice has gone somewhere? That was definitely her car. I heard her phone is shut off, though, so nobody knows for sure.

Mae clicked on Alice's name and tapped out a message asking if she was okay anyway, and then waited for a response. When none came, Mae sent a message to Evelyn.

Look what I just read. She added the link. *Did you hear this? Think Alice is okay?*

After a few minutes, Evelyn hadn't responded, so Mae clicked her phone off and put it back on the counter. She tried to ignore the worry pressing down on her. She made herself a cup of coffee and drank it standing up. When it was almost gone, she tipped her head back to get the last sip, then put the mug in the sink and grabbed her keys.

For the rest of the morning, she focused on her errands —grab some wine for dinner that night, pick up a library book she had on hold, get her eyebrows freshly shaped, buy some new ballet tights to replace the ones Ruby had torn a hole in. Life would go on as normal for Mac, as if the most natural thing to do when police were searching for your friend was to get your eyebrows done.

Mae couldn't stop thinking about the article, though. She ran through the details and facts in her head again and again. She tried to remember specific features on Alice's face—what color were her eyes? It bothered her that she couldn't recall. Alice's face was fuzzy in Mae's mind, like Mae had never really seen her at all.

Chapter Sixteen

WHAT MAE KNEW about Alice lately could be reduced to only a few facts: her car had been found, her phone was likely shut off, and her husband wasn't talking. It wasn't enough. Mae needed something else, or someone else, who could help her connect the dots. Her need to find Alice and make sure she was okay made her muscles ache. She was so tense she decided to try and calm herself by writing everything down to make sense of it.

Mae pulled out a notebook and organized what she could remember about Alice. She scribbled down facts from the article, things Evelyn had told her, and anything else that might help. At least she was doing something. When she was done, she closed the notebook and tucked it away into her purse so Drew wouldn't find it. She didn't want to explain yet. First, she had to collect all her thoughts.

Later that afternoon, while she waited for the school

bell to ring, Mae made her way to the edge of one of the Riverpark Mom groups to try and listen in on their conversation.

"—her husband is doing everything by himself," one woman said. She had on a light jacket that didn't look like it would be warm enough for the October air. Her voice was thick with concern, as if it was foreign to think of a grown man taking care of his children without a woman's help.

"I heard the police think he might be involved. It's pretty common for it to be *the husband*." Another woman, one wearing a winter hat that was clearly more for style than for purpose, spoke up. She lowered her voice on the last two words. Mae thought of Alice's husband and the few times she tried talking to him. She wouldn't have guessed he was the type, but you never know. God, she wasn't certain of much anymore.

"Listen to yourself," the woman with the impractically light jacket chastised. "You sound like this is a twisted mystery or something. I heard her phone was turned off. Why would you jump to accuse her husband from that? First of all, she was seen walking away. Secondly, that kind of stuff doesn't happen in Burlington. There are no sinister secrets here." She crossed her arms over her chest.

"That's not what I heard. People are saying she drowned at Waterfront Park."

"Why hasn't she been found, then?" Another woman, this one with beachy waves and dressed in all black, shot back. "This is a stunt. She's looking for attention."

Mae moved away, disgusted by what they were saying.

Their cruelty was breathtaking. When the girls came out of school, Mae gave Ruby and Isla a quick hug and turned to walk home. They must have noticed she didn't ask who they ate lunch with and what they played at recess. Mae learned long ago that asking how their day was in the generic sense yielded few detailed reports. Instead, she knew to pose questions in a way that couldn't be answered with a yes or a no. Today, after she hadn't spoken for over a block, Ruby uncharacteristically slipped her small, smooth hand into Mae's. Mae looked down at Ruby and squeezed her hand in three short bursts to indicate all was fine.

"Did a marching band come to your school today?" she asked.

Ruby smiled. It was their inside joke. Last year, when Mae was bustling around the kitchen one evening doing the dinner dishes, a pot lid clattered to the ground, clanging loud enough to make Mae wince.

Isla had been standing close to the stove and looked down at the lid. "That sounds like the cymbals we heard today in the band."

"What band?" Mae asked, bending over to pick up the lid and put it into the soapy water in the kitchen sink.

"The band that came to our school today to do a presentation. They were big." At this, a grin stretched across Isla's face. "They marched all through the hallway and then into the big gym and played for us."

Mae glanced at Drew, who shook his head in confusion.

"A marching band came to our school, and we had an assembly," Ruby said, casually shrugging. "It was cool."

Mae stood at the edge of the sink, trying to understand. She put one hand on her hip, her fingers edging the front of her shirt where it was wet from leaning up against the counter. "We've been home for *hours* now and talked all throughout dinner. When I asked you how your day was, you didn't say a word about a marching band."

"I forgot," Ruby said as if it were a minor detail, something commonplace and perfectly normal. Mae burst out laughing, and Ruby grinned up at her, pleased she had made her mother laugh.

"No," Ruby shook her head now as they walked. "There was no marching band today." Her shoulders relaxed, no longer tight around her small ears. They walked home the rest of the way in comfortable silence, but Ruby kept her warm hand in Mae's, never letting her grip loosen, and Mae held on tight in return, liking how Ruby grounded her.

"How was your day?" Drew came in the front door that evening and flipped through the mail. Then he tossed the envelopes onto the counter, grabbed a mini chocolate bar from their Halloween stash for handing out the next night, and looked up at Mae and smiled, all lips and no teeth. It was casual and familiar, the kind of smile you give someone you know almost better than you know yourself. He reached for Mae, and she leaned into him, the warmth of his touch a comfort.

"I don't know," Mae said. She closed her eyes, trying to compose herself before speaking. "I feel a little numb."

"Numb?"

When she could see Ruby and Isla were preoccupied in the next room and wouldn't overhear, Mae told Drew about Alice's car and the latest details of the police and what she overheard at the school.

"Wow." He pulled away from their embrace and stood with his arms dangling at his sides for a second. Then he hooked one of his arms around her neck and gently pulled her forward into a hug. Mae could tell he cared about her feelings but wasn't overly concerned about the details of Alice. She knew how his mind worked—he likely thought that the police would take care of everything. Drew was trusting of the law and of people in general. Besides, it wasn't his nature to have big reactions. He would internalize it, think about it, but never really react.

Drew went into the bedroom, and Mae followed. He flopped down onto the bed on his back, closing his eyes and resting his hands on his stomach. Mae took a seat at the edge.

"I guess I have to wait to hear something," Mae said. Drew remained silent. She glanced over her shoulder at him. He was perfectly still, like a corpse; not even his face moved. She wasn't sure if he had heard her. "Drew?"

He released a long, slow breath from his parted lips. Then he rubbed at his closed eyes. Mae bristled at his reaction. He didn't need to say a word; she already knew he wanted her to leave it alone and let the authorities solve it.

"I think that's all you can do," Drew said.

Mae didn't say anything, but she felt like there was definitely more she could do.

"Why don't you come here? Sounds like you need to

destress." Drew reached his arm out to the side, searching for Mae. She lay back onto the bed. Even though her mind couldn't stop whirring, she nestled herself into the crook of his arm and stayed there, listening to his steady, low breathing.

Chapter Seventeen

THE COFFEE SHOP WAS BRIGHT, with floor-to-ceiling windows on one half that allowed large swaths of sunshine to flood the space. The nutty, rich scent of roasting coffee beans enveloped Mae, along with the low hum of people chatting. It was the morning after Halloween, and Mae grabbed her library book, its plastic cover crackling at her touch, and made her way here for a few quiet hours alone. It would be the perfect way to relax after the buzz of trick-or-treating and too much candy last night, plus it would help her shrug off the unease of the last couple of weeks.

The last time Mae was here for coffee, she was with Alice. They dropped in after taking the kids to school and each decided to grab a fat, buttery scone to go with their morning coffees. Mae remembered it well, because she was glad Alice had chosen the scone first instead of the little egg white bites that most of the women in this area got to go with their morning coffees. They sat making small talk until Alice suddenly opened up.

"Do you ever worry about who your kids are?" Alice asked.

"*Who* my kids are?" Mae tilted her head.

"I mean, I didn't have a lot of stuff when I was growing up, so I find it hard to understand what they'll be like when they grow up with all this around them." She looked around her. "I worry that if they turn out to be spoiled kids, I'm going to have a hard time with that. You know—will they be generous? Will they be kind? Will I like them?"

Mae glanced around the coffee shop as if she would find the answers at the table next to her or behind the counter where teens were foaming milk and pressing buttons on the cash register. It was an odd thought. It had never crossed Mae's mind to question if you liked your children. She loved her kids, and, of course, it was awful when they had tantrums or when they were irrational, but she couldn't imagine disliking them.

Alice's eyes clouded over, and her face went slack. Eventually, she said, "I—I hope I always do."

"Alice—are you okay?" Mae asked. "What's going on?"

"I had a hard time ... liking my daughter in the beginning," Alice said. "Breastfeeding was difficult. She had colic. She cried for hours on end. For eight weeks straight, I had to hold her upright and sleep on a chair, which I know you're not supposed to do, but it was the only way she wouldn't cry." Her mouth turned down when she spoke. "I didn't like her very much. It took me time. I didn't fall in love with her as quickly as I think most moms do."

Mae's heart hurt. "A lot of moms take time to bond with their kids," she said. "It's natural."

Alice shrugged. She looked up at Mae and then away. "I'm now at a place where I really like my kids. I don't want to ever not like my daughter again. I have so much remorse about that. I want to be proud of who she is. I don't want her to be mean or bad, you know?"

"Of course, she'll turn out well," Mae said. "She has you for a mother." She thought she was saying the right thing, but Alice looked as if Mae had wounded her. Alice changed the subject then, and the rest of the conversation was a little stilted. Shortly after, she said she had to run.

Now, Mae tried to focus on her book, but she couldn't. She rifled through her purse, looking for lip balm but found her notebook instead. Mae took it out and began jotting down more notes about Alice, this time pulling from the conversation she overheard at the schoolyard. She tried to arrange them chronologically. After a while, a familiar voice called her name. Leah's husband, Jeff, was at the entranceway, looking at her with a smile, his arm held up in the air. She hadn't seen him since the book fair. She hoped the smile on her face was believable, but if she was honest, as nice as he was, she wasn't in the mood for company.

"Hey! Funny to run into you again." Jeff approached Mae's table and stood over her, his hands on his hips. The sun shone through the large windows behind him and highlighted his silhouette, shining over the tiny hairs on his large hands. He smiled at her and the skin around his eyes creased. *He's a nice person. He's just trying to be friendly.* She tried to let the guarded feeling go.

"Hey," Mae said. She put the palm of her hand onto her notebook, hoping she appeared casual. It failed. Jeff looked down at her book and held his gaze there for a beat before his eyebrows scrunched together into a knot, so Mae closed it up and placed it into her purse before he asked questions. "How are you?"

"I'm good, thanks. I'm meeting someone here in a bit." He looked around the coffee shop. "Mind if I join you while I wait? I didn't interrupt your work, did I?"

"Not at all," Mae answered. She watched Jeff as he went to grab a coffee and then forced a smile again when he made his way back to her table.

"So, the book fair went well, hey? Kids love the magic of it, don't they?" His enthusiasm was palpable. Jeff was the kind of guy who seemed like he was always positive. A 'salt of the earth' type that everyone loved. Mae still struggled to understand how he and Leah ended up together.

"It seems that way. My girls loved it."

He ran a hand over the greying hair at his temple. "How are things with you?"

"Good. Same old, I guess."

Things weren't the same, but Mae wasn't about to tell Jeff her doubts and worries. As good of a person as he seemed to be, Mae knew better than to say something that could be repeated—even well-intentioned—to someone else. She spent her childhood learning how to say the right thing and make the right moves, and she wasn't about to let it unravel now because she liked the way Jeff's eyes crinkled when he smiled.

"That's good." He sipped his coffee and then placed it in front of him. When he looked up, his eyes flitted from

Mae's face back down to his coffee cup. He smiled almost shyly and opened his mouth like he was going to say something but then shut it again. Mae wasn't sure what to think.

The front door to the coffee shop tinkled and chimed as it opened, a rush of fresh air entering and reaching Mae's exposed hands, encircling her feet. Jeff turned toward the doorway and then raised his hand at the man standing there.

"That's my meeting."

The man waved back and then came toward them. Mae was waiting for Jeff to stand up and leave in search of another table, but he didn't.

"Hey, Rick. Nice to see you." Jeff leaned forward in his seat. "This is my wife's friend, Mae."

Rick gave Mae a smile. "Nice to meet you." He turned back to Jeff. "I'm going to grab a coffee; mind if I leave my stuff here?" He had several notebooks and a newspaper in his hand, and he placed them on the table in front of Mae before making his way to the long lineup at the cash. Jeff didn't have a chance to respond.

"Sorry. We'll find another table." Jeff glanced down at the pile of things in front of them. His back stiffened, only a slight hint of a change in his body language, but Mae caught it. She followed his gaze down to the newspaper in front of him. It was the local paper, the *Burlington Free Press*. Scrawled across the top on the right-hand panel was the headline Mae read the other day about Alice's car.

Jeff's eyes went back to Mae's. She nodded at the paper, acknowledging it.

"I think that's about Alice, isn't it?"

His forehead crinkled. "Yeah."

She reached for the paper and then scanned the story quickly.

"It's confirmed that it's Alice's car?" Mae tried to keep her tone light, but her heart thrummed inside her body.

"I'm not sure. I heard she's okay, though. Resting up in some kind of wellness center."

Mae straightened in her seat. She allowed the information to settle into her mind before responding. *Resting up?*

"What's a wellness center? Like a retreat? Or rehab?"

"Something like that." Jeff shrugged. "I don't really know."

"Oh. But you know she's there? And she's okay?"

"That's what Leah said. Apparently, that's what the police are saying. I have no idea where Leah gets her info from, but it's almost always right."

This was a lot to process all at once. If she was at a retreat, why hadn't Alice returned any of Mae's calls or texts?

"Although," Jeff went on, "Leah said that nobody was sure it was Alice for a while because she checked into the place under a different name."

"What name did she use?" It was an insignificant detail. Mae wasn't even quite sure why she asked it, but she thought she noticed Jeff's back stiffen again at the question.

"Tessa Neele." He shifted his gaze around the room and then back to Mae. She met his eye. She'd never heard the name before and was waiting for him to say something more.

"Is she still there? Isn't she going to come home?"

Jeff grabbed his shoulder with the opposite hand, wrenching it like he suddenly needed to stretch and massage it. He looked uncomfortable for the first time. "I don't know. I should probably go grab a table." He hesitated, like he wanted to say more, but decided against it. "Nice talking to you, Mae."

Mae watched him go, wishing he would stay and tell her more.

She picked up her phone and opened her message thread to Alice. Still nothing. Maybe Alice needed space. Maybe she wasn't even allowed to use her phone at the center.

Mae put her phone away and then opened her library book up to read, placing her palm onto the cool pages, her eyes trying to make sense of the words while her mind was fragmented into a million confused little pieces.

Chapter Eighteen

On Thursdays, there was pizza. Lunchtime was a joyous event at school then, but Mae couldn't quite grasp what the pleasure was in cold cheese pizza when the girls knew Mae and Drew could almost always be convinced to order in on a Friday night after a long week. Mae gave in, though, and ordered them each a slice for that semester.

That Thursday, Mae walked down the school's hallway, surrounded by the smell of warm dough and cheese and the tang of tomato sauce. She had to give it to the girls; it smelled incredible. Parent volunteers buzzed around in one corner of the hallway with pizza boxes, paper plates, and lists.

Mae avoided them and pulled on the office door handle, bracing herself to meet the two women behind the desks inside. The few times Mae encountered them, their mouths were often turned down, their eyelids half closed when they glanced at her. The sheer annoyance of a parent's presence was unmistakable, but Mae tried to give them the benefit of the doubt. She could only imagine what the parents around here were like when it came to their children and the requests they made. Mae once saw a woman bringing in a take-out order of sushi for her son's lunch and insisted the women in the office get it to him immediately or it would spoil.

Today, Ruby and Isla had routine doctor appointments and needed to leave only for a couple of hours before coming back again. Mae suspected this would also irritate the women in the office, but she forced herself to be cheery.

"Hi there. I'm here to pick up Ruby and Isla Roberts." Mae tapped her fingers on the counter in front of her.

One of the women nodded, her short bob shaking around her thin face. She said nothing but picked up the phone and called into a classroom.

"Excuse me? Please send Ruby down to the office. She's being picked up early." She paused, listening for a moment, and then spoke into the phone again. "What?"

Mae waited.

"Her pizza." The woman's voice was flat. She sighed and then turned to Mae, her hand over the receiver. "Go to the pizza station and tell the volunteers you need to get your pizza for both your daughters. You can take it with you since we're about to break for lunch now anyway."

Mae nodded and turned to exit the office. At the pizza station, a handful of mothers bustled around frantically with box after box of pizza and class lists to cross-reference with the number of pizza slices. Mae made a mental note never to volunteer to help on pizza days.

Several of them were familiar, as a few had been at

Evelyn's house the night of the dinner party, but there was nobody Mae knew well enough to call by name. She stood in front of them and raised her hand into a half-wave. When it was clear that they weren't going to acknowledge her, Mae spoke up.

"Hey. Yeah, sorry—the office told me to come here and get my daughters' slices of pizza because we're leaving early."

One of the women stopped moving and stared at Mae, blinking. "I'm sorry—what?"

This was not okay. Mae had gone and thrown off their groove.

"I have to take my girls out of school early, so they told me to come to get their pizza."

The mom in the middle of it all, the one who looked like she was Main Pizza Mom, put one hand on her hip and used the edge of her other wrist to swipe at some hair that was in her face. "This pizza is going down to the classrooms right now."

Mae stared. She shoved her hands into the pocket of her jacket. "I was told—"

Main Pizza Mom shook her head and narrowed her eyes at Mae like she was studying her and suddenly recognized her. Her mouth was tight and thin. "Are you Mae?"

"Oh—um, yes." Mae was brought up short by the fact that this woman knew her.

After a pause, the woman grabbed a class list. "What room number are your kids in?"

Oh God. Mae had no idea. Who knew all the room numbers in the school?

"I'm not really sure—"

"Hey, Jen. Can I help?" Corinne appeared next to Mae, her hands in the pockets of her coat, speaking casually to the woman in front of her. She turned to Mae. "I know how complicated this pizza delivery can be. I used to volunteer."

Jen, a mom with dark brown hair tied into a tight bun at the nape of her neck, picked out two slices of pizza and handed them to Mae while looking at Corinne. "No, it's okay, but thanks." She turned back to Mae. "Take this. We'll figure it out later."

Mae thanked them, apologizing again. She turned to Corinne and held the plate of greasy pizza up as they walked to one side of the hall, away from the pizza station. "Thanks."

"No worries. I know how they can be." Corinne shot a look over her shoulder.

Mae turned to see a couple of the women watching her. The nape of her neck prickled. She swiveled back around to Corinne. "I don't get it. Why do they seem so annoyed by me?"

Corinne leaned her shoulder up against the smooth interior wall of the school. "Some of them have *rules*." She rolled her eyes as she said it. "But some of them can be really nice. You need to find the ones who are more like you."

"Like Evelyn," Mae said. She lowered her voice before she spoke again. "I'm not so sure about Leah, though."

Corinne raised her eyebrows and then looked away, down the hallway, averting her gaze from Mae.

"What?" Mae asked.

"They wouldn't want me telling you this, but it's not

fair," Corinne sighed. "There's a rumour that's just started going around about you. Leah's been telling people that you're 'inappropriate' when you're around her husband." She made air quotes when she spoke. "She said you seem really interested in him. You know, ask him a lot of questions, lean in when you're talking to him. She said you asked him to go for coffee?"

The words sent a cold wave over Mae's body, like a glass of ice water had been poured into the top of her head and cascaded down to her toes. "*What?*"

"I know. Ridiculous. I told them you weren't having coffee with Leah's husband."

Mae's mouth dropped open. "I was reading at the coffee shop yesterday, and he happened to show up at the same time, so he joined me—"

Corinne's mouth turned down. "Really? Someone must have seen and told Leah."

"But—it was nothing. He was there when I was there. It wasn't planned." Mae's head was fuzzy like she couldn't form rational thoughts, and her legs grew restless. She shifted her weight and shook her ankle as if she could expel the anxiety through her toes.

Corinne spoke in a hushed tone. "I'm sure it wasn't. But from an outside perspective, it probably looked like two married people on a coffee date without their spouses. The other mothers around here can be judgmental, and if Leah says something, they believe it."

Mae barely knew any of these women, and now she was the school's homewrecker? What did this mean? Would the consequences trickle all the way down to Ruby and Isla? She thought of Drew. She knew he didn't want her making waves with Evelyn because of Evan and work, but she would have to tell him about this as soon as she could. What a messed-up place.

"I'm happily married." Mae tugged at the collar of her jacket. It was warm in here. She needed out. "I didn't do anything."

Corinne glanced behind Mae and then focused on her face again. "Were you at Alice's house with her husband?"

Mae's mouth fell all the way open now. "Last week—I was trying to ask him something about Alice. Why?"

Corinne's face was full of sympathy. She tilted her head a little before speaking. "They said something about that, too. Listen. Just forget it. I know you're a good person."

"But am I tarnished because Leah said so?"

Corinne's face was serious, but her eyes were kind when they looked at Mae. "She has power here. The thing is, most people know she can be a bit—dramatic, but they won't admit it out loud. This should blow over."

A deep wave of embarrassment washed over Mae.

"This isn't right." Her bones buzzed. It wasn't fair to her, and if her kids were going to be ostracized because of it, it wasn't fair to them either.

Corinne reached out and touched Mae's arm. "I know. I'll see if I can help."

Mae thought about Corinne's purse, and the way she had so easily reached out to take a look inside of it. Her face burned. She didn't deserve Corinne's help. Before Mae could say anything else, Ruby came down the hallway, walking quickly with her flowered backpack slung over one arm. She had a huge grin on her face and something in her hands. Mae squinted and saw that Ruby was carrying a paper plate with a slice of pizza on top.

"I've got to run," Corinne said. "I'm on crossing guard detail for lunch. See you soon?"

Mae gave a half wave and turned to Ruby as she approached. She pointed at the paper plate. "Where did you get that?"

Ruby looked down at her pizza and then up at Mae again. "It's my pizza. My teacher didn't want me to miss out." She smiled. There was an excited flash in her eyes, as if getting to take your pizza with you was a special treat. It softened Mae for a moment. If only we could all see the world the way a nine-year-old kid does.

"Hang on. I've got to return this, then. Wait here." Mae went back toward the pizza station with her plate in hand. She hadn't touched it yet, so it could be given to someone else. The mothers were still frantically whisking slices off to each classroom. Their backs were turned, and they didn't see Mae coming.

"—yes, but she should really be more aware, don't you think?" One of the women said to another. "People like her—"

"Like who?"

"The new one." The woman's voice was low.

Mae stiffened. She held her breath, listening.

"Women like her end up getting in trouble."

"I almost want to warn her," another woman said.

"Right? Except—no thanks. Don't get me involved. I don't want my kids suffering."

"Your kids?" One of them asked, her head cocked.

"You remember, don't you? It's the kids who get the worst of it when the mom crosses a line. Poor things."

One of them glanced over her shoulder and saw Mae. Her eyebrows shot up to the middle of her forehead. She nudged the woman next to her.

Mae cleared her throat. "It turns out one of my daughters already got her slice. We have one too many now."

Jen stared at Mae as Mae held the pizza out to her. When it was clear she wasn't going to take the plate, Mae put it down on the table in front of them, turned and walked away.

Isla came trotting down the hall, no paper plate with pizza, thankfully, and went to take Mae by the hand. Mae hurried the girls out the door, a deep need inside her to get them away from those women. What she overheard could be nothing more than gossip from a bunch of nosey Pizza Day Moms, but it felt like more than that.

"Ow, Mommy," Isla said. "That pinches. You're holding my hand too tight."

Chapter Nineteen

"LET's get out of here for the rest of the afternoon," Mae said to Ruby and Isla. They had been there so long their bodies were melting into the couch. Mae let them flake out in front of the TV after school while she washed up their snack containers and repacked them with fresh vegetables and fruit for the next day. Now, she paced around the kitchen with a jittery feeling in her stomach. She needed to go somewhere. She needed a change of scenery.

Ruby looked up at her. "And do what?"

"I don't know." Mae shrugged. She hadn't thought that far. "How about we go to Grandma's? I bet she's home. She'd love to see you."

Isla's eyes lit up. It was sweet the way she was still young enough to get excited by the thought of seeing Frankie. "Yes!" Isla shouted. Ruby just nodded and stood up, making her way to the front door.

The drive took forty minutes, which was a little quicker than usual thanks to light traffic, but when they arrived at Frankie's, they got out of the car and stretched like they had taken a long summer road trip.

Frankie was at the front door waiting. When the car doors slammed shut, her arms went up into the air, and her entire face brightened.

"Hello, my favorite girls!" she called. Ruby and Isla were already running for her.

They stood on the front step, Frankie's head bent over, her cheek resting on the top of Ruby's head and her arms around Isla's small body. Mae liked the simplicity of their joy. To have someone's face light up simply because you showed up.

Mae leaned in for a kiss on Frankie's cheek and then followed them into the warmth of Frankie's small house. It wasn't one of the homes Mae had grown up in, but despite the fact that there were no memories on the walls or the creaky hardwood floors, it made her feel safe. It was homey here because it held her mom and dad and all of their things. The knick-knacks nobody ever collected anymore—little ceramic figurines that stood in their dining room hutch, a wooden rack for gardening magazines, decorative plates that hung on the wall. It was busy and full in contrast to Mae's minimal home with clean lines. Now Mae couldn't recall why she ever thought having stuff was a bad thing.

"Do you guys want anything? A snack, maybe?"

Ruby and Isla both nodded. "Do you have cookies?" They rarely had cookies at home. It was such a 90s thing to do, in Mae's opinion, to always keep a bag of store-bought cookies in the house. Besides, they wouldn't last. The girls could eat six at a time without blinking.

"Of course I do. Chocolate chip, the ones you love," Frankie answered. She turned to Mae. "I haven't changed all that much since you were a kid. I didn't bake then; I don't bake now."

Mae smiled. She actually loved to bake—probably because she hadn't had much of it when she was growing up. Frankie was busy working a nine-to-five job, raising kids, and doing all the things women and mothers were still trying to do in a day. In the last few months, Mae found she liked to bake for the girls, things like whole wheat bread, black bean brownies, and applesauce muffins.

"How are you doing? What's wrong?" Frankie asked Mae in a low voice once the girls had settled at the kitchen table with their snacks.

"Have you got a sixth sense?" Mae said. "How do you know?"

"You're pale. Besides, mothers know these things." Frankie's eyebrows drew together. She leaned in closer to Mae and reached over to place her warm, smooth hand on top of Mae's. Mae could tell that when Frankie saw Mae with anything but cheeks full of color and a smile on her face, she worried, even now that Mae was an adult. Mae supposed the worrying never stopped. It was one of the cruel things about motherhood: if you let yourself think too much about everything wrong with the world, you could get so scared you couldn't function. It never went away.

"I'm okay."

"Mae." Frankie's voice was stern. "Tell me everything."

Mae told her most but not all. While the girls tore up and down the stairs, playing with whatever they could find and exploring the basement, Mae filled Frankie in on the details of Alice and her car and of the note and the rumours about her and Jeff. She left out the conversation she overheard earlier that day from the Pizza Moms. There was no sense in making Frankie worry sick about her grandkids' safety when Mae didn't even know what those women had been talking about.

Frankie listened, her lips pursed, while Mae talked. When Mae was done, Frankie's back straightened.

"What on earth? What kind of place are you living in?"

"I don't know," Mae said.

"Have you met anyone you like? You're such a good person; you must know someone there who you can trust. Someone who can vouch for you."

It was a typical mother thing to say, and it was sweet. Mae gave a non-committal shrug. "There are a few nice women."

The truth was, Mae was no longer so sure about any of them. Doubt had planted itself inside the rational half of Mae's brain, and she couldn't ignore it as much as she wanted to.

"Do you remember what I used to always tell you growing up?" Frankie said.

Mae looked at her mother with confusion. "What?"

"You're only stuck if you want to be."

"And? What does that have to do with this?"

"I told myself that when you were young and things were much harder so that I had something hopeful to cling to, and I believe it even more now." Frankie reached out and touched Mae's arm. "You can do anything now. I know we had a rough time when you were little but look how far you've come. Your dad and I are so proud of you. You've made it this far without a lot of extra help, and you can figure your way out of any problem now. If you have an issue with someone, do something about it. You're a doer, Mae. You make things happen."

Mae smiled at Frankie as if she believed everything her mother was saying, but she knew it wouldn't be that easy. Burlington was complicated.

"Hey, Grandma!" Isla called out. The girls were coloring with thick markers and sharp pencil crayons. "Do you like my picture?" Isla held it up.

A smile stretched across Frankie's face. "I love it! Let me get a better look." She made her way around the counter she had been leaning on, stopping to run a hand over Mae's shoulder first. Mae looked over at Isla's picture and then stiffened.

"What is that a drawing of, Isla?" Frankie glanced at Mae; her forehead creased.

"It's me at school."

Mae studied the picture—a stick figure all alone in the middle of a big field. There were dark colors everywhere. No sun or blue sky. No light.

"Where are your friends?" Mae asked.

"I play alone."

"Why's that, sweetie?" Frankie went over to Isla and touched the top of head, smoothing some hair out of Isla's face.

Isla shrugged. "The other kids don't really want to play with me, so I walk around by myself."

Mae wouldn't look at Frankie or Isla. She didn't want them to see her eyes welling up. Instead, she looked past Frankie and the girls and out the window. She studied the tips of the bare branches. They looked like sharp, gnarled fingers that were pointing out to her, telling her to do something, but Mae hadn't yet figured out what.

On the drive home, Ruby's voice came from the back seat with a hint of concern. "What were you and Grandma talking about?"

Mae's eyes darted to the rear-view mirror and met Ruby's. "What do you mean? When?"

"I heard you say someone said something bad about you," Ruby said. "Why would they do that?"

Mae breathed out, thinking about how to approach this one. "Some people can be unkind at times."

"But why would they say something about you? You're a grownup."

"I know. You would think grownups would know better and do better, but sometimes we don't." She glanced into the mirror again. Ruby's mouth was pointed down.

"It doesn't make sense."

Ruby was right. There wasn't a clear way to explain it, but Mae didn't want to leave it at that and have Ruby worrying about her. Her shoulders tightened. "I know, but it's not a big deal; it's okay, really."

"What if other people start believing that person and side with them instead of you?"

"That kind of thing doesn't happen so much when you get older."

Ruby looked out the window, her face expressionless like she was thinking about what Mae had said.

"I'll be fine, Rube. I've got you guys, and that's all that matters."

Isla chimed in. "I love you, Mommy!" Her high-pitched voice was so small and cute that it never failed to bring a smile to Mae's face. She lightened the mood just by being her sweet seven-year-old self.

"Thank you, Isla. I love you, too." Mae glanced back at the girls through the rear-view mirror again and found Isla grinning. Ruby appeared to be still deep in thought. If only Mae could see what was running through her daughter's mind.

"Ruby, honest. Everything's okay."

Now, if she could only believe her own words.

Chapter Twenty

AFTER PICKING up a few groceries the next day, Mae sat in the driveway inside her car, searching wellness centers in the area on her phone.

The list was long, and Mae quickly realized she couldn't call them all up and ask if Alice was there. She was certain the police would have done that, anyway. Instead, she searched for news reports on Alice and devoured everything she hadn't already read. Nothing stood out. It was the same information she had heard before.

Mae put her phone in her pocket and went inside. She wanted to cry, but the groceries needed to be put away.

Later, the sight of Leah at school made Mae recoil with anger. She stood with a group of women Mae recognized from pizza day and the dinner party. They were all huddled close, bundled up in thick coats and hats with enormous pom-poms on top. It was a cute trend, but Mae thought it looked ridiculous on grown women, especially many women huddled together. It reminded her of when she was a teen, and most girls used to dress the same as one another for fear of appearing as an individual. Then again, what did Mae know about being a part of a group? Her entire life had been fraught with difficult female friendships, and when girls were running around school hand in hand, dangling friendship bracelets off one another's wrists, Mae didn't have that. There was nobody close until she met Grace.

And here she was again, alone and feeling like an outcast. Except she wasn't dejected, she was angry. She spotted Evelyn a few feet away and went to her side.

"Hey," Mae said. "Do you think we could talk? Alone."

Evelyn's round eyes widened. "Of course. What's up?"

"Some odd things have been happening. I'm sure you've heard what Leah's been telling people about me."

Evelyn glanced down at her feet. When she looked back up, she held a hand to her chest and spoke in an overly sympathetic tone. "I've heard."

"I don't know what that's all about, but it's not true." Mae lowered her voice. "I think Leah has a big problem with me, and it's getting out of hand."

Earlier, when Mae had been thinking about the note again, she recalled Evelyn's words at Leah's house. *Leah mentioned you've been asking about Alice.* Mae started to put it all together.

"I doubt she has a problem with you," Evelyn said. "I told you she's great. Maybe it's that she doesn't know you very well yet."

Mae tilted her head to one side, unsure if she heard Evelyn right. "She's spreading rumours about me."

"Why don't we try to clear this up?" Evelyn raised her arm in the air and waved it back and forth until she had Leah's attention. She motioned for her to come over.

This wasn't what Mae meant. She said she wanted to talk to Evelyn alone. Mae fidgeted with a loose thread at the edge of her coat sleeve. Her mouth went dry.

"What's up?" Leah said, her voice cold and sharp.

"We were chatting, and Mae seems to think you two really got off on the wrong foot," Evelyn said.

Leah opened her mouth to say something, but Evelyn cut her off.

"That can't be the case, can it?" Her voice was cool and firm. Something unspoken passed between Leah and Evelyn. Mae tried to get a read on the exchange but couldn't. There was a flutter in her stomach when she turned to Leah.

"I'd like to clear up whatever it was you may have heard or what you might be thinking about me and—uh—me and—"

"My husband?" Leah said.

Mae flinched. There was no Mae and Leah's husband. She pulled her hands out of her pockets. "Yes. I ran into him at the coffee shop when he was waiting for someone, so we chatted for a bit." Surely, Jeff had already explained this to Leah.

Leah didn't move, and her expression didn't change. One of her fingernails tapped the edge of the phone in her hand.

"I'm not sure if you had someone watching me," Mae

continued. Her mouth was awkward as she moved her lips.

Leah laughed. "Oh, my goodness. Can you hear yourself? Why would I have someone watch *you?*"

Mae's face warmed. She looked down at her feet where her toes were curling in her shoes. "I don't know. Because of the group, the MOB. You watch people."

"Don't be so paranoid. I wouldn't have someone follow you." She shifted now, crossing her arms over her body. She gestured at Evelyn with her chin. "She likes you."

Mae glanced at Evelyn, grateful that she was there. Evelyn nodded encouragingly. "There's got to be some misunderstanding," she said.

"Right. The confusion about Jeff and I—" Mae stopped. She realized later that it must have been the way she coupled them: *Jeff and I* that made Leah's eyes flicker with anger.

"There's no confusion. You need to back off from other people's husbands, and you need to remember Pearl."

"I'm sorry?"

"Pearl." Leah sighed as if Mae were slow. "It's an acronym. Please Engage in Acts Resembling a Lady. It's our code."

Mae froze in place, unsure what to do with her face. They couldn't be serious. It sounded like something you would say in the 1950s. Acronyms to instruct one another on how to behave?

"Cozying up to someone's husband is definitely not Pearl-like," Leah said. "I'm sure you can see that."

"I wasn't cozying up to anyone."

"Whatever it was you thought you were doing, the thing is, it matters more how it looks to everyone else. Not what *actually* happened."

"How it looks?" Mae repeated. How could that be true? The more Leah said, the more Mae wondered if the conversation was really happening. Anger bubbled up inside of her again.

Leah shifted her position and went to stand directly beside Evelyn now. "Appearance is everything around here. You should know that. It can get to people. Alice—"

Evelyn reached an arm out to her side to stop Leah from talking. She glanced sideways at Leah and then opened her mouth, but Mae spoke first.

"I don't give a crap about anybody's appearance."

Leah's head jerked back. Evelyn closed her mouth. Mae almost wished she hadn't said it. Almost.

"Stay away from Jeff, and we'll be fine," Leah said with finality. The conversation was over. She gave a slight nod and then left.

Evelyn pinched the bridge of her nose. "That didn't go the way I wanted. Sorry. I'll go catch up and talk with her." Then she left too, leaving Mae alone and steaming, wondering what the hell just happened.

Chapter Twenty-One

MAE AND DREW called a sitter and went for dinner the next night at a restaurant called Bobby's Hideaway. Evan told Drew about it, so Mae wasn't sure if it would be too fancy, but it ended up being perfect. It was a cozy, narrow room with a long bar that stretched across the right side and plush booths down the left. It was intimate and dark; exactly what they needed.

They were both so caught up in their own lives lately —Drew with work and Mae with Alice—that it suddenly dawned on Mae that it had been a few days since she had let him in on everything. He had no idea about the rumour Leah spread or how Mae was asked to check in on Corinne. It struck her as odd that so much was happening in her life, and she hadn't immediately told her husband. He used to be the first to know anything and everything going on with her; now she couldn't remember when she decided to pick and choose what to tell him about.

At the table, Drew shook his head while he glanced down at the menu. "These prices."

"What?" Mae took a long, slow slip of her wine. "We can afford it."

"Yeah, but I guess we need to be a little careful with our finances."

"We do?" Mae's back stiffened. "What's going on?"

"Nothing. But everything is more expensive here. Our mortgage, the girls' activities, and with you not working."

A stab of guilt shot through Mae's insides, deep in her gut. "I thought we didn't need my income."

"We didn't. We don't." Drew shook his head.

"We didn't?" Mae put her wine glass down and locked eyes with Drew. "Seriously. What are you getting at? Are we having money issues?"

"There's less in the account than I expected. Maybe we should be careful about some things."

Mae hadn't looked at that account in ages because it was still in Drew's name. She kept a separate account, always had. They shared bills and expenses but never got around to starting up a joint account, and Mae didn't have a reason to check.

"Do we need to worry?" Mae said.

Drew shook his head. "No. Forget I said anything. We're fine. Anyway, how's everything been going? You don't seem yourself today."

Mae chewed at the fleshy part inside of her bottom lip and then flopped back into the booth. "I guess I'm okay."

"But?"

He knew her too well. "I don't know. It's Leah. Evelyn's friend."

"What about her?"

"She gave me a warning. She told me not to talk to her husband."

"What?" Drew's mouth went slack. "Why would she do that?"

"I was volunteering at the book fair, and her husband was there. Then I ran into him again at a coffee shop the other day and we sat and talked for a bit. Someone told Leah about it, and I guess she thinks something was going on."

Drew scratched at his jaw. "Why?"

"I have no clue. She doesn't like me. I feel like I'm trying, but they're too different from me. They told me to remember 'Pearl.'"

"What the hell does that mean?" Drew asked.

"It means to Please Engage in Acts Resembling a Lady." Mae widened her eyes for emphasis, silently trying to impress upon him how odd it was.

"That's so weird." Drew put his knife and fork down onto his plate. "Avoid her as much as you can."

Mae sighed. It wouldn't be that simple. Leah was everywhere and knew everyone. She wasn't the type to be ignored. "I'm not sure I have a chance here. Did you know most of the women get wife bonuses?"

"What are those?"

"Exactly what they sound like. Money for performance."

"Jesus." Drew shook his head. "That's ridiculous. We're not doing that."

This was one of the many reasons why Mae loved Drew. He was on her side of this, her partner, and he felt the same way as she did. They were equals, which meant there was no way he would ever attempt to *give* Mae something that was already both of theirs.

"I know. Anyway, what do you think we should do?" Mae asked.

"What can we do other than ignore them? It's not easy to do something drastic like leaving. We bought a house, we moved the kids, and they're settled in school. I've got a good job now. But if things get worse, we should definitely figure out our options and decide what makes the most sense. In the meantime, is there any chance you two can sit down and work this out?"

"I'm not the problem," Mae snapped. It wasn't the answer she wanted to hear. She wanted him to still be on her side, not suggest she fix it herself. All the things he said were true, however. She couldn't deny that none of it would be easy.

"I know," Drew said. "Of course I know that. The people here can definitely be ... odd. I'm struggling with some things at work, too."

"You are?" Mae sat up straighter. "But you've never said anything."

"It's not a big deal at all, and I didn't want to worry you. I know you've got enough on your plate."

"What are you having issues with?"

Drew frowned. "It's Evan."

"Evelyn's husband?" Mae asked.

"Yeah. He says things that strike me as odd."

"Like what?"

"Oh, I don't know. He asks a lot of questions. Personal ones, like he wants to know about my background. He even asked if we've got lawyers or police officers in the family. He seems to want to know a lot about me, but I can't tell if it's genuine or not. I can't get a read on him."

"Strange," Mae said. She sat back in her seat and studied Drew's face for a moment. "We need to keep talking to one another."

Drew nodded. "I know. We will. That's what we're here for."

Mae glanced around the dim restaurant. Everything was dark and shadowy. "Maybe I'll try and find some other women to get to know." She would have to avoid Leah, and she supposed that meant avoiding Evelyn, too.

WHEN MAE WAS A KID, Frankie had given her some motherly advice that really stuck with her. "Never end up financially dependent on someone else, Mae. You have to be able to support yourself. Always. You never know where life will take you." Frankie would wave a long finger in Mae's direction as she said this. She would touch the top of Mae's small head and run her hand through Mae's hair and down her cheek. "I want to protect you. I want you to be happy."

Mae always listened to her mother, certain she would grow up to be a doctor, a dentist, or one of those other jobs where you were admired, a job that afforded you all the opportunities to aim higher and strive for more. She began to equate happiness with having money. But when it became clear to Mae that she didn't want to be a doctor, she set her sights on another path that would earn her a good salary. If she were really honest with herself, she would admit that she wanted to go to college to study English literature, but she chose a business degree instead. English literature didn't translate into a job. And that was what she had her sights set on: a good job, so she wouldn't have to worry.

During elementary and high school, even somewhat at college, Mae was constantly aware of the things she didn't have that everyone else did. In the tenth grade, everyone was wearing jeans with a little red triangle. Mae had asked Frankie about them, but Frankie only shook her head.

"I don't even spend that much on jeans for myself, Mae."

Instead, Mae had to make do with the no-name pair, the boxy and stiff ones that weren't the right color and had no rips in the knees. One day, she took a pair out front of their house to the driveway and ran rocks over top of them. She did it over and over again, hoping they would get that distressed look to them that the other girls had.

In high school, the vice principal came into their classroom a few months before prom carrying a stack of flyers. She wanted to share them with the class, she said to Mae's teacher. They were about a special program. Something to do with prom dresses for low-income families.

"You should take this home," the vice principal said to Mae. She smiled when she spoke. She thought she was helping. Mae took the flyer and shoved it into her backpack so it would be out of sight. She was the only one who got one.

It wasn't that she was angry about her lot in life. Mae simply wanted to blend in until the day that she would no longer be reminded of how different she was. So, when she got her first job in advertising, and there were multiple zeros on her paycheck, Mae could hardly believe it. She sensed things were finally changing. By then, she had met Drew—his family had three cars and lived in a big house with actual land—and even though he never brought it up, as if he hadn't noticed it, their childhoods had been very different. She got a glimpse of what her adult life could be and what she could provide for her own kids one day.

Here, in Burlington, Mae should have finally belonged. She did it. She went from having not much to helping build a life for herself with Drew and the girls. She had so much privilege now she didn't even have to rely on that paycheck with all the zeros. They could get by on one. Drew was great at his job, the girls were mostly happy, and Mae could afford whatever jeans she wanted. Everything had fallen into place by all appearances.

It made no sense that she could have everything and still feel wrong.

Chapter Twenty-Two

A FEW DAYS LATER, Mae decided on a whim to visit Drew at work. She got into her car and drove straight there instead of calling him first. She didn't want another phone conversation with him where she couldn't see his facial expressions when he spoke. This fragile anxious feeling was new to her, and she needed to be in person with him now.

She stood in front of the locked door on his building's floor that led into the offices. Mae went for her phone to text Drew that she was there when someone came out and pushed the door aside for her to enter. Perfect. Now to find his actual office.

The floor was large, and the layout was complicated for someone who hadn't been there before. Mae went down one hallway, suddenly self-conscious about not calling Drew first and being out of place, when she heard a familiar voice.

"Mae?" It was Evan. He stood behind a desk inside an office, looking at her with his eyebrows raised. He gestured at her. "Come in. You're here to see Drew?"

"Hi," Mae said, walking into his office. "Yeah, I don't know where he sits."

"I can show you," he said. "But first, I have to run this over to someone. Wait here, and I'll be back in a second." He held up a few papers as he spoke and then moved toward the doorway. Mae watched him leave and then turned around, eyeing the things in his office.

A framed photo of Evelyn and Evan at their wedding sat on one corner of his desk. Mae moved closer to get a better look. She loved wedding photos—the couples always looked so beautiful and radiant. In this one, Evelyn was laughing, her eyes closed and her face relaxed and happy. Evan was smiling at her, holding the edge of her veil. God, they were a stunning couple.

Mae went to stand upright again when something caught her eye. It was the corner of an envelope, mostly hidden under a notebook. Only an edge of it peeked out, but it was the edge that caught Mae's eye. It had a name scribbled very small at the bottom right-hand side.

Alice.

Mae went cold. She glanced at the doorway. Still empty, and the hallway was silent. Evan wasn't on his way back yet. She turned to the envelope and reached out to move the notebook so she could touch it, pulling the edge of the envelope closer to her and then sliding it open with one finger. There was money inside of it. Mae couldn't tell how much, but it looked like a lot.

She put it back in place with shaking hands. Her mind raced. What did it mean? She had to move away from the desk before—

"You ready?" Evan's voice came from behind Mae.

"Yes," Mae said, head whipping around. "Thanks so much."

"I didn't interrupt you, did I?" There was a darkness in Evan's eyes that gave Mae a twitchy, quivery feeling.

"No. Not at all."

"That's good. I wouldn't want to have to harm you if you knew too much." He laughed, a barking type of sound, and nudged Mae's elbow. "I'm kidding. Follow me."

Down the hallway, they turned a few corners and then stopped. "Right here." Evan knocked on Drew's open door. "Look who I found wandering around." He gestured toward Mae.

Drew looked up from his work. "Mae! Hey."

"I'll leave you two. Nice to see you, Mae." Evan turned, and Mae watched him until he was out of hearing range.

"What are you doing here?" Drew asked. He stood up and came out from around his desk, moving toward Mae.

"I wanted to see you." She leaned into his hug.

"This is good timing," Drew said. "I have some great news."

Mae wanted to tell him about the envelope with Alice's name, but Drew was beaming. He exuded a raw energy that was palpable.

"What is it?"

"I'm up for a big promotion," Drew said. He held his

hands out wide, his palms facing upwards like he couldn't believe his good fortune.

"That's wonderful!"

"This is big. Like, a huge leap in my level here, which also means big increase in pay. It could be fantastic for us." He spoke rapidly, his voice slightly raised. Drew deserved this.

"When will you find out for sure?" Mae asked.

"Evan said he'll be reviewing everything in the next few weeks and will let candidates know by the end of the month."

Evan.

"Evan's making the decision?"

"I report to him." Drew was still holding onto Mae's arms, but he let go now. He grinned at Mae. "I should have a good shot. I know it seems I've got an advantage because of you and Evelyn being friends and the four of us socializing and all that, but he's professional at work. It'll be a fair decision. And I've earned this."

"Of course you have," Mae said. She hadn't seen Drew like this in a while. She couldn't recall the last time his voice held so much hope. He must have forgotten what he told her about Evan the other night at dinner. "I thought you weren't sure about him?"

Drew waved a hand. "Oh, that's not a big deal. I can separate business from personal stuff. Besides, I really want this job."

Mae scraped a hand through her hair.

"Was there something you wanted to talk to me about?" Drew asked. "To what do I owe this unexpected pleasure of a surprise visit?"

Mae shook her head. "No specific reason. I wanted to see you." She nestled her head into his chest when he pulled her closer.

Now was definitely not the time.

Chapter Twenty-Three

MAE WAS on her knees in the basement, rooting through boxes that hadn't been unpacked yet. She pushed a piece of hair away from her face when the phone rang. It was Evelyn.

"Can you drop by my place real quick?" Evelyn's voice was warm, which struck Mae as a little odd after the conversation the other day with Leah.

"Um—" Mae hesitated. On the one hand, she was glad they were going to forget whatever the tension had been previously. On the other, Evan and the envelope of money still weighed on her mind. It could be nothing, or it could be easily explained. In fact, maybe Evan was helping Alice. Or it could be something else.

"I can't. I'm really busy today."

"Please? A few of the girls are coming over for coffee. We need you. Be here in ten minutes?"

Drew's excited face came to mind, and Mae's lips pressed together into a grimace. Despite her hesitation,

Mae agreed and clicked the phone off, placing it down on the floor beside her. Was this how it worked with them? One second you were being warned, and the next you were part of the group again as if nothing had happened? Mae heaved her body up to standing and went to fix her hair. She wanted to know what was going on, but everything would have to wait until after Drew heard about the job.

When she reached Evelyn's porch, the door swung open. On the other side, Evelyn stood, wearing jogging pants and a fitted t-shirt, with her hair up in a bun on top of her head. She leaned in for a hug, and Mae inhaled a woody and smoky scent, like cedarwood and vetiver oils. The sound of chatting and laughter came from inside the house.

"Come in," Evelyn said.

Mae followed her into the kitchen. Leah stood at the table with two other women. They were all in regular clothes—joggers with hoodies that were meant to be casual, but they made the casual look effortlessly fashionable.

After accepting a mug of coffee, Mae took a seat, enjoying the warmth on her hands.

"You remember Kelly and Jen, right?" Evelyn said, gesturing at the women across from her. "We were talking about the Fall Harvest Social coming up. Are you volunteering?"

It didn't feel like a question.

"Sure," Mae said.

"Great! I'll put you down for decorations?"

They talked about what this would require, how much

they needed new, what they could still use from last year. Leah was cool with Mae, but nothing out of the ordinary. Mae half-listened, wondering why she had been asked to come here.

At one point, Evelyn glanced in Leah's direction and held her gaze. Leah eventually nodded. "We need to talk about Lisa," Evelyn said.

Leah shifted in her seat and tucked her smooth hair behind her ear. "She's been so—different—recently."

Kelly and Jen murmured and nodded, their shining locks shaking around their faces like curtains in a summer breeze. They frowned as they cradled their cups of coffee.

Lisa? Mae searched her memory for which one was Lisa. Most of the women were still a homogeneous blur, but something sparked in her mind. Evelyn had once introduced them. Lisa was short, with dark brown hair and a kind face that was almost always free of any makeup. She was plain, for lack of a better word. Mae had seen Lisa with Corinne a few times.

"I feel so bad for her," Leah continued. "I mean, who knows what's going on behind closed doors."

Mae could sense there was a 'but' coming.

"But I think it's clear that she's been strange lately. Almost like she's acting out."

"I heard she's telling everyone about the therapy sessions she's taking." Kelly said it as if therapy were a bad thing. "She's not keeping anything to herself. And she's stopped coming to our get-togethers. Have you noticed?"

The way they were speaking made Mae's skin tingle. She shifted in her seat and gripped her coffee mug tighter.

"We're not going to ignore the elephant in the room, are we?" Jen asked.

"What?" Mae couldn't help herself.

"Her *drinking*." Leah put an emphasis on the word like it was dirty. "She came to a get-together and got drunk. That's so embarrassing."

"It was only two glasses; I'm not sure she was drunk," Evelyn said, but Jen spoke over her.

"It's like she's giving everyone the middle finger."

That was overly dramatic, in Mae's opinion. What was going on here? It felt like this was much more than gossip. Like it was building to something.

"She's too unpredictable," Leah said. "We can't associate with her, in my opinion."

A wave of unease crested within Mae.

Evelyn sat up straighter in her seat. "I don't know. I think we should give her one more chance. Somebody should have a talk with her, see if we can rein her in, you know?"

"You're much more forgiving than I am," Leah said. Evelyn laughed.

"Who should talk to her?" Kelly picked up her mug of coffee and looked around the table.

"I will. But someone needs to come with me," Evelyn said. "Mae? Do you mind?"

Mae's head swivelled around. "Me? I don't know her. I'm not even sure what you mean."

"I think it would be better if you were there, too. You're not biased. Lisa will understand we're not picking on her, but there's a real problem that you see, too."

"But I don't see a problem," Mae said. "Shouldn't one of you go?" Her eyes scanned the other women.

"Listen, we all feel for Lisa, but she's not listening to us and she's getting out of control," Leah said. "She's too comfortable with us, I suppose. It's not okay. It has to stop." There was an edge to Leah's voice, one that made Mae's mouth go dry.

"I don't know. It doesn't seem right. Especially because I don't know her."

Leah shot a look at Evelyn that Mae couldn't help but notice. Her stomach flipped. What was she supposed to say or do here?

"It'll be fine. Lisa needs some encouragement, and you're the right person to come with me. I know it." Evelyn smiled. She was so sure of herself. "She might not even realize how she's acting. We want to help her."

Controlling someone's behavior was a strange way of helping, but Mae couldn't find her voice to say it.

"I'll come have lunch with you," she said eventually. "But I'm not comfortable saying anything to Lisa."

"No problem. I won't ask you to do anything you don't want to." Evelyn's voice was cheery.

"Okay, it's settled. Lisa has one more chance." Leah pushed her chair back from the table and stood up. The other women got up and shuffled around, getting ready to leave Evelyn's kitchen. None of them looked uncomfortable as they moved, gliding through the room, touching one another's arms and smiling like they hadn't agreed to pick on a friend and make her feel bad for being honest. Mae's pulse quickened. She wished she hadn't been roped into it all.

"Mae, text me when you're free, and we'll pick a date and time." Evelyn waved her fingers in a casual way. "Oh, and by the way, I found something out about Alice. I know what wellness center she's at."

Mae did a double take. Her heart sped up. "You did?"

"Yep." Evelyn grinned, pleased with herself. "Why don't we go visit her together after our lunch with Lisa?"

A floating sensation went through Mae, the kind that came with relief.

Chapter Twenty-Four

ON THE MORNING she was supposed to go with Evelyn to give Lisa a stern warning, Mae felt sick. It could have been a coincidence, but either way, her head throbbed, and her throat felt like it was closing.

"I don't think I can go," Mae said to Evelyn over the phone.

"I really need you." The disappointment in Evelyn's voice was evident. It reminded Mae of when she was a kid, on those rare occasions when she had disappointed her mother. It was much harder to handle than anger.

"Are you sure you can't? We were going to check out the center for Alice afterward, remember?"

Mae found herself eventually saying yes, despite her gut telling her the restaurant was a bad idea. Before leaving, she did the things she needed to do: take a couple of Advil for her headache and chase them with a glass of water, put the breakfast dishes into the dishwasher, and run a brush through her hair again. Afterward, when there was nothing left to distract herself with, Mae grabbed her jacket and stuck her arms into it, putting her phone into her pocket and leaving her tidy home behind.

They were meeting at a local restaurant where it was busy and noisy. The perfect place for giving out bad news. Bliss Kitchen was a unique spot in Burlington. It was designed to look quirky and one-of-a-kind. Outside, the building was made up of red brick, with long, narrow windows that rounded in an arch at the top, and a door of thick wood sat in the middle of the building front. A small chalkboard sign held messages each day like, "*Romaine calm & carrot on.*" Inside, small maple tables were accented with chairs painted bright teal and white. On one wall, a large set of shelves held work by local artists, small potted plants, and a few books. The menus boasted that everything was made with locally sourced ingredients, all gluten-free, naturally sweetened and vegan. It was a cute and homey place to grab cauliflower wings, curry bowls, kimchi burgers, and smoothies with blue spirulina or activated charcoal. It was always busy.

Mae arrived first. She sat at a booth big enough for the three of them in one corner and hoped Evelyn wouldn't be too long. Lisa might not even remember Mae. This was what made it all very uncomfortable—Mae was there to help deliver awkward news to someone she barely knew.

After a few minutes, Lisa was at the side of the table. "Have you been here long?" Her voice was stilted.

"Hi," Mae said. "No, just got here. I'm waiting for Evelyn."

Lisa smiled briefly before taking a seat. Her hair was

shapeless, and her clothes very casual. Mae liked that about her.

"Well, thanks for asking me."

"Of course. Nice to get to know you." *Oh god.* This was so awkward.

While they waited for Evelyn, they ordered bubbly water and made small talk: what streets they each lived on, which teachers their kids had. They talked until Mae realized she was thoroughly enjoying herself and had lost track of the time. She looked down at the screen of her phone.

"I'm not quite sure what happened to Evelyn." She was an hour late. No text messages either.

"That's strange," Lisa said. "Why did she want to talk to me anyway? She was kind of mysterious about it."

Mae looked at the door desperately, as if she could will Evelyn to appear. She didn't want to come here in the first place, and now Evelyn was late. Mae wasn't sure she could stall much longer.

"Oh, I don't know. I think it would be better if Evelyn were here to explain."

"But she's not," Lisa said. "I have a feeling she's not coming. She's done this kind of thing before."

Mae's heart sped up. *Shit.* There had to be some explanation. She looked down at her phone and then at the door, but after a while, she knew there was no point.

"What's all this about?" Lisa asked again.

Mae clenched her jaw. She had a headache forming at the base of her skull. How dare Evelyn do this? She didn't even care enough to send a text and explain or give some notice. Mae picked up her phone and looked at the screen once more. Blank. By now she was so irritated, she decided to tell Lisa the truth. Evelyn would be forced to explain herself later.

"Evelyn and some of the moms at the school were saying you've been ..." Mae paused and smoothed a piece of her hair behind her ear. "Not yourself, lately."

"They were talking about me?" Lisa's face fell, and then her mouth scrunched into a tiny bow.

Mae rubbed at her forehead. She hadn't thought about how to say this so it wouldn't hurt Lisa; she was only thinking about blaming Evelyn.

"No. Well, I guess they said some things." She tried to deliver the next part as softly as she could. She gave Lisa an edited version of the conversation in Evelyn's kitchen the other day while her face and neck grew hotter. Why the hell had she agreed to any of this?

"They're mad at me? But I thought everyone liked me." Lisa's tone was incredulous.

"I think they wanted to give you a warning—" It slipped out before Mae could think about what she was saying.

"Warning?" Across the booth, Lisa's eyebrows furrowed. "They're giving me *a warning*?" She shook her head.

"They said ... about your drinking ..." This was awful.

Lisa's eyes looked like they were going to bulge out of her head. "My drinking? Are you kidding me? I only had two glasses of wine that night, and I had skipped dinner." Her face went pale, and she glanced at the doorway of the restaurant as if she expected Evelyn to show up now—as if she wanted her to.

"You know, they could have told me to my face what they were thinking," Lisa said sharply. "I thought I was different. I thought they were my friends. I haven't done anything wrong."

Mae looked down at the table in front of her to avoid Lisa's stare. She wasn't sure what to do or say next. Something uncomfortable clawed at her throat.

"Why did Evelyn ask you to come here?"

"I don't really know," Mae said. "She didn't explain." She fumbled over her words. Why had Mae agreed to do this was a better question.

The restaurant's espresso machine let out a loud whir and sizzle. Lisa turned her head to watch the barista for a moment. When she looked back at Mae, her eyes were glassy.

"If they've decided that I'm a problem, it's going to be uncomfortable for me now. My kids are going to have a tough time. I've seen this happen before."

Mae shifted in her seat and glanced down at her sparkling water. "I'm sure it'll be okay." She knew she should look up, but in that moment, she couldn't bear the eye contact. "It'll blow over." It was another lie, and Lisa probably knew it.

Lisa moved and shifted her body to slip out of the booth. Mae finally forced herself to look up.

"This was a pretty shitty thing to do," Lisa said. She could have been talking about what Evelyn had done or about Mae's part in it all. Mae had no idea. Lisa threw some money down on the table and left.

When Mae got home, she tried calling Evelyn, but there was no answer. She put her purse on the couch and went downstairs to rummage through the unpacked boxes, desperately searching for something. She picked through old yearbooks, folders filled with paperwork, trophies, and medals from her youth. She wondered why they bothered packing those up and bringing them to the new house only to sit in a box for the next twenty years. She had no idea what she was looking for until she ran her hand over the cool, waxy cover of an old photo album. Mae opened it up and placed her palm over the pages.

There was Mae when she was just a little kid, with wild hair that stuck out into wings at her temples. In one photo, she was standing in front of their townhouse wearing old shorts and a t-shirt that was too big with a giant picture of a loon across the front. Mae flipped it over, reading *Mae, eight years old,* before she placed it back under the filmy clear sheet. It wasn't until the photo was in front of her that Mae knew she needed something physical —the innocent, little-kid smile on her face, the gentle loop of her mother's letters on the back of the photo—to ground her.

Back then, she never would have imagined that friendship could still be this confusing all these years later. She thought of Evelyn and Lisa and wondered how many times she was going to have to do things she was uncomfortable with and if that was the price she had to pay to be in Evelyn's circle. Was this even worth it? Who knew how long it would be until Mae potentially ended up in Lisa's place? Or, heaven forbid, Alice's. All Mae wanted was to be a good mother and a good person, but the more time she spent with these women, the more she found it hard to remember how.

Chapter Twenty-Five

THAT SATURDAY, nothing had been scheduled—no play dates or activities for the girls, no errands to run. Most of the laundry was already done, and their fridge and pantry had been restocked with groceries. Mae was still getting used to the feeling of not having to cram every task into one weekend.

She woke early that morning because she couldn't sleep. During the night, Mae dreamed of Alice inside a strange house somewhere along the edge of a lake. Mae could see her from the outside and could sense Alice was in danger, but Alice couldn't hear when Mae tried calling out to her. Mae wanted so desperately for Alice to duck, to hide, to do something, but it was too late. The next thing she knew, Alice was dead, her body limp and bruised, pale and purple at the same time. Mae woke with a start in the darkness, her hairline damp. She stayed in bed for a while, staring up into the empty darkness, assuring herself that Alice was fine, she was at a wellness center, and Evelyn knew where. It would all be okay. Then, when she knew there was no way she'd fall asleep again, she got out of bed.

Ruby and Isla were lounging in the living room in their pajamas, eating cereal and watching TV. The laziness of slow weekend mornings suited them. In her bedroom, Mae found Drew buried under the covers, eyes closed. Every spare minute he could get, he would stay in bed, drifting between asleep and awake, dozing in and out until he finally had to get up. Mae went around the room, grabbing her running socks from the drawer, a pair of leggings, a long-sleeved shirt, and her sports bra. She snapped a hair elastic off the door handle.

"You going out for a run?" Drew's voice mumbled from bed, his eyes still closed.

"Yeah. I need one. Only a short one, though. The girls are in the living room watching TV. Keep an ear out for them, okay?" A run would clear her head

Drew grunted and rolled over. Mae fumbled into her clothes, went to the bathroom to pull up her hair, and then laced up her shoes in the front hall. She waved at the girls from the open doorway.

"I won't be long. Don't open the door for anyone, and go get Daddy up if you need anything." The girls halfheartedly waved, their eyes set firmly on the television.

Outside and alone, her feet steadily pounded out a rhythm below her. She didn't bring her earbuds this time; she needed silence, not music. Instead, she replayed every thought she had about Lisa and their conversation yesterday. She thought about Leah and Evelyn and Alice, everything that was bothering her, all set to the low beat of her feet on the pavement.

When her phone buzzed, Mae pulled it out of her pocket to check. It was Evelyn.

Can you stop by today? Are you free now? Need to chat.

Mae's right hamstring tightened, a slight twinge caused by an injury from years and years ago when she used to take ballet lessons. She slowed to a walk and bent over at the waist to stretch, grabbing at her toe. She stood up straight and bent to one side, stretching her hips before considering what to text back. She was still angry about how she'd been left to handle Lisa on her own. Not to mention they missed their chance to see Alice. Mae wasn't sure which bothered her more.

Her phone buzzed again. It was a series of smiley faces. She wouldn't be able to avoid Evelyn forever. She texted back that she'd be there in five minutes, and then she shifted her direction to make her way toward Evelyn's house.

When she arrived, Mae was led to the living room, where she took a seat on the edge of the couch, not wanting to set her sweaty back on the smooth, expensive-looking fabric. Evelyn disappeared into the kitchen and came back with a glass of water even though Mae hadn't asked, and then sat down across from Mae in an oversized, cushy chair.

"I haven't heard from you. How did it go with Lisa?" Evelyn asked.

Mae's mouth fell open. Wasn't she going to explain? Or apologize?

"Why weren't you there?" Mae demanded. "That was *not* okay to leave me like that."

Evelyn's neck jerked back like she hadn't been

expecting Mae to be so direct. "I was hung up at an appointment and couldn't get out. There was nothing I could do. I feel terrible."

"It was uncomfortable," Mae said. "Extremely uncomfortable. Anyway, Lisa doesn't seem so bad. I'm not sure any of that was necessary. It seems mean."

Evelyn let out a sharp laugh. "Trust me. It was necessary."

Trust. Mae was no longer sure what the word meant. Evelyn hadn't given Mae much to show that she should be trusted.

"I'm not doing that again." Mae turned her face away from Evelyn. "I'd appreciate it if you wouldn't put me in that situation in the future."

Evelyn placed two fingers on the lines that had formed between her eyebrows. "Mae, there's a role you play when you're a Riverpark Mom. We rely on each other to keep things in check. We have one another's back; I told you this."

One of Mae's eyebrows arched as she considered what Evelyn was saying. "Like you had Lisa's back?"

"I'm not sure why you're so *hostile.*" Evelyn's expression turned cooler now. She leaned back in her seat and crossed her arms over her chest.

"I'm not hostile. I'm only telling you that I'm not okay with you ditching me and leaving me with the task of telling someone they're no longer welcome around you." There was a lot Mae wasn't okay with. The rumours, the threatening note, the lingering anxiety of never knowing what the hell was going on around here. It was too much.

This thing with Lisa was the straw that broke the camel's back.

"I didn't force you to do anything, Mae. I just didn't show up. You're the one that still said whatever you said to her."

Mae's throat was stuck with things she didn't know how to say. She suddenly wanted to be at home, spending time with the girls and Drew. They could play a game, watch a movie, and pop some popcorn. At home, she was safe.

"I have to go."

Evelyn leaned forward in her seat, uncrossing her arms. She looked directly at Mae, her gaze unflinching. "I thought you were my friend. What's the deal?"

"No deal. But I can't be played around with. I'm not going to do whatever you want me to do."

"Then we have a problem."

Mae's back stiffened. She stood. "Okay, I'm leaving for real." She shook her head and turned to make her way to the door.

"Think about what you're saying," Evelyn called. "It can be pretty damn lonely when you have no friends around here. There's safety in numbers, Mae."

Mae turned back around. Evelyn's expression had changed. There was a hint of desperation, but mostly her face was pinched like she was annoyed.

"I don't give a shit."

Mae made her way outside and then set off in a jog again on shaky legs. When she got home, she kept the argument to herself. She buried it deep, hoping she could shake it off and forget it all.

On Monday evening, after Ruby and Isla had gone to bed, Mae and Drew sat in the dimness of the living room, their feet on the ottoman in front of them. Drew was flipping through Netflix shows relentlessly. Mae wanted to ask him to choose one already.

"Did anything happen with you and Evelyn?" Drew asked out of the blue.

"Me and Evelyn?" Mae repeated. "We got in a bit of an argument, I guess. Why?"

"Evan said something to me at work today." Drew put the remote down. He turned his head and looked at Mae now. "It was hard to tell what he meant, though. I couldn't tell if he was joking around."

"What did he say?" Mae sat up, shifting her position so her whole body was facing Drew.

"He asked me if I could have a chat with you. He said it would make his life easier if Evelyn wasn't stewing over whatever it was that was bothering her."

Mae's body went still. "What?"

"I don't want to get in the middle of it, but it sounds like Evelyn got Evan involved, so—do you think you could talk to her?" Drew said. He went to pick up the remote, but Mae reached out and stopped his hand from moving.

"Wait. What kind of a talk did he want you to have with me? I mean, what kind of a wife does he think I am? A little woman who can be handled by her husband?"

"Whoa—Mae, I didn't say that, and neither did he. I'm asking you to maybe try and smooth things over."

Mae sat back in her seat and let the words roll through her head.

"And if I don't want to?"

Drew shrugged. "Then don't. It's okay. It doesn't matter."

Except that it did. Drew's promotion was being decided soon. It mattered to Drew, even if he wasn't admitting it right now. Even though it was a business decision, it would be easier for Drew to get on Evan's good side if Mae and Evelyn were on each other's good sides too.

"I'll try and fix things with her," Mae said. Drew smiled, but it was tired, like he didn't want to get into it any further. He reached out and squeezed Mae's hand lightly. He was about to say something when Isla came into the living room, her curly hair wild with bedhead, rubbing her eyes.

"I can't sleep," she mumbled.

"I'll go," Drew said. He hopped up off the couch and went to Isla's side like he couldn't get out of their conversation quickly enough. Drew took Isla's hand and murmured something to her as they went back to her bedroom.

Mae sat alone, staring into the dark.

Chapter Twenty-Six

A COUPLE of days before Thanksgiving, the night of the fall social arrived. It was like a fun fair, held in the evening at the school with craft stations, pumpkin and apple-themed games, and face painting. You had to buy tickets to get everything—the cold hot dogs, the popcorn in the tiny paper bag, the juice and soda Mae rarely let her girls drink. Two girls hopped up on that much sugar at bedtime was not ideal.

Ruby and Isla begged Mae and Drew to go. They hated missing out on fun things like this, events that the kids would be talking about over the next few days at school. Since Mae had to be there as part of the commit-tee, they decided to go as a family. It wouldn't be the best setting to try and smooth things over with Evelyn, but she could try and make it work.

Despite the initial annoyance and anger, Mae *did* want to smooth things over. There was a heaviness that came with being angry. The weight was too much to bear, and with time, her anger always dissipated. It was so much easier to forgive. Hopefully, Evelyn would feel the same.

The committee had spruced up the gym that night. Mae provided decorations, but she hadn't been inside since it was all set up. It was clean and snazzy, rather than dull and dusty. The smell of freshly popped popcorn and warm pizza filled the air. Ruby and Isla's mouths hung open when they first walked in, then smiles tugged at the edges of their lips.

"I'm going to find my friends!" Ruby called, racing off. Mae's instinct was to stay together—the room was crowded and hot, busy with people everywhere, but they were at the school, the place where Ruby came and did things independently all day long. Mae had to let go a little.

Isla looked up at Mae and Drew and asked for tickets and treats immediately. Drew was good at these kinds of things, letting the regular rules slide out the window like a breeze. He went with it, wherever it was, usually following the girls around, letting them have their fun.

"Sure," Drew said to Isla, and then to Mae, "I'll go with her and grab tickets for Ruby, too."

Isla grinned in that way she did, wide and full, teeth showing, and then grasped Drew's hand, tugging him forward.

Mae stood alone and took the scene in. Kids were happily running around, and parents lined the gymnasium wall holding coats and juice boxes, looking a little tired, but mostly content. Mae spotted Corinne standing in one corner. She was frowning, her eyes a little distant. Mae approached.

"Hey, Corinne. How's it going?"

"Oh, hi."

"Kids having fun?"

"Yeah, it's great." Corinne's voice was dull, not at all her usual bright demeanour.

Mae moved a little closer. "Is everything okay?"

Corinne had a look about her, like she had just woken up. She blinked. "Sorry. A lot on my mind."

A loud and boisterous group of women were standing off to the right and Corinne watched them with a faraway look in her eyes. Then she hauled her body off the wall she had been leaning on.

"I should run," she said. "But listen. Are you free tomorrow? I know it's almost the holidays, but maybe we could get together for a quick visit—at your house?"

"Sure." It threw Mae off. She would have to give the bathrooms a quick wipe-down earlier than she had planned. "What are you thinking?"

"I need to talk to you, but I can't get into it here."

"Okay." Mae didn't understand what she was getting at, but Corinne was already turning her body to leave.

"Great. See you then. I'll text you." Corinne called over her shoulder and then started for the gymnasium doorway. Mae watched her for only a moment before she sensed someone approaching on her right.

"Can you help with the ticketing?" Leah asked, approaching Mae. She wore jeans and a crop top that revealed a sliver of her smooth stomach. An unusual choice for a kids' party, Mae thought, but that was Leah.

"Uh—I think I have to find the girls."

"You're on the planning committee, aren't you?" Leah asked. "We all help one another out."

That reference again, about having one another's backs. Evelyn mentioned it as well, but Mae had yet to get the feeling that anyone was watching hers. She glanced around, her mind working over an excuse, but there was no easy way out.

"Sure," Mae said. She rubbed at the side of her arm.

"Follow me." Leah directed her through the crowd of parents and kids until they got to the front entrance. She motioned to a chair at a long table. "If you could sit here and sell tickets as people come in, that would be great."

It was the last thing Mae wanted to do, but she nodded. She pulled out the chair and sat down, adjusting the money box and roll of tickets in front of her.

When Evelyn came over to talk to Leah, Mae's stomach soured. She straightened in her seat and tried not to stare. As much as she didn't shy away from confrontation, and as much as she wanted to forgive and forget, she hated being face-to-face with someone who was mad at her. It made her skin tingle with discomfort.

When Evelyn turned and looked at Mae, she pushed down the uncomfortable feeling and took her chance.

"Hey. I've been thinking about it and was hoping we could forget about our conversation the other day?" Mae tried smiling convincingly. "Sorry about all that."

"Of course," Evelyn said. "No worries."

That was it. It was over. It wasn't the most enthusiastic of responses, and Mae wondered if Evelyn was going to apologize, too. Leah moved in front of Mae then, in between the table and Evelyn. She turned her back to Mae to talk to Evelyn, cutting Mae off.

On the table in front of Mae sat Leah's phone. The

screen was lit up, covered with dozens of small squares: apps for Starbucks and Instagram, banking and music. Mae never left her phone on and open like that, but her mother did it all the time, too.

After a minute, the screen went from dim to bright, lighting up with a message. Mae glanced down and caught Corinne's name at the top of the message bubble.

No I don't. What does that mean??!?!?

Mae's eyes flicked up to where Leah was standing. They weren't looking. Her gaze went back to the phone. It was right in front of her; all she had to do was click on the message to make it bigger.

She stretched her arm out slowly from where she sat and pressed on Corinne's message, glancing at the thread. Up above Corinne's message was a single line from Leah.

You know what you did.

Chapter Twenty-Seven

IN HER EMPTY HOUSE, Mae tried to quiet her racing mind with chores. She listened to a podcast while she cleaned the bathrooms ahead of the holiday, threw a few loads of laundry on, and made herself a salad and toasted a bagel for lunch. She prepared the salmon to be cooked later for dinner, all the while waiting to hear from Corinne. There had been no mention of when she would text, and before Mae knew it, most of the day was gone.

Three o'clock in the afternoon came quickly when your mind couldn't stop running. After seeing Leah and Corinne's text message exchange last night, Mae had barely managed to focus on selling tickets. Her body vibrated all evening. She eventually made an excuse to leave the ticketing, found Drew with the girls, and ducked out of the social without crossing paths with Evelyn or Leah again.

What did you do, Corinne?

She wanted to text or call Corinne immediately, but

she tried to let it simmer first. *Give Corinne a chance to tell you. Don't jump to conclusions the way you normally do.* But then the note came back to Mae for the first time in a while.

You ask too many questions.

An uncomfortable sensation washed over Mae, like the feeling of being completely alone in the woods. Outside the window, the dull grey sky hung low overtop, signalling late afternoon in November. She would have to go pick up the girls now. Maybe Corinne had her days mixed up, and that's why she hadn't texted yet.

Hey! Mae messaged. *Were we going to meet up? Maybe after the holiday? I'm free all weekend.*

Then she swapped her maternity sweater out for one of her winter jackets and left to get Ruby and Isla from school.

Once the bell rang, the children were released like zoo animals set free of their cages. Ruby and Isla ran toward Mae and gave her a quick hug before they started the walk back home. Their constant chatter with one another meant Mae didn't need to engage in conversation. Just as well. She had trouble focusing on the present.

"Madelyn wasn't in class today," Isla told Ruby. "Ellie said her family is sad."

Mae's ears pricked up. "Madelyn who?" Mae asked.

"Madelyn Miller."

Corinne's daughter. A slight shiver went through Mae's torso. She pulled her jacket tighter around her body.

"What happened? What do you mean her family is sad?" Mae said.

Isla looked up at Mae, her small eyebrows bunched

184

together. She shrugged. "Ellie said it was something about her mom."

Mae stopped in her tracks. Isla sometimes got her stories mixed up. She pulled out her phone and sent Corinne another text.

How are you? Everything okay?

Mae waited, but no response. She put it back into her pocket, hoping she would hear from her soon.

For the rest of the afternoon, Mae's world was off kilter, teetering back and forth like a ship balancing on rolling waves. She walked the rest of the way home with Ruby and Isla, helped them unpack their bags, washed up their lunch containers, then prepped some of the vegetables for their small Thanksgiving dinner the next night, all the while moving from task to task in silence, but her mind was elsewhere.

There were too many strange little coincidences. Corinne's mood at the social, the text from Leah. As soon as Drew got home, Mae told him she needed to run an errand. She would explain later once she got some answers.

She got in the car and started driving. Mae had seen Corinne turn down a street often enough to know it was where she lived. She just didn't know which house. Still, Mae gave it a shot anyway.

She turned right and slowed to a crawl on the court in front of her. A few kids were out, but for the most part, it was quiet. She stopped in her tracks when she saw a police car parked in front of one of the houses. There was no fanfare, nothing unusual, except for the fact that you didn't often see a police presence around here. The hairs at the nape of Mae's neck stood up. She stretched forward to try and see someone or something at the house—but there was nothing.

Mae pulled her phone from her pocket and opened the message to Corinne again. Still no response. Her stomach quivered. Even if it wasn't her business, Mae didn't think she could sit by idly.

She got out of her car and scanned the road around her. There were no adults walking dogs or out chatting with neighbors. Mae went to the door of the house with the cop car out front. She knocked and then waited. After a minute, she peeked into the window but couldn't see anyone. She was about to turn around, maybe glance into the backyard if she could, when voices came from around the side of the house. Mae froze, as if remaining perfectly still would help her hear better.

"Thanks again," a voice said.

"Of course. We'll let you know if we find anything, but honestly, try your best not to worry. We've seen this happen before. She'll probably come back."

"It's not like her," the first voice said.

There was a mumbling Mae couldn't make out, and then a man and two police officers came around the corner. They stopped in their tracks when they saw Mae.

"Oh, um." Mae fumbled. Her face grew hot. "I was looking for Corinne?"

"She's not here," the man, presumably Corinne's husband, said. "Who are you?"

"Are you a friend of Mrs. Miller?" one of the police officers asked.

Mae nodded. "Our kids go to the same school."

The man looked down at his feet; he rubbed the back of his neck and winced. "She's gone."

"Gone?" Mae's stomach lurched.

"She's missing."

A dizzy feeling swept over Mae from head to toe. She needed to sit down. Instead, she put a hand out to steady herself on the edge of the brick wall.

"It's a little early for us to know that for sure," the police officer interjected. "But we're fairly confident she'll come back soon. These things happen. Do you know anything about where she might be?"

Mae shook her head. The muscles in her shoulders were so tight.

"When did you last see her?" The other officer asked.

"Last night. At an event at school."

"The fall social thing. We were there." The man turned to Mae. "I'm her husband, Rick. If you hear anything, could you let me know?" He gave Mae his number, and she punched it into her phone with shaking hands. Then she put her phone into her pocket and ran her damp hands down the side of her jeans.

"We'll do our best," the police officer said to Rick. She nodded at Mae and walked back to her cruiser.

Mae left, too. She got into her car and watched Rick walk to his front door. She took a deep breath and tried to process what was happening. Then she put her car into drive and got the hell out of there before anyone else could see her.

Chapter Twenty-Eight

For the rest of the evening, Mae barely spoke. She made dinner, helped Drew clean up, bathed the kids and got them to bed in fresh pajamas, all slowly and methodically, trying to ensure the illusion of normalcy wasn't shattered. It wasn't until the girls were in bed and she was certain they were asleep, their breathing steady and eyelashes fluttering on their soft cheeks, that Mae fell onto the couch next to Drew. She crossed her arms over her chest.

"Tough day?" Drew asked, reaching his hand to rub her leg. His eyes remained on the television. They had finally found a show they could agree to watch together, and Drew was starting it up for them, but Mae was too agitated to sit and absorb mindless television.

"My friend Corinne is missing."

Drew's head shot sideways. "What?"

Mae thought about the facts: Alice had disappeared, and there were so many rumours about where she was, but nothing was confirmed. Now Corinne. What the hell kind of a place were they living in? This sort of thing happened in movies, not in suburbia.

"I don't know what's going on," Mae said. They thought they had moved to where the grass was supposed to be greener, but now Mae wasn't so sure. She wasn't sure of anything. Her body started to shake.

"Hey, come here." Drew pulled Mae in close and wrapped his arms around her shoulders. "Damn, this is so wild."

"It's terrifying," Mae said. "What if something happens to us?"

"We'll be careful. We can take some extra precautions." Drew pulled away from Mae but kept his hands on her legs. His touch was reassuring.

"Like what?" Mae said.

"We can check in with each other more often during the day, and we'll make sure the girls stay together and are never outside alone. I'll look into an alarm system for the house."

"You think all that is needed?" Mae didn't know if the measures were a bit much or if this kind of thing would be their new normal.

"I don't think we need to panic, but it won't hurt. Let's keep our wits about us, okay?"

Mae nodded, and Drew pulled her into his chest again. "Hopefully the police will find something soon."

That night, Mae slept poorly. She kept waking up, worried she was going to miss a text message or a phone call. Whenever she closed her eyes and was about to drift off, her mind went to the last time she saw Corinne and the look on her face. Mae stayed in bed most of the night, flopping over from one position to another, willing herself to sleep. At some point, she drifted in and out, but when she woke up, her eyes were heavy with exhaustion.

AFTER THEIR RELATIVELY QUIET Thanksgiving weekend, and once the girls had gone back to school, Mae opened her laptop. The unsettled feeling hadn't budged; in fact, it had moved from low in her belly up to her lungs, making her chest feel tight. She needed to find answers. She clicked the button and watched her laptop hum to life.

Her first thought was to start by googling Leah and jotting down whatever she could find in her notebook. Leah, with her air of mystery and contempt, had to be like everyone else in some ways. She was a person, after all, with feelings and concerns and needs, but something about her gave Mae pause. She assumed she could find answers if she looked hard enough.

Mae wrote Leah's name in large letters and under-lined it three times, then left a space below for every little detail she found. She cracked her neck before bending closer to the laptop. Her shoulders were hunched, and her eyes squinted as she scanned the screen in front of her, hoping to find out what she and Drew had gotten into by moving here.

After a quick search of social media, Mae learned the basics: Leah had grown up in the same area she lived now, no surprise there, and she and Jeff had been married for thirteen years. She jotted that down. Mae also discovered that Leah ran her own business for a while as a personal stylist but appeared to let it fizzle. This surprised Mae, but only because Leah's old website, which had not been updated for years now, listed one of her services as 'Etiquette Consulting.' There was a market for grown women to seek out etiquette consulting? Mae shook her head and then wrote it down as well before clicking the corner of her screen to close Leah's website.

She went to shut down all the screens on her laptop, including the social media sites that contained something about Leah, but stopped when she saw it. Leah and Mae had a mutual friend. Mae's head tilted to one side. Small world.

Minjoo Chen was an old acquaintance of Mae's from her first job in advertising—back when Minjoo briefly lived in Montréal. They had worked together in the city when they were young and eager, and Mae and Minjoo had clicked instantly. Mae recalled Minjoo was stylish, living in a glossy condo in the city with her older sister. The two were single and had money to spend on dinners out and great clothes and were always up for trying something new—hang gliding lessons or cooking classes. Despite how different they were, Mae and Minjoo were close back then, but they hadn't spoken in years. She was one of those acquaintances you could lose touch with, and before you knew it, ten years had gone by, and you wondered how they remembered you.

Mae leaned in closer to the screen and clicked on Minjoo's name. It only took a few messages back and forth for Mae to learn that Minjoo had moved to New York and was doing well. She was still working in advertising, and still living an exciting life. Mae brought up the fact that they shared a mutual friend, and Minjoo filled her in on the rest. It turns out Minjoo knew Leah through her sister from when they were back in college, and they all used to run in the same circles.

Mae opened up and read Minjoo's last message.

Hey! I'm going to be in Montréal later this week for work!! It's been so nice catching up, you're not free for a lunch, are you?

Mae responded yes. They agreed on a time and a place, and Mae mentally picked out something to wear. This would be nice. Or, at the very least, a reprieve from everything happening around her.

WHEN SHE GOT THERE, the inside of the restaurant was bright and warm, with tables covered in white linens lined up tight and close to one another. The scent of garlic, fresh bread, and smoked meat welcomed her. Minjoo was already seated, a glass of white wine and a tall bottle of water in front of her. Her eyes were cast down, scanning the menu, her black hair falling to one side of her slender neck.

Mae felt a familiar stab of momentary self-consciousness. It passed quickly, though, and she smoothed her hands over the front of her black turtleneck.

"Hey!" Minjoo stood and smiled broadly. She moved forward and enveloped Mae in a hug like no time had passed.

"How are you? God, it's been forever, hasn't it?" Minjoo sat back down and leaned forward, pouring some water into the empty glass in front of Mae.

"I've been great, thanks. Busy with the kids and all that, of course."

"I've seen the pictures. So cute." Minjoo smiled again. "Where are you working now? You mentioned you're out of the industry?"

The industry. Advertising was exciting when Mae first got into it as a writer. Client parties and big presentations. Late night brainstorming over beer at the pub. It was great for a twenty-something with few responsibilities, and the money was more than Mae could have hoped for at the time, but she never quite fit the way Minjoo did. The schmoozing and boozy lunches grew old quickly.

"Actually, I'm taking a break to focus on my family life."

There was a pause. An unbearably awkward silence surrounded their table for a few beats, loaded with judgment.

"Oh yeah?" Minjoo averted her eyes when she spoke. "And where are you living now? Did you say Vermont?"

"Burlington." Mae sipped her water. "That's how I met Leah, remember?"

Minjoo nodded. "Right. You said that. So, what's she up to these days?"

"Kind of the same as me," Mae said, nodding at the waiter when he arrived at the side of their table. She asked for the same glass of wine Minjoo was having and then turned back. "I don't know her that well, though. I can't read her. She's a tough nut to crack." Mae laughed lightly.

She was being careful, not revealing too much, waiting to see what Minjoo would say first. Maybe Minjoo was doing the same thing.

"Really? I remember her being like an open book," Minjoo said. "Almost to a fault. She talked and talked about everything in her life, like the attention had to be on her at all times, you know? She had this need for everyone to adore her, to be the most popular. Or, at least, that's what I thought then. Is she still like that?"

"I guess you could say that. Although, to be honest, she's a bit of a mystery to me."

Minjoo nodded and sipped her wine. "My sister liked her, but I remember always thinking she was a bit strange."

Mae wrinkled her nose. She wondered what Minjoo meant by strange. Leah was so many things in Mae's opinion, but who was she to others?

Minjoo laughed. "I'm sorry, I sound like such a gossip, don't I? I swear I'm not."

The conversation switched to the old days, then. They talked about the people they used to know, the work they used to do. Minjoo was still in advertising but had risen in the ranks. They laughed about the fact that she was now one of the big wigs they used to think were old when they had first started. Their conversation was easy and comfortable, and Mae remembered why she and Minjoo used to get along so well.

Afterward, when their lunch was done and the coffee had arrived, Mae wanted to prod a little further. This might be her only chance.

"Hey, so you said you're still in touch with Leah from

time to time. Do you know any of her friends? Did you ever meet any of them?"

"I think so. A few of them came out with us a couple of times."

"You don't remember who, do you?"

"Now you're the gossip," Minjoo chuckled. She picked up her cappuccino, took a sip, and put it back on the table before giving a little shrug. "Why?"

Mac shook her head. "I'm not trying to get dirt; I only want to understand them. Some of the women seem so different from me, but others seem great. It's a really odd mix."

"They probably *are* different from you. Leah is, anyway." Minjoo's tone was gentle and kind. "Actually, now that you mention it, I do remember one of them stuck out from the rest. She didn't fit the mold."

"Who was that?"

"Theresa?" Minjoo looked up above her until her eyes lit up. "No, Tessa! Tessa Neele. Have you met her?"

It sounded familiar, but it took a moment to come back to Mae. Then she remembered: it was the name Alice had given at the wellness center she had checked into. Mae froze, trying not to react physically, but her mind was swimming. She shook her head.

"I wouldn't worry about not understanding those women if I were you," Minjoo said.

Mae nodded, and then, unsure how to press further, she let the conversation change direction. They chatted about their homes, vacations they had taken, where Minjoo had been traveling and where she was going next.

After the coffees were done and the bill was paid, they stood up, and Minjoo leaned in for another hug.

"This was nice. We shouldn't wait so long until the next time."

Mae agreed.

"Oh, and tell Leah I say hi," Minjoo said.

Mae smiled and waved goodbye. There was no way she was going to tell Leah about any of this.

Chapter Twenty-Nine

A FEW DAYS LATER, Evelyn dropped by Mae's house. She stood at the front door with a sheepish look on her face. "We haven't spoken much at all since our little disagreement." She stuck her hand out and offered Mae a coffee. "I picked up a latte for you to say sorry. Can we forgive and forget?"

Mae accepted the cup, although she no longer had a clear sense of what she should do, and what she shouldn't. All she knew for sure was that she was growing tired of drama.

"Can I come in?" Evelyn said.

"Okay." Mae stepped to one side and made room for Evelyn. They went to the living room to sit and drink their coffee.

"You were right about the whole Lisa thing. I shouldn't have left you there."

Mae nodded, noting that Evelyn wasn't actually apologizing. "What was all of that about? Lisa seems harmless."

"You don't know the whole story. Lisa needs to be guided, in my opinion."

"But why?"

Evelyn looked out the window to her right. She sighed heavily before turning her head back to Mae. "Some people need extra help to stay in their lane, to make the right choices. I know she's an adult, but I can see it coming from a mile away when someone's spiraling in the wrong direction, and I like to try and help. Lisa needs help before the rest of the women around here ostracize her."

Mae shifted in her seat. This didn't sound like the way Mae would choose to help. "Oh?"

"They can be tough. I try not to be." Evelyn shrugged. "That's what I meant when I said we watch out for one another. Anyway, I feel so bad about potentially ruining things between us. I don't want to wreck our friendship over this, which is why I came by today. With gifts." She held up her latte and smiled.

"Thank you. I appreciate it."

"Of course. It's important to me."

When Evelyn and Mae first met, Mae instantly warmed to her, and now she was reminded of why. She had a pull, a gravitational force that was hard to resist. Evelyn had an uncanny ability to make Mae want to forget about anything that had come before.

"Helping others has always been important to me," Evelyn said.

"Why's that?"

"When I was a kid, my mother was useless. She didn't know how to take good care of me, and I was her only child. I guess she didn't have that gene or something. It couldn't have been *me*." Evelyn laughed, but there was hurt in her eyes.

"I'm sorry to hear that," Mae said.

Evelyn shrugged. "Eh, after a while you get used to being told you're nothing." She said it like it wasn't a huge deal. "She was also super controlling. She always wanted me to do whatever she said, no questions. So, once I was old enough, I got out of that house and vowed never to be like that with my relationships. I've always tried hard to be helpful rather than a control freak. The last thing I want is to be like my mother."

"Mmm." Mae's response was non-committal and perhaps not thoughtful enough, but she wasn't sure what else to say.

"Anyway, now we're estranged. She lives right here in Burlington, but I haven't seen her or spoken to her in ages. She only met my kids once. Sad, isn't it?"

"We've all got our issues," Mae said. She had a hard time imagining what that would be like though. It was almost impossible to know why a mother couldn't love and protect the little beings that were part of her. It was instinctual, wasn't it? And what did that do to a person for the rest of their adult life?

"Now, your turn," Evelyn said. "What are you hiding?"

Mae spluttered, almost spitting out her sip of latte.

Evelyn laughed. "Relax. I'm kidding. Besides, I always know what's going on around here. I don't need to ask to find out. Anyway, we're good?" Evelyn stood up, quickly and abruptly.

Mae pushed her lips together into a closed-mouth smile. "Yep."

"Great. I have to run, but I'm glad we had this chat."

Before Mae could rise to walk her out, Evelyn disappeared down the hallway toward the front door.

Chapter Thirty

A GUST of wind brushed across Mae's face. She stood in the school yard early the next week, deliberately apart from the Riverpark Moms in their heavy coats and those hats with the pom-poms. Her hand went to the hat on her own head and felt the soft pom-pom between her fingers. Mae spotted one at Target the other day and picked it up. She needed a new hat anyway.

Evelyn walked past Mae with a group of women and stopped. Her high cheekbones were pink from the cold air.

"Are you coming to my place Thursday night?"

It sounded like one of those things you say that slips out accidentally. Like when you're casually trying to say goodbye to someone you're stuck making small talk with and you make a promise you know you won't keep. *Let's get together for lunch!* Or *Text me when you're free!*

"Thursday night?" Mae said.

"I'm having a few friends over. Can you come?"

Resistance bloomed in Mae, but Evelyn was so good at

making Mae feel a part of something. Evelyn smiled encouragingly, the way she always did.

"Sure," Mae said. "Sounds good."

That Thursday night, Mae sat on Evelyn's couch with a glass of wine in hand and legs crossed in front of her. She fiddled with her extensions. They were itchy now and her scalp ached when she touched them, but she wasn't due to go back to the hairdresser for a few more weeks. She couldn't wait to have them removed.

Little pockets of conversation swirled around her. Leah was an expert at steering and directing the conversation, but now, a woman across the room with shiny dark hair started talking loudly about how she wanted a wife. It was a joke—the things you could get done in a day if a wife had another wife.

"Wouldn't it be nice to have a wife to keep track of the kids' doctor and dentist appointments?" the woman said. A murmur went through the room.

"And to keep track of mine, too!" Jen interjected. Everyone laughed.

"I want a wife to cook—not just food, but healthy, unprocessed meals for everyone in the family. And keep the kids clean while they're at it. Oh, and my wife needs to do all the laundry and clean the house." This time it was a woman with a blonde ponytail who spoke. Mae had trouble keeping track of who was who. They were mostly all in black or jeans, tight t-shirts and long hair that fell to the middle of their backs.

"They also have to be the one to take care of the kids when they're sick because I can't miss out on anything that's important to me," Jen spoke again. Mae laughed out loud, surprising herself. She hadn't seen this real side to the women before. Mae would never have imagined they could admit to needing help.

Kelly, the one who was at Evelyn's the day they gathered to talk about Lisa, chimed in from across the room. "My wife has to arrange for *everything* to do with the kids —school, activities, birthday parties, appointments, play dates. And don't get me started on Christmas." She counted on her fingers as she spoke.

"My wife needs to keep track of that damn Christmas gift spreadsheet for me," Mae added. Another laugh rippled around the room, and Mae smiled.

They passed the wine around and kept the joke going —they wanted wives to drop off and pick up the kids, hustle them around everywhere, and put them to bed every single night. They wanted wives to be sexually attentive—to do the work on the days when you're so worn out you can't even begin to think about having the energy to please someone. The conversation turned almost solely to sex soon after. The needs their husbands had.

"I will always say that Evan is a great man. He's a fantastic husband and an excellent father," Evelyn said. "But why is it that there's some unwritten rule that he will always be satisfied? It can never be only my turn." Evelyn sipped her wine and glanced around the room. "God, I'm not alone, am I?" She looked directly at Mae.

"Heck no," Kelly laughed. "Mine is the same way. Amazing guy, and I love him dearly, but if he gives me the 'you've let me down' look one more time when I tell him I'm too exhausted—"

Mae shifted in her seat. She placed her empty wine

glass on the coffee table in front of her. Her head was woozy. She knew three glasses were too much to handle. Were they waiting for her to say something? She had no problem chiming in about all the work she did in a day, but Drew was way too personal.

"Patrick left me." It was the woman with the business degree, from the afternoon when they told Mae about wife bonuses, who blurted it out. Her words were slightly slurred. Mae suspected she would regret her honesty tomorrow. "He told me he doesn't love me the way a man should love his wife."

Leah went to her side and rubbed her arm. "Oh, Rosie. I'm so sorry."

Rosie's face collapsed. She stared down at her lap. "I feel so ... lost."

"You'll be fine because you've got us," Leah said. Rosie looked up at her with appreciation and then closed her eyes, her face returning to the sad, sunken way it looked before. When Leah closed her eyes as well and breathed out a deep shudder of a breath in one long exhale, Mae was oddly touched. She didn't realize Leah had it in her to feel compassion.

Then Leah opened her eyes back up again and looked at Rosie with a glimmer of something mischievous. "What happened? Did you see it coming?"

No, Mae silently warned. *Don't tell them*. Mae didn't know Rosie from the next person, but she remembered what Corinne said. *Once they know something about you, they can use it later*. Rosie would be another Lisa. It struck Mae then that she already had three glasses of wine and not a lot of dinner. She could end up another Lisa herself if she wasn't careful.

"He shouldn't get away with it," Rosie said, opening her eyes now. Her tone was bitter. "I should do something that would embarrass him."

"Don't go getting rash," Leah said. She sat up and shifted on the couch.

"But why should he be allowed to say something like that? To ruin everything after all I've done for our marriage. After all the work I've put into him and our kids. It's not fair."

"Life's not fair," Leah said, a sudden sharpness in her voice.

"It's fair for *them*," Rosie said. "The men around here make millions while we're giving away the skills we honed in graduate school for free. Think about it. We're organizing galas, running the school, and throwing fundraisers for nothing."

"It's not for nothing. Besides, our husbands are the good guys. They treat us well because they love us," Leah said. It seemed like a dig at Rosie.

"Oh, they act like good partners, I know. But we're still dependant on them, and they can change their minds at any time. Look at me." Rosie stood up.

"He'll come running back to you as soon as he realizes his clean underwear won't materialize in his drawer. Somebody actually *washes them*?" The woman with shiny black hair joked. A few women laughed. Rosie didn't.

"Think about it. Your husband could decide to give you a bonus or not. It's all up to him."

"Rosie, what are you implying?" Leah asked. "That all of our husbands are jerks?"

"I'm saying, if we want any kind of power, we need to earn our own money. Otherwise, aren't we a lot like mistresses? We're dependent. We need to do something. To challenge the status quo. Remember what's-her-name? Used to live here a while ago—"

"Okay," Leah said, standing up. "This evening is not supposed to be so heavy. Let's move on." She looked across the room at Evelyn, her eyes flashing.

Something clawed at Mae's throat. Her fingers tingled with anxiety.

"Tessa!" Rosie said, triumphant.

Mae's stomach suddenly dropped. The mood in the room shifted. A few women lowered their heads and looked at their hands, another coughed. What did Rosie mean?

"Has anyone heard more about Alice?" the woman with the shining dark hair asked.

"There's nothing new." Leah's jaw clenched and unclenched after she spoke.

"I'm not taking my chances. First Alice and then Corinne? It makes me really uncomfortable. I had Wes install a top-notch security system in our house," the woman said.

"You don't need extra security," Leah said. "Nobody's going to come and kidnap you." There was so much disdain in her voice when she said it. Mae cleared her throat. She wanted to get out of here.

"Everyone needs to calm down." Evelyn stood and reached for the bottle of wine. She topped up Kelly's glass.

"There's no kidnapping going on. We all know both Alice and Corinne were unstable. It's unfortunate, but when you're mentally unwell, you're bound to fall apart. Bad things happen sometimes."

Mae didn't think Evelyn was right, but she didn't dare say it.

"More wine?" Evelyn appeared next to Mae now. Mae shook her head. How much had she had already?

"Hey, are you okay? You don't look so well." Evelyn placed a hand on Mae's arm. "Do you want to get some air?"

That was probably the wise thing to do. Her body was so hot. A single trickle of sweat ran down the middle of Mae's shoulder blades to the waist of her pants. She nodded and stood up, following Evelyn to the stairs. When she glanced back at the room, she caught sight of Leah watching them leave.

Outside, it was a relief to breathe in the cold air. Mae took it in in gulps, letting the November chill cool her cheeks and the nape of her neck.

"I like you, Mae, but I don't get you." Evelyn was leaning on the edge of the post out front.

"What do you mean?"

"I wanted to get to know you, and I thought we were becoming good friends, but sometimes you seem really uncomfortable around me. Around most of us. Do you want to hang out with us or not? I can't tell if you're in or you're out."

"I've had too much wine. I'll be okay." Mae sat on the edge of the front porch step, her head bowed.

"Fair enough." Evelyn took a seat next to Mae on the

cement step. "Do you want me to call you a cab or something?"

Mae shook her head again. She opened her mouth slightly but said nothing. Evelyn was close now. Her hair smelled like lavender. Under the porch light, her skin was gleaming and dewy.

"Poor Rosie," Evelyn said. She looked out at the darkness in front of them. "Sounds like she's going off the rails. Then again, can you imagine your husband telling you he doesn't love you anymore? That's painful."

Mae didn't want to imagine it. One minute, you're living a perfect life, and the next thing you know, your husband doesn't love you, and what next? Rosie would somehow be expected to just keep up with the life she'd built but without any support. And she was right. It wasn't fair, the way she was reliant on her husband, the way all of them were giving away everything they had worked at for free. Yet nobody wanted to admit it could happen to them, too.

Mae thought of Alice and Corinne and shifted from her hunched position, straightening her back. She forgot about them both momentarily. While Mae was sitting in Evelyn's den, sipping wine, Alice and Corinne were still out there somewhere, but Mae was too caught up in herself. Her head felt cloudy, despite the fresh air. She was too tipsy, and now she regretted it.

"Poor Alice. And Corinne," Mae said. "I wish I knew what was going on."

Evelyn's face remained unmoving as she stared out at the dark lawn and quiet houses in front of them. "I told you already. They both have issues. Who knows what's going on with them, but if I were you, I'd forget it."

"It's kind of hard to forget about," Mae said. "How often do women you know disappear?"

"What does that mean?" Evelyn's head turned sharply.

"Nothing—it means I'm worried. That's all." Mae blinked. She felt queasy now. She needed some water.

Evelyn put a hand on Mae's knee. "It's nice of you to worry, but I don't think you need to."

The text message Mae saw between Leah and Corinne came to mind. Before she could think rationally, Mae blurted it out.

"I saw Leah's phone at the social," Mae said. "She texted something weird to Corinne. She said Corinne knew what she did."

"You're reading Leah's personal messages?"

"I didn't mean to." She did, though, and now she couldn't cover it up. It was all out in the open, exposed. "It was right there. I couldn't help but see it."

"Mae, that is an invasion of privacy!" Evelyn's eyes narrowed. She stood up, her arms crossed over her chest.

"I'm sorry," Mae mumbled. And then, as if she had no control over her actions or her words, Mae blurted again. "But, what if Leah did something?"

"There's nothing going on, Mae. It's a coincidence, and you sound super paranoid," Evelyn snapped. "We aren't living in a sinister neighborhood. It would be best if you could remember that. I think you've had too much wine."

"I need a glass of water."

"I'm going inside," Evelyn snapped again. She turned and disappeared through the doorway while Mae sat on the porch, head throbbing. Mae waited only a moment and then went back down into the dimness of the den to get her purse. She needed to get out of there before she said anything else.

Chapter Thirty-One

MAE TAPPED her fingertips on the edge of the windowsill in her living room as she waited for Grace. They made plans for Grace to come by early for a visit the next day, but a few minutes ago, Grace called to say she was stopping to grab bagels and coffee first. "Like how we used to do on Saturday mornings," Grace had said.

When Grace pulled into the driveway, she got out of the car and walked slowly, balancing the coffees and a paper bag in her hands. She stuck the tip of her tongue out the corner of her mouth in concentration the way she used to when she was studying in university, and Mae was struck by the familiarity of her friend. Having Grace here again was exactly what Mae needed. Mae swung the front door open and wrapped Grace in a tight but careful hug so she wouldn't knock the coffee to the ground.

Grace whistled as she took in the high ceilings, the ornate light fixtures, and the shining hardwood floors in Mae's entrance.

"This is gorgeous. Very fancy." She followed Mae to the kitchen to set the food down. She ran her hand over the granite counter. "I can't believe you have this stunning house settled on top of a hill in a beautiful neighborhood, and I haven't been here to see it yet."

"I know. And, thank you. I think I need some more accent pieces, though, to elevate the room a little."

Grace stared at Mae and then nodded slowly. "Uh huh. It could use some elevating in here."

Mae laughed, though she had been serious. She remembered the open house when they first walked through this place. The couple who lived here before were great at decorating. Mae tried to keep it up.

"How are you?" Grace sat down, peeling her jacket off and placing it on the back of the chair next to her. She opened the bag of bagels and handed one to Mae.

"I don't know. Okay, I guess," Mae said. Where did she even start? She was still uncomfortable after the way things were left at Evelyn's the night before, and when she had gone back inside after talking to Evelyn, Leah was there, asking questions like she suddenly cared about Mae.

"Hey, you okay?" Leah had asked. She was sitting back on the couch, one leg dangling over the other.

"Yeah, thanks. Just getting some air," Mae said.

"You haven't had too much wine, have you?" Leah smiled, but it didn't reach her eyes.

Mae had pushed down the annoyance she felt. Leah was too much.

"No, I'm good. But I have to get going."

"Wait—I was hoping we could talk."

"About what?" Mae had turned back around to try and read Leah's expression.

"Evelyn said you opened up a while ago. About your friends growing up. I want to hear about where you came from too, Mae." Leah's face was neutral, but Mae was wary. She fumbled over an excuse and left, hoping the brisk air would help clear her head. There was no way Leah cared about Mae's life before Burlington, and there was no way Mae wanted Leah, of all people, to know about her past. Leah was digging for something else, but Mae wasn't going to stick around to find out what.

Now, at the kitchen counter, Grace didn't wait for Mae to elaborate before she continued talking.

"I should have brought burgers. Remember how we used to go to Honest Fred's to get those sliders and fries?"

Honest Fred's was a tiny, hole-in-the-wall kind of a place where all the college kids would go after a night of drinking for a limp piece of brownish meat with ketchup and one sad pickle in between a flat bun. The kind of burger you could only love at one in the morning after a night of drinking booze, but everyone did love them, including Mae and Grace. Mae couldn't remember the last time she had a burger, now that she thought of it.

"I remember," Mae said. "This is perfect." She held up her cup of coffee and took a sip.

"You probably can't even get a regular old burger around here, hey? They're most likely all the *elevated* kind with avocado and garlic confit or something." Grace raised her eyebrows and grinned at Mae. "Did you do something different to your hair?"

Mae shot a hand up to her long, fake locks. She twirled

an extension around her pointer finger. "Yeah. Do you like it? I got extensions."

Grace stopped mid-bite of her bagel. "Really? What for?"

"To add a bit of body. For something a little different, you know." She scratched her scalp where the extension was attached. "I'm having them taken out soon though."

"They look nice," Grace said. She took another bite. "What's the plan for today?"

"Actually," Mae said, "I was hoping you could come do something with me." She hadn't really thought this one through, it was more of a spur of the moment kind of idea, but she could use Grace for moral support.

"What is it?"

"You'll see," Mae said, hoping Grace would understand.

HALF AN HOUR LATER, they were in Mae's car, parked just within viewing distance of Leah's house and partially hidden by a tree. It was mid-morning now, and Mae suspected they wouldn't have to wait much longer. Leah had plans with Evelyn today. Earlier last night, Mae overheard them discussing it at Evelyn's house. For some reason, it bothered Mae, the way they were whispering, almost hissing at one another. They had a tense conversation, and Mae only caught the part where they agreed to meet up. Something told Mae that this might be her chance to find out what the hell was going on with Leah.

"What are we doing?" Grace asked.

"There she is," Mae said. She gestured to Leah, who was walking with purpose down her driveway. She got into her car and started to pull away. Mae put her car into drive and followed at a safe distance.

"Are we going somewhere with her? Why didn't you say hi?" Grace's voice changed from lighthearted to concerned as her eyes followed Leah's car ahead of them.

"That's Leah," Mae said, nodding ahead of her as they drove. "She's meeting up with Evelyn, and I want to check out what they're doing."

"I don't understand."

Mae had intended on telling Grace about everything long ago: the details about Alice and Corinne, the anonymous note in her mailbox, the way she suspected Leah was dangerous. She had planned to unload it all, but she hadn't yet, and now it seemed like so much all at once. She told Grace what she needed to know while they trailed behind Leah's car.

"Wait. You think that the rich woman club you told me about—your friends—are involved in the disappearance of two women?" Grace tilted her head, waiting for an answer.

"I think so. And Leah's not my friend."

"Mae—are you sure about this? That's a serious accusation you're making. You shouldn't say those kinds of things unless you know." Grace had always been straightforward in her delivery. Still, Mae's shoulders tightened up.

"Something's up, and I want to find out what."

"Why aren't you leaving it to the police?"

Mae frowned. "They're looking for both Alice and

Corinne, but nobody has drawn the connection to Leah yet."

The car went quiet. Mae turned to catch a glimpse of Grace. Her eyes were narrowed like she was deep in thought.

"Okay," she said after a while. "If you think something's not right and want to look into it, I'm in."

"Really?"

"Of course. When have we ever not been there for each other?"

Mae smiled. "We won't be long. I promise."

Leah stopped her car out front of Evelyn's house. Mae pulled over. She nodded in Leah's direction as Leah went to the door and knocked. They watched her stand and wait until Evelyn opened the door, and they both disappeared inside.

Mae knew how it looked. It looked like two friends meeting up, nothing more, but Mae's instincts told her that Leah was up to something. There were too many incidents, too many alarm bells that Mae couldn't ignore. If she could find out what the hell Leah was doing or how she might be involved, she could tell Evelyn the truth.

"I'm going to go to the door."

"And do what?" Grace asked. There was a hint of surprise in her tone.

"I don't know." She hadn't thought about that yet.

"Maybe you should come up with a plan first," Grace said. "Why don't we go back to your house? We can talk about it."

It would be easy to let it all go, to ignore whatever Mae's instincts were telling her for a little longer, but she couldn't. She was so certain Leah was in the middle of this mess. She had to know what was going on with Alice and Corinne, and she was sure Leah knew.

"One sec. I'll be right back." Mae exited the car and strode up to Evelyn's front door. She was about to knock, but she took her hand back, realizing she had nothing to say to their faces. Mae placed her palm on the doorknob instead. She turned it slowly, then gently pushed the door open enough for her to lean forward and listen.

There was a low murmur, two distinct voices, but Mae could only make out parts of the conversation.

"They're just *kids*."

A muffled sound came next. And then an angry tone. Mae couldn't make it out until she heard, "—the ravine. But that story is so old."

More low murmurs. If Mae could get a little closer ...

"You were there, *Leah!*"

"Don't you dare blame me—"

Behind her, a car horn honked, loud and high-pitched. Mae spun around. Grace's eyes were wide as she pulled her hand away from the driver's side. Mae's head snapped back around to the open door.

"What the—" Leah's voice came from inside.

Mae turned and raced back to her car, her breath uneven. She fumbled into the front seat and ducked down. Grace did the same.

"What the hell?" Mae hissed at Grace as they wedged against the center console. "Why did you do that?"

"It was an accident," Grace said. "I was trying to lower the window."

"I could have been caught. Jesus, Grace," she snapped,

a little harsher than she intended. Mae knew she shouldn't get angry, Grace was only trying to support her, but the feeling was still there, rolling in her stomach, causing her heart to race.

"I'm sorry," Grace said. She raised her head and pointed her chin in the direction of the front window. "Your friends are driving away."

Mae sat up and watched as Leah's car pulled away from her house with Evelyn in the passenger seat.

"I have to follow them."

She put her car into drive and inched her way out again, keeping her eyes on Leah. After a short while, Mae knew where they were going. They were heading in the direction of Waterfront Park.

"This is where Alice's car was found," Mae said to Grace when they got there. She pulled into an empty parking spot and watched Leah and Evelyn from afar.

"It's also a public park," Grace said.

"But it's suspicious, don't you think? When they were at Evelyn's, I overheard them say something about a ravine. It sounded like they were arguing, but there's no ravine here that I know of."

Grace studied Mae from her seat. There was a pained look on her face. Maybe it was a mistake for Mae to bring her here.

By now, Leah and Evelyn had walked to the edge of the water and stood shoulder-to-shoulder. Mae couldn't get a read on their body language. She leaned forward in her seat and rolled down her window so she could tilt her head outside to try and listen.

Leah turned. Her face was red and contorted, and she

waved her arms around when she spoke. Mae couldn't see Evelyn's face, but she watched as Evelyn gestured wildly with her hands.

"I think they're fighting." She cracked open the car door a sliver and considered getting closer to try and catch some of what they were saying.

"I feel like this is getting a bit weird now," Grace said. She placed her hand on Mae's leg. "Seriously, what's going on? Are you okay?"

"I'm fine." Of course she was fine. She only wanted to get to the bottom of all of this. Grace, of all people, with her journalism background, should understand.

"Maybe we should talk to Drew. We could sit down and have a chat, the three of us. I'm sure we could help you."

"I don't need to talk," Mae said. She glanced sideways. Grace was staring at her, eyebrows drawn together. Her presence in that moment annoyed Mae. She said she was in, but all Grace was doing was doubting her.

"Just a few more minutes, okay?" Mae looked back in front of her where Leah and Evelyn had ceased their arm waving though they were still speaking.

"Mae." Grace spoke sharply, unlike her. They weren't the kind of friends who used that tone with one another. "I think we should go home."

After a pause, Mae conceded. "Fine. We can go."

The drive back was mostly silent and uncomfortable, with bits of stilted conversation. This entire day wasn't the way Mae intended it to go.

"I should get going," Grace said shortly after walking through the door of Mae's house. She grabbed her purse and turned but then stopped, looking at Mae for so long Mae started to squirm. "You're sure you're okay?"

"I'm fine. I don't know why you keep asking."

Grace reached out and tapped the side of Mae's arm. "Think about what you're doing, Mae. You're not yourself. I barely recognized you today." She went to the door.

Mae followed and stood out front of her house, arms folded across her chest, watching Grace go. She stayed there long after Grace's car had disappeared around the corner, standing outside on her porch in sock feet, chilled by the wind and wondering if there was some truth to what her friend had said.

Chapter Thirty-Two

THE NEXT MORNING, after showering, Mae applied moisturizer to her legs as Drew sat on the edge of the bed putting on his socks.

"Grace was really strange yesterday," she said.

"How's that?"

"She kept asking me if I was okay and was acting like I was being paranoid about Leah. She said she barely recognized me," Mae said. "You don't think I'm acting different, do you?"

Drew stood and looked above him like he was thinking before he spoke. "Maybe a little." He shrugged one shoulder.

Mae stopped moisturizing. That wasn't what she had expected to hear. "What? No. How?"

"Well, I guess you seem preoccupied at times."

"You mean with Alice?"

"With all of the women," Drew said. He came over to her and put his hands on her waist. His touch was gentle, as if he worried she might break. "There's a lot going on. Maybe you should be less involved?"

"Don't you think *anyone* would want to know what's going on when two women they know go missing?"

"Of course. But it's more than that."

"What do you mean?"

"Mae—I don't want to get into this right now." Drew's forehead wrinkled, and his eyebrows merged together.

His dismissal of the conversation stung. "You don't want to get into *what*?"

"Things with you. How your priorities seem to have changed." He looked around the room and ran a hand through his short hair. "I don't know. Maybe you should look into going back to work. Some kind of regular routine, like you used to have, so you've got something to do."

"I don't want to!" Mae said. Working at an unsatisfying job wasn't what she wanted. Then again, she had no idea what was satisfying to her, but she wasn't about to admit that. "And what do you mean my priorities have changed?"

"Forget it. We can't do this now. I have things to do."

"Drew!"

"Do you really want to do this? Do you want to insist we fight?"

Ruby came into the room, eyes wide. "What's going on?"

"Hey, Rube. Nothing much. How are you? Have a good sleep?" Drew's expression softened, the way it always did when he talked to the girls. He grinned down at Ruby. She hesitated, her eyebrows furrowing for a moment, but when Drew held his arms open to her, Ruby went to him and buried her face into his chest.

"I have to run. See you in a bit." He kissed the top of Ruby's head and turned back to Mae, running a hand over her back before disappearing out of the room.

On Monday, after the girls were at school, Mae pulled out her notebook and sat at her kitchen table. Christmas was only two weeks away, and she welcomed the distraction. Thankfully she was organized and had been buying gifts for the girls for weeks already. Now, she jotted down a list of last-minute things to do: order the turkey, go shopping for stocking stuffers, and clean the floors and the spare room for when their families visited. She paused and considered the timing of dinner, the yearly attempt to get everything hot at once, when the doorbell rang.

Mae looked out the window and froze. On the other side of the door, Leah stood with her head cocked to one side, like she knew Mae was home and didn't appreciate having to wait.

Damn it, Mae thought. Her nerves were too on edge for this. She made her way to the door even though she would rather pretend she wasn't home.

"Hey," she said, attempting a neutral tone.

"Can I come in for a second?" Leah asked.

Mae couldn't very well say no. She held the door open wider to let Leah in. They made their way to Mae's kitchen, and Mae busied herself behind the counter, putting the bread that had been left out back into the cupboard, placing dishes in the sink.

"I thought we could have a talk about some things," Leah said, her tone light. She smiled unconvincingly as she stood on the other side of the counter, placing her palms down on the surface.

"Yeah?"

"If you don't mind. I would really like for us to get along, but I feel like it's been a bit ... bumpy."

The melodic ring of Mae's phone came from the bedroom where she had left it on her nightstand.

"One sec," Mae said. She left the room and went for the phone, where she found her mother's name splashed across the screen.

"Hey, Mom, can I call you back?" Mae said in a hushed tone. "I'm a little busy."

"Oh, sure." Frankie said. "No problem. I was calling to talk about the holidays—"

"Sounds good, but I'll call you right back, okay?" Mae spoke quickly and then said goodbye before Frankie could keep talking.

When Mae returned to the kitchen, Leah was standing over the table. Her notebook was open, and Leah's head was pointed down, examining it. She didn't look up until Mae cleared her throat.

"What are you doing?" Mae asked.

"What the hell is this?" Leah's voice was angry and dark. She looked up and jabbed a finger at the page in front of her.

"Why are you reading my notebook?" Mae moved closer and glanced down at what Leah was reading. The book was open to the page where Mae had taken notes when she was creeping Leah's profiles, looking at her website. Mae moved closer and grabbed the book from the table, snapping it shut.

"Why are you writing shit about me?" Leah asked, her voice high and shrill.

"It's nothing," Mae said.

"It doesn't look like nothing. It looks like you're weirdly obsessed with me."

Mae gripped the book tight. She glanced around the room, waiting for something to come to her. An excuse, something to make sense of this for Leah so she could forget it and go away.

"Who asked you to do this?" Leah shouted. "Who told you to watch me?"

"Nobody! It's nothing; I was curious about a few things. I swear, it's not a big deal."

Leah looked around the room like she was searching for answers, her eyes wild. Mae didn't know what to say. She took a step back, dread seizing hold of her arms and her hands, radiating down through her fingertips.

"I have to go. I need to get out of here," Leah said in a sharp tone. She refocused her gaze on Mae, her face angry and confused as she pointed at the notebook. "Throw those notes out. That's messed up, Mae. And trust me, you don't want anyone else to find them. It will end badly."

She left, slamming the door behind her, leaving Mae standing alone in the middle of her kitchen. Mae looked down at her notebook and the pages filled with things about Alice and Leah. It was innocent enough, though she knew how it must look.

She moved back to the kitchen table and sat unmoving except for the light shake of her body. Adrenaline. She wanted to right this before it got out of hand, tell her side of the story before Leah got to Evelyn first, but she had no idea where to begin.

Chapter Thirty-Three

MAE HADN'T BOTHERED MAKING the bed that morning. Her bones ached, her body was creaky, and all she wanted to do was crawl back under her flannel sheets and stay there. She wanted to pretend the past few days hadn't happened. But that wasn't reality, and responsibility forced Mae to stay up that day, keep the house running, do all the things she was supposed to do.

After pulling the duvet taut across her mattress and smoothing her hand over the freshly made bed, she sat on the edge and tilted her head back. Her eyes went to the ceiling, where she noticed a small water stain in one corner of the room that she had never seen before. She would have to get Drew to take a look at it before it got bigger. That tiny imperfection had the potential to grow and swell until it ruined the rest of the ceiling. When she didn't want to look at it any longer, she rolled her shoulders and pushed herself off the bed.

Next, she went to the grocery store for a quick shop

and then came straight home to put the food away. She crossed her arms and looked around her empty, clean kitchen. She had no other errands to run, but there were still a few hours left until she needed to pick up the girls, so Mae went to her closet and grabbed a long-sleeved shirt to run in. She found some leggings, laced up her shoes and, at the last minute, decided to leave her phone at home. The notifications and distractions had been aggravating lately.

Without intending to, Mae made her way down to Waterfront Park, where Alice's car had been found. She moved slow and steady at a light jog, breathing deep, until she came to the edge of the lake and stopped. She could watch the water for hours. There was something so calming about the vast blue space stretching out for miles in front of her.

Her body was damp with sweat, and the cool air chilled her. Mae turned to continue her run down the lakeshore but stopped when she saw a familiar figure up ahead and to the right of her. Sitting on one of the benches that lined the path was Lisa.

It would have been preferable to avoid her after their last encounter, but they made eye contact for an awkward beat before Mae raised a hand in the air to wave.

"Hey! How are you?" She went toward Lisa, rolling her shoulders and stretching her arms.

"Hi." Lisa's voice was cool, with more than a touch of bitterness to it. Mae supposed she deserved that. After all, Lisa hadn't done anything, but Mae went along with Evelyn's request without question.

"I've been meaning to apologize to you. For the way I

said things at the restaurant that day. I shouldn't have implied anything was wrong with you or that you needed to change. I shouldn't have said anything at all."

Lisa's eyes flashed with surprise. "Okay." Her voice trailed off like she was waiting for the catch.

Mae opened her mouth to add something, but Lisa cut her off.

"I have to run." She stood up and fumbled with her purse before mumbling about needing to be somewhere and turning to leave. Mae figured she deserved this dismissal, too.

BACK ON HER STREET, Mae stopped at the base of the hill below her house and looked up. One last push of energy, and she would be done. That was all she needed. She willed her tired legs to carry her up the incline, knowing she would enjoy the endorphins afterward.

She was right. Inside her home, Mae let the lightness radiating through her limbs carry her from room to room. She made her way to the bathroom and peeled off her clothes. She turned on the taps for the shower and went back to her bedroom to toss her clothes in the hamper when she noticed her phone on the nightstand where she had left it, only now the screen was lit up with messages.

Five missed calls from Drew and several texts asking her to phone him. Her heart pounded. She dropped her clothes into the hamper and steadied her shaking hand so she could dial Drew.

"What is it? What happened?" Mae demanded, pulling on her robe. "Are the girls okay?"

"The girls are fine. There was some news. I heard it at work today from Evan, and I wanted to speak to you first."

"Drew? What are you talking about? Is everyone okay?"

"It's your friend, Alice," Drew said. His voice was quiet, choked. "She was found dead."

The bedroom floor shifted and tilted beneath her. Mae had to sit down. Her vision narrowed, but she found the edge of the bed and collapsed onto it, shoulders hunched.

"Are—are you sure?"

"Yes. She was going to come home, apparently."

"But what?"

"She called her husband and said she was ready to come back and start over. She asked him to pick her up at a hotel where she was staying. When he got there, she didn't answer the door. They had to get hotel staff to let him in." Drew's voice was low and soft, different than usual. "They found a bottle of pills."

Rushing flooded Mae's ears. It took her a minute to realize she had become hyper-attuned to the shower, still running. She turned off the taps and then stood by the edge of the bathroom sink, gripping it with white fingers, bent at the waist to brace herself. She straightened up and pushed her shoulder into the wall, trying to steady her shaking body. How was she going to get to school to pick up the girls without coming undone? She couldn't see anyone from Riverpark right now.

"No." Mae shook her head. No, this wasn't real. She had never known anyone this had happened to before; she couldn't process it. "Why would she call him and say she wanted to come home?"

"There was a note."

"What did it say?"

"Mae—" Drew started.

"What did it say?" Mae demanded.

"Something about changing her mind. How she was sorry. She was so sorry, but she couldn't do it." Drew's voice was pained. He sounded so far away.

Mae slumped to the floor of the bathroom. She was shaking now, but she couldn't tell if it was from the cold tiles on her bare legs or the shock. She heaved, and acid burned at her throat.

Not Alice, please. Mae would have given anything to see her again, to have a chance to talk to her. How could this happen? It didn't seem like the Alice she knew. The amount of pain she must have been in. Mae should have known. She closed her eyes tight, trying to will everything away, but her throat was thick now, like it was closing over.

"I—I can't talk."

"I'll pick the girls up from school," Drew said. "I love you. I'll see you soon."

An hour later, he appeared at Mae's side. She had stayed in the bedroom, lying under the covers in her bed and staring at that water stain on the ceiling again. Drew sat next to her and pulled her close to him. He lifted her body and wrapped his arms around her. They stayed that way until the girls came into the room and asked them what was going on.

"Mommy's not feeling great, but she'll be fine after

some rest," Drew said over his shoulder. Mae mustered everything she had within her to smile at them.

"Come on, we'll order a pizza," he said to the girls. He turned to face Mae again and left his hand on her leg, his head hanging.

"Let's go, Daddy," Ruby said.

Drew's gaze moved to Mae's face, and he studied her with a watery gaze for a minute longer, then stood to reach for the girls' hands. His movements were slow like his body was being weighed down.

Later that night, after the girls had gone to bed, Drew came back into the room and stretched out onto the bed next to Mae.

"Are you going to be okay?" he asked into the darkness. He reached for her, brushing his thumb against the back of her hand.

Mae pretended to be asleep. She couldn't talk, not even to Drew.

Chapter Thirty-Four

For the rest of the week, Mae thought of every little detail about Alice she could remember. When she was putting the cereal box back into the cupboard, she thought of Alice's face, of her mannerisms. When she was stepping out of the shower, she thought of the way Alice fiddled with her watch when she was distracted, how she walked briskly on the way to school but always so slow on the way home. Part of Mae wanted to write it all down in her journal before she forgot the little details forever, but she didn't. The journal reminded her of Leah.

She drove to Alice's street and sat in the car outside her house on Friday afternoon. It wasn't like Mae expected Alice's husband to come talk to her, but she wanted to be there. She brought a tinfoil-wrapped meal for his freezer, like that could make up for losing your partner. Afterward, she called Corinne again and again. No answer.

At ten minutes to three that afternoon, Mae made her

way to the edge of the schoolyard where her daughters usually came out of class. When kids started pouring out of the building, Mae saw Isla first. Her small face had a blank expression, her eyebrows slightly furrowed as she scanned the sea of parents. Mae could pinpoint the second Isla found her because her entire face lit up into a wide smile. It was one of the best feelings Mae had experienced since becoming a mother. The intensity of love those little ones had for you was overwhelming and incredible. All Mae had to do was show up. She couldn't bear to think of Alice's daughter, so she kept her eyes down, focused on the ground, instead of scanning the sea of children further.

"Hi Mommy." Ruby walked up to Mae from the left and wrapped her arms around Mae's waist, the way she always did after school.

"How was your day?" Mae asked, placing a kiss on Ruby's head before she could protest.

"Good."

Mae put her hands on Ruby's freckled cheeks, studying her daughter closely to examine her face for signs that something was off. 'Good' wasn't much to go on. Had news spread among the kids about Alice?

"Can I hang out here for a bit?" A couple of girls were waving Ruby over to the edge of the school's playground. Isla was already running in another direction, chasing another little kid up the slide. Mae nodded at Ruby and placed the girls' backpacks on the ground in front of her. She lifted her face to the wind. It was mild and gusty for December; a welcome change. There was nothing as peaceful to Mae as the feel of the breeze, so she closed her eyes.

She only opened them again when she heard someone approaching. Leah and Evelyn had been on the other side of the playground, talking with their heads close together, their shoulders almost touching, but now they were making their way over to her.

"You heard?" Evelyn said to Mae. Her expression was solemn. Something caught in Mae's throat. All she could do was nod.

Leah's face was pale. She glanced everywhere but at Mae.

"It's so awful," Evelyn said. "I had no idea she was that broken."

Mae turned her head away from them. She couldn't stand here in the playground talking about Alice in this way, but Evelyn didn't take the hint.

"I feel like it came out of nowhere. There were no signs, were there? Did she ever talk to you about anything? Like, why she was so depressed or anxious?"

Mae noticed a small shift in Leah when Evelyn said this. Her back went rigid, and she cast her eyes down at her feet. Mae couldn't recall ever seeing Leah this way now that it was right in front of her.

"No, she didn't mention it," Mae said.

"I need to go." Leah shoved her hands in her pockets and shifted her weight from one leg to the other. "Are you coming?"

"You can go," Evelyn said. "I'm not keeping you here. I want to stay and talk with Mae."

Leah's mouth turned down even more until it looked odd, like her face was melting. She kept her eyes on Evelyn for too long.

"Fine," Leah said eventually. It felt almost indecent for Mae to witness the desperation in Leah's tone. Mae wanted out of there, but Leah left first.

Evelyn watched Leah go before turning back to Mae. She pursed her lips like she was thinking very hard, and then sighed. "She's taking it hard. Actually, I better try and talk to her." Evelyn hurried to catch up with Leah. Mae watched them for as long as she could, until they disappeared from sight.

Back at home, Mae went through the motions. She put her keys down on the table, helped Isla get her backpack off and emptied it of the library book that was inside, along with her class folder filled with artwork and poems, and a permission slip to fill out. She took out Ruby's lunch containers and washed them, and then started on dinner.

Mae jabbed a knife into the potato she was cutting up, sticking it into the side with force and then sliding it all the way through, until she accidentally nicked her finger. She jerked her hand back and put the knife down so she could grab hold of her finger. A bead of blood formed, growing and growing until it began to run. Mae pulled a paper towel off the roll and held it to her finger, watching the dark red seep through the flimsy paper. It made a pattern, snaking its way through the soft towel. She held it there for a minute and then pulled the paper towel off, investigating the cut. It was small—she thought it might not even need a Band-aid—but the bead of blood kept pooling. As quickly as Mae wiped it away, it was there again, growing, building, until it spilled over and ran down her finger like there was no stemming it. It would run and run until Mae did something about it. She held her finger directly over the drain in the kitchen sink, watching and waiting for it to stop.

Later that night, Mae took her phone from her pocket and sent a text message.

Can we talk?

Grace texted back. *Yes.*

Chapter Thirty-Five

MAE AND GRACE hadn't spoken in a week. It was hard to remember why, now that Mae was numb most of the time. She spent most of her days walking around in a fog until Grace popped into her mind.

"How are you?" Mae asked when Grace answered the phone.

"Not bad. How about you?"

Mae sat at her kitchen table and looked out the window next to her, examining the bare branches that stretched skyward like fingers. "I've been better."

There was a silence, a pause that lasted so long Mae wasn't sure who was supposed to speak next. "Alice is ... gone," she said eventually.

"Still missing?"

"No, she died." Mae didn't like using that word. It was too harsh and ugly, but a euphemism didn't seem appropriate.

"What? Oh my god, what happened?"

Mae told Grace about the news, and about Evelyn and Leah the next day in the school yard. "This place is so screwed up."

Grace took a deep breath in over the phone line. "I'm sorry. Things sound hard, and I want to be there for you. How can I help?"

Relief moved through Mae as she leaned back in her chair. "Are you still writing that article? The one about women in their forties?"

"We're almost done. It's going to be published soon; why?"

"Could you fit me in? I mean, if you still want to talk to me."

"Of course."

"Thanks," Mae said. "But can we do it in person?"

They made plans for Mae to come back to Montréal again in a couple of days and then ended their conversation. Mae clicked off her phone. She would do it. She would be honest with Grace and with herself about the women in Burlington, but most of all, she would tell Grace about Alice and about the kind of woman she was.

There was no way Mae would use any real names or reveal anything too private, but she wanted to give Grace a peek into the way the Riverpark Moms lived. People should know about women like Alice. If it helped even one person out there who was on the verge of cracking under the weight of expectations and pressure, it would be enough. She hadn't done enough to help Alice, but maybe she could help someone else.

AT GRACE'S OFFICE BUILDING, Mae was met with a strong hug. "You okay?"

Mae nodded. "I will be."

They went down a corridor until they reached Grace's brightly lit office. Mae sat down on one side of a desk, Grace on the other with a notepad and a laptop, her hands already clicking away on the keys by the time Mae settled back into her chair.

"Okay, I'm going to go ahead and launch into some of my questions. Here's how it works. We start with a survey, so we ask everyone this first set of questions which are designed to get an overall sense of where women in their forties are. Then we'll get into the more personal stuff." She stopped typing and looked directly at Mae. "And whenever you can, you can give me some insight into the women around you as well."

Mae pushed a piece of hair behind her ear.

"But no pressure," Grace said. Mae could tell she was being careful, probably out of concern for how Mae was feeling about Alice.

"Okay. So. How often do you and your partner have sex?" Grace kept her eyes on the screen of her laptop while she spoke.

Mae sat up straighter and choked on the saliva at the back of her throat. Grace poured a glass of water and pushed it toward Mae.

"Grace!" Mae said.

"What? Was that question too much? I told you they're meant to get to know women in their forties better."

"Right," Mae said. "But you already know me."

"I know, but I didn't want to answer for you; I might get something wrong. Maybe we can switch to questions about work first. We'll go to sex and health after."

A nervousness crept over Mae, and she wondered whether she had made the right choice in doing this interview. How honest would she have to be?

"Would you say, when you were working—" Grace's eyes flicked to Mae's, and her face flashed with a hint of something Mae couldn't read. "That you ever fantasized about quitting your job?"

"Sure. That's why I did quit."

"How often did you think about it? Every day? At least weekly? At least once every month? Rarely ever?"

Mae looked at the ceiling for a second and then back down at Grace. "Every day."

Grace's nails clicked away on the keyboard of her laptop. She nodded and then looked at her notes.

"And—how important is ambition to you?"

"Like, work ambition?" Mae asked. Grace nodded in response. Mae took a heavy breath in while she thought about it. "You know, I kind of hate saying this, but I think ambition is more of a younger woman's game."

Grace's eyes widened. "You're only forty, Mae."

"I know. But when I was starting out in my career, I didn't push myself hard enough. I had a vague desire to get that corner office, but I didn't really try. Then life took over. You know, the marriage and the house and the kids. I let work slide a little, and that corner office didn't seem worth it."

Grace nodded, her eyes never leaving the laptop screen. "How do you feel about it now?"

"Work?" Mae asked. "Well, I'm not working."

Grace waited.

"It was my choice; you know that." Mae ran her hand over the arm of the chair. The office was bare bones—a desk and two chairs, two large panes of glass alongside the edge of the door.

"What about the women in your neighborhood. Do any of them work?" Grace asked.

"Sure. Of course."

"Most of them?"

"Well, no. I would say most of them don't work. A bunch of them have business degrees."

"What do they do all day?" Grace asked.

Mae pointed her head to the left but kept her eyes squarely on Grace. "They do a lot. It's regular life stuff that has to get done—laundry and dishes and groceries and little things the kids need, but it all adds up. And before you know it, the day is over, and you're picking up the kids from school again. Then it's making dinner and bathing them and getting them ready for bed."

"And do you think they're happy?"

"I'm not sure." She thought of Alice. "Actually, no, I don't think they are. I think they just want you to think they are."

Grace pulled her hair over one shoulder and smoothed it down. "What do you mean?"

"I think they've got problems like most other women, but they don't like to admit to it. It's tough when you're a mother, and you have to focus on your kids and making your partner happy. But then society also values you more if you're thin and beautiful and have lots of money. So, these women do everything they can to take care of their skin as they age, and their hair and their bodies." She let out a puff of air. "Even their god damned feet. Heaven forbid you wear sandals with toes that haven't been freshly pedicured."

Grace tapped on her keyboard as Mae spoke.

"I mean, it feels like kids need so much, and you're always getting it wrong. Don't let them have too much screen time; get them outside because that's better for them. But don't let them go outside alone, as that makes you a neglectful parent. Feed them healthy food, even if you can't really afford organic vegetables. Oh, and that cereal they really love? It's the worst possible breakfast you could feed them." She crossed an arm over her body and then continued. "Don't yell at them because that's bad, as we all know, but hey, wait—don't turn them into lazy, precious snowflakes by doting on them. When you're a mom with a kid in Riverpark, you can't admit to any of your issues, though. You have to put your face on, do your hair and keep posting shiny, happy pictures on social media, waiting for hundreds of people to admire your carefully curated life."

Grace's eyes widened again, but her voice was gentle when she spoke. "Mae. Are you sure you're okay?"

"I'm fine."

Grace reached out a hand and placed it on Mae's arm. It was warm and comforting, and when Mae looked at her friend, she saw compassion. Mae made a split decision to fill Grace in on everything. She told her about Corinne still being gone, about Leah finding Mae's notes. She talked about Evelyn and how she thought she was a kind, caring person, the opposite of the rest of them, but now she was confused because she couldn't read Evelyn anymore. In fact, everything had confused her about the women in Burlington. Eventually, she turned to talking about how the women in her neighborhood were relentlessly putting this inordinate amount of pressure on each other and it was impossible to live up to. And how it must have gotten to Alice.

"The women are all gorgeous, with expensive clothes and big cars and handsome, successful partners. Their nails are always manicured and faces always done up with makeup. They have loads of money, and they are never *not* put together. They look untouchable. And yet, under the surface, I think they feel like most women. They find life hard, but if you show it, you're cast out."

"Cast out?"

Mae mentioned her discussion with Lisa. "Maybe Alice had the same warning, and I didn't know it." She fiddled with the edge of her glass of water.

"What do you think is going on with Corinne? Do you think it's connected to what happened to Alice?"

"I don't know." Mae couldn't talk in absolutes. She had no idea. She was in the dark.

"Have you asked any of the women what they know?" Grace asked.

"No. I don't think they'd tell me much."

Grace tapped on her keyboard as Mae spoke. This was getting uncomfortable. Mae wasn't here to give specifics and names. She wanted to help other women who were suffering, but this didn't feel like the way.

"When did Alice first go missing again? And how soon after did Corinne disappear?"

"I don't know—and, uh, I'm not all that comfortable with those kinds of questions. Can we get back to the survey?" Mae tried to make her tone light.

"Oh. Sure." Grace took her hands off her keyboard and pointed them up like she had been caught. She looked down at her notes. "I'm almost done."

"Can I take a look at this before it gets published?" Mae asked. "Maybe I can add a few words of my own. You know, give it my voice." Grace knew Mae had the experience and talent. She had been writing in advertising throughout her career, but Grace, rather than agreeing, put her hands back on the keys of her laptop and kept her eyes on the screen.

"Let me see how it goes. The Editor in Chief has to review it, and she's pretty particular about the way she likes it," Grace said. "So, why do you think the women separate themselves from the men in the way they do? At the dinner parties."

"I think they prefer it that way," Mae said. "It's a choice."

"Sex segregation over dinner. It's a strange choice," Grace arched an eyebrow. Mae shrugged. She hadn't considered it as anything other than odd, but now that she thought of it, what choices did these women have? They chose some things—like what happened around Riverpark, or where they worked out and went for lunch—but how much of their lives were really in their control? What choices did Alice have?

"I think the more hierarchical the society, and the

more sex-segregated, the lower the status of women," Grace said.

Mae's chest fluttered. It was a valid point. Why hadn't she seen this before? God, what if the men were behind some of this? Behind what happened to Alice.

After they wrapped up, Mae stepped outside into the cold. She walked briskly with her coat open to let the sharpness of December air cool her hot body. It was so warm in Grace's office. Outside, along the edge of Mae's forehead where her hairline started and at the nape of her neck, tension dissolved. She ran her fingers through her hair and stopped when they got stuck on the tape of the extensions.

Fake hair. Mae shook her head. *What the hell have I been thinking?*

Chapter Thirty-Six

MAE CIRCLED THE ROOM, not knowing who to look at or what to do. Everyone at Alice's visitation was in dark clothing with sad faces gathered in groups, but she hadn't seen Alice's husband or kids yet.

In front of her was a table full of framed photos on display. Mae got closer. There were photos of Alice smiling, Alice laughing, Alice holding onto her children's small hands and grinning directly into the camera. The back of Mae's neck grew hot and sticky. Her stomach cramped. She needed to sit down. It would have been better if Drew had been there, but he stayed home with Ruby and Isla. She had come alone, and now she didn't want to be.

"Mae."

Evelyn and Leah appeared beside her. Evelyn's smooth face was white and her mouth pointed down, the little wrinkles at the sides of her lips standing out.

"I was just leaving," Mae lied.

"Wait." Evelyn hugged her arms to her body.

"What?"

"This is awful, and we all need each other right now, don't you think?"

When Mae was a kid, she thought she needed so many things—the cool jeans all her friends were wearing, the expensive shoes so she could fit in. She wanted to blend in and be accepted. It's what most kids want. Most adults, too. Mae recalled the stirring she had when they first came to Burlington; it was a flutter low in her stomach at the idea that all this could be hers. She would do even better than blend in; she would be a part of a life she would never have imagined she could be a part of.

Now, standing here, Mae didn't want it anymore. When you took away all the flashy things, Mae was still the same. Burlington didn't make her life easier or more comfortable in the way she had been certain it would.

"I'm going home," Mae said. She left the smaller room where Alice's pictures and memories were held and stood by the front doors of the building. Evelyn and Leah followed her.

"You can't just—leave." Evelyn's tone was incredulous, like she couldn't believe what Mae was saying or doing.

"Yes, I can."

"I want to talk to you," Evelyn said, emphasizing the "I" at the start of the sentence. In some ways, Mae was envious of the way Evelyn demanded whatever she wanted. She wasn't pretending right now. Leah, on the other hand, fiddled with the ends of her hair and crossed her arms over her chest, shifting her weight. It was unlike her, odd enough, in fact, to draw Mae's attention to it. This wasn't the Leah Mae knew. Mae thought of what Minjoo had said when they met for lunch—how Leah had a need for everyone to adore her, to be the most popular. Now she was meek. Mae wanted to tell her to stop fidgeting.

"But *I* don't want to talk," Mae said. "So now what?"

Evelyn's jaw clenched. When Leah looked at Mae, it was with a stony expression. Mae wondered if Leah had told Evelyn about the notebook. It didn't matter. Mae was a little dizzy at her own bravado. She couldn't remember the last time she was this honest, standing in front of them with her chin raised ever so slightly.

"I'll see you around." Mae put her hand out, searching for the door handle so she could leave the visitation, but stopped when another woman came into the building.

"Excuse me," the woman said. "Is this for Alice Christie?" She gestured to the room behind them. She was tall and thin, even under a bulky winter coat, with a long face and pin-straight hair. She was the kind of person who looked like they commanded attention when they walked into a room, but unconsciously.

Mae opened her mouth to tell the woman she was in the right place but was cut off by Evelyn.

"Tessa?" Evelyn's voice was curt. "What are you doing?"

"Excuse me," the woman said to Mae again. She brushed past Evelyn and Leah, refusing to look at them, and went into the visitation, disappearing into the room.

Mae turned back around to Evelyn and Leah, but they were already walking away, heads bent toward one another.

She wanted to follow Tessa into the visitation. She wanted to ask who she was and how she knew Alice. Tessa was the name Alice gave at the wellness center. The person Minjoo mentioned, and the name Rosie blurted out. Mae's head was swimming. She had to go in and find out more. But her phone dinged with a text message. It was her mother.

You better read this.

Chapter Thirty-Seven

LATER, sitting cross-legged on top of her bed with her computer in her lap, Mae read the headline on the screen for the third time.

This is 40: The Secret Lives of Suburban Women

Frankie had sent it to Mae, but she didn't explain what she meant by her text. Mae already scanned the headline and images on the way to her car but didn't have a chance to read it in detail until now. She took her time, studying the collage of women's faces used as a featured image to the article and spotted herself. She had sent Grace one of her favorite photos of herself—smiling and close-up, but not too close, wearing a black shirt. She looked at the other women's faces. There was a wide representation of women—different sizes, skin tones, and hair colors. A refreshing contrast to her neighborhood.

She leaned forward, craning her neck, and scrolled down to read the introduction of the article.

Our editors at Blaze *asked just under 1,000 women on*

both sides of 40 in-depth questions about love, sex, work, women's bodies, money, and ambition. We've gathered all of it together into an eye-opening synopsis as well as profiling a few of these fascinating women below.

Mae's eye scanned the next few paragraphs and studied the images. There were so many women's faces smiling at her. Confident-looking women with bright, bold lipstick and average-looking bodies. They had glasses; some had on hats; others wore scarves. They looked like regular women.

Mae stopped when she saw her face again, and this time, the photo was larger. Her first name was displayed in bold, all capital letters, and used as the heading over the top of a few paragraphs. So, she *had* been chosen as one of the profiles. Obviously, Grace didn't get the chance to send this to Mae before it was published. Mae's pulse sped up.

Mae told us about her affluent neighbourhood, where the women are hellbent on perfection. The mothers have gorgeous hair and bodies, lots of money, and well-behaved kids. Married to rich men, most of the women have no need —and no desire—to work outside the home. Instead, they toil away at what we refer to as 'intense mothering,' exhaustively enriching their children's lives by virtually every measure.

Mae's body went cold. She placed a hand down on the mattress to steady herself. Yes, she meant the things she said, and yes, she wanted to help Corinne—or anyone— but now, placed in front of her in neat font, Mae was no longer so certain this was the way to do it.

Mae herself admitted to having almost no ambition

when it comes to work outside the home, having recently quit her job. "I had a vague desire to get that corner office, but I didn't really try." Then came marriage and the house and the kids, she told us. "I let work slide. That corner office didn't seem worth it. Ambition is a young person's game." We wanted to know—is this how most women in their forties feel?

Mae ran a hand over her face, pulling on her eyelids and her cheeks as her fingers swept downward. Her words were out of context. She read further and saw that Grace had switched back to talking about the women in her neighborhood. Mae scanned phrases like *sexless marriages* and *wildly unhappy.* She described the kids as 'lazy, precious snowflakes.' Those were Mae's words, but she didn't use them that way exactly. An icy wave went through Mae's limbs and bloomed outward. She could only hope that nobody would see this. *Blaze* wasn't *The Times* by any stretch. Maybe this wouldn't get out around Riverpark.

When Mae read a little further, a phrase a few sentences down caught her eye.

The Queen Bees. The Ringleaders. Her eyes hungrily scanned the next several lines. Grace took some creative license, but it was clear who she was talking about. Evelyn and Leah. Mae remembered that she hadn't held back in the interview, and now her head was foggy and dizzy with her own recklessness.

She sat upright on her bed, reading the entire thing two more times, thinking about what she had done. What had been Mae's purpose? She could barely remember now what she had been trying to say.

She closed her laptop. She wanted to talk to Grace, but she was numb. The article was good. It was well-written and flashy and juicy. It wasn't meant to hurt Mae, but it would. She typed out a quick text and sent it to Grace.

You didn't hold back. I think I'm screwed.

Her phone buzzed a minute later.

I've been meaning to call you. My Editor in Chief wanted to go with a different angle. I tried to soften it, but she had the final review and took some creative license with it. It was so last-minute already that I didn't see it until it was too late. I'm sorry.

Mae closed her eyes for a moment, collecting herself before opening them again to respond.

It makes me and the women around here sound so terrible.

Mae waited but didn't get a response right away. After a while, a bubble appeared.

I'm really sorry! I mean it. But they're mostly your words, aren't they? I have to go. You did nothing wrong!

Mae clicked on the keypad and jabbed Corinne's number into the phone, this time trying to call instead of text. No answer. It had been weeks of no answers now. Just like with Alice. Mae put her phone back onto the bed in front of her and looked out the window. The sky was grey today, which made everything appear lonelier. She told herself she would focus on something else now, anything other than what the consequence of this was going to be.

WHEN SHE SAT in her car, Mae's eyes flicked from the road in front of her to the rear-view mirror where she could see both Ruby and Isla's faces. She picked them up after school instead of walking today, and now Isla's gaze was pointing down, studying a craft she made in school that day. Ruby was facing the window, but Mae could still see the frown on her daughter's small mouth.

"How was your day?" Mae asked.

When Isla didn't respond, Ruby shrugged. "It was okay, I guess."

The tone of her voice made Mae tense. "Just okay?"

"Yeah."

Ruby didn't offer anything else. Mae glanced in the mirror, eyes narrowed, as if that would help her to read her daughter. "How come?"

"Some kids wouldn't let me play manhunt with them."

"Why not?" Mae asked.

"They said they're not allowed to be friends with me." There was a quiver in Ruby's voice then. Mae's stomach flipped.

"What did you do? Did you find someone else to play with?"

Mae's eyes flicked to Ruby again as Ruby shook her head. "I walked around by myself."

"You did?" Mae tightened her grip on the steering wheel. "For the entire recess?"

"No. For the whole day."

Mae blinked furiously. She wouldn't let Ruby and Isla see her cry. Isla always got so worried, and Ruby would think it was her fault. They drove the rest of the way home in silence.

THEY WERE MAD AT MAE.

The Riverpark Moms sent icy glances her way, and they gave her the cold shoulder. Plus, the texts from Evelyn had completely stopped. Evelyn sent a few messages after the visitation, trying to make nice, asking Mae what was up with her, wondering if she could do anything. Even though Mae wanted to ask about Tessa, she didn't respond to Evelyn. Now there would be no coming back from the article.

Years ago, when Mae was in ninth grade, a new girl moved to the neighborhood and started at her school. Mae thought it might finally be a chance for her to make a friend before this girl heard what everyone else thought of Mae. Maybe she would see Mae for who she was.

It sort of worked. Mae and Jane sat next to one another in math, and Jane thought Mae was funny. They talked a lot, but only when they were in class. Still, Mae liked how kind Jane was. She was a talented artist and doodled a picture of a bird with its wings spread on a piece of paper one day and then handed it to Mae with a grin. Soon after that, Mae worked up the courage to ask Jane if she wanted to hang out outside of math class. Maybe they could go to the mall or watch a movie.

At least Jane had the decency to look uncomfortable when she said she couldn't. She kept saying it too, a different excuse every time, until Mae stopped asking. After the school year ended, they never really spoke again.

When Mae thought of herself back then, her face burned with the memory. The way she asked Jane repeatedly to hang out, completely oblivious to the cues Jane was giving her. Jane had nothing in common with Mae except for when they were in math. Outside, in the hallway, Jane was popular and well-liked.

For years, Mae would think of that doodled bird, broad wings, in flight. Free. Mae wanted that feeling so desperately, and here in Burlington, she felt like she could have it for a short period of time. She thought Evelyn might make up for what Mae had missed, but maybe Evelyn had been more like Jane all along. Mae hadn't seen it.

Mae thought of the bird as she stood alone in the schoolyard, desperately wishing she could feel that freedom. The wind in her hair, the gentle air gliding over her body. Mae knew she had made the right decision to talk to Grace, to tell the story and hopefully help someone else who might need it, but she also realized that she had clipped her own wings. And now it appeared she had clipped her daughters' wings by association.

Chapter Thirty-Eight

HER DREAMS that night were of Evelyn and Leah. It felt so real, the way they stood, the way they reached out for her and held down her arms so she couldn't move. Mae couldn't have done anything if she wanted to, as the muscles in her body wouldn't let her move no matter how hard she tried. After she woke up, Mae could still smell them, the earthy scent of essential oils that Evelyn sometimes gave off, Leah's shampoo. It took her a while to realize that none of it was real.

Over the next few days, Mae went through the motions, but she didn't feel grounded. She didn't know if she should try and find out more about Tessa or leave it alone. She didn't know how to get a hold of Corinne and, for some reason, felt like she was running out of time.

On the morning of the last day of school before the Christmas holidays, Drew called her from work as Mae was making the bed. His voice was strangely low but steady.

"What's going on?" Mae asked.

"I'm being let go."

She stiffened and then lowered herself onto the edge of the bed. "What? What's the reason?"

"They no longer have the need for my position. Too many managers, they said." His tone was even, but it sounded distant to Mae. Far too distant for this kind of a problem.

"Right before Christmas?" That didn't seem right. "But what about your promotion?" Mae asked. Right after she said it, she realized it was a dumb question.

"It's gone. Everything's gone."

"Where are you?"

"On my way home," Drew said. "I'll be there soon. You'll be home, right?"

"Yes. Of course." They hung up, and Mae set her phone down on the night table. Her mind raced. What the hell would they do now with no income? Could she get another advertising job? Could Drew find something fast enough? They had savings they could dip into, but Drew didn't like to touch them. He was always so worried they would need the money one day and it wouldn't be there.

When Mae was a kid, there were so many whispered conversations between her parents when they thought she couldn't hear. It was always about the bills, about the clothes she needed, the food. The heavy creases on their foreheads and the frown lines around their mouths seemed permanent then, a constant reminder of the burden Mae put on her parents. She would never let Ruby or Isla know anything was wrong.

Mae stood and went back to making the bed. She

thought of Evan telling Drew he was no longer needed. A protective jab pierced through her. Evelyn and Mae hadn't talked since the article had come out. Mae stopped pulling at the bedsheet. It couldn't be a coincidence, could it? A knot formed deep in her stomach.

LATER, after Drew came home, they sat together on the couch, facing one another. Mae kept her hand on Drew's leg as she spoke with a surprisingly calm voice.

"Are you okay?"

Drew shook his head. "I don't know. I guess?"

"What happened?" Inside, Mae already knew. It had to be her fault.

"I don't know. Everything was fine, until—it wasn't. They said there was no need for my role, but I had been doing great. I was the frontrunner for that promotion."

Now it was all gone. Everything Drew wanted—over. Mae was dizzy.

"I think we should sell the house," Drew said. "This place isn't right. We can find something smaller. Maybe we should go back to Montréal?"

Mae straightened in her seat. "What? I don't know. Let's not make any hasty decisions. We don't have to tell anyone about it yet. Let's take the time over the holidays to think about this." At least everything for Christmas was already planned and paid for.

"There's not much to think about. You said yourself that shit is getting weird here."

He was right. Things had been weird since they first

got here, but could they find a cheaper house in Montréal? Could Drew even get another job there?

"Let's look at our finances and figure this out for the short term before we make any drastic decisions," Mae said.

Drew agreed, but he didn't seem convinced.

Chapter Thirty-Nine

MAE WENT to the coffee shop and ordered a regular coffee instead of the expensive latte she would normally buy. She needed a minute alone to think, and Drew was busy looking at their expenses and savings. When she went to get a seat, she scanned the room and saw it was fairly full, with people sitting and chatting, sipping coffees. One of them was Jeff.

The skin under his eyes was faintly purple today, his face covered with a mask of stubble. He was well dressed though, in dark jeans and a fitted sweater. Mae was worried she might see Leah with him, but he was alone. She took her seat and lowered her head, busying herself with her phone and hoping he wouldn't notice her.

No luck. She could see out of her peripheral vision that he was approaching.

"Hey, Mae," Jeff said. His smile seemed forced.

"Hey," Mae said. The polite thing would be to make conversation with him now, but she wasn't in the mood.

"Look, I won't bother you, but I'm actually glad I ran into you. I had a feeling I might find you here one of these days."

Mae arched an eyebrow. "You did?"

"I've been meaning to give you something." Jeff fumbled in his back pocket. He pulled out his wallet and retrieved a worn, folded piece of newspaper. He placed it on the table.

Mae looked up at him and tilted her head. Jeff frowned and glanced around the shop.

"I have to go." He left without giving Mae a chance to ask any questions.

Mae opened the newspaper and smoothed her palm over the top of it onto the table in front of her. It was a clipping from three years ago in the *Burlington Free Press*.

A YOUNG GIRL *has drowned in Kettle Creek in south Burlington. Police said the victim was a nine-year-old from the community. They were called to the area at 4:30 p.m. on Wednesday after a group of about six kids had been gathering at the creek earlier in the day.*

"One female child was located and pronounced deceased at the scene," police said in a release. "It is a tragic circumstance, and our thoughts are with the family and community regarding all the kids that are involved."

MAE READ it twice and then folded it up and put it into her pocket. It made no sense. Especially coming from Jeff. She wished she had his number so she could call him and ask what it was all about, but she didn't, so she sat there and read the article over again.

Our thoughts are with the family and community regarding all the kids involved.

Mae shivered.

BACK AT HOME, Mae opened her laptop and searched drownings in Burlington from three years ago. She scanned the headlines and clicked on one that appeared to be what she was looking for.

THE DEATH of nine-year-old Sarah Neele has been ruled a drowning, and there were no signs of foul play.

Her mother, Tessa Neele, and friends gathered at the edge of the creek to grieve. Sarah Neele's brother, Riley, shed tears as he stood with close friends who were all mourning the terrible loss.

"She's beautiful on the inside and out. She's very caring and loving," Tessa said before collapsing at the scene. She had to be helped away.

MAE STOPPED READING, stunned by the words on her screen. She tried connecting the dots but couldn't understand what Jeff had to do with this or why he would give her a hint. She put her head in her hands. Then she sat back, her fingers quivering as she tried once more to call someone who might know.

Answer, Corinne. Please answer.

"Hello?" Corinne's voice on the other end was like a tiny bloom of hope, despite its dull tone.

"Corinne?" Mae gasped. "Corinne, where are you? Are you okay?"

"I'm not allowed to use my phone much," Corinne said.

"Are you okay?" Mae repeated.

"Kind of. I'm at a place called The Ranch. It's a mental health treatment center. They have me working on a farm and getting therapy."

"A farm?"

"I know. It sounds weird, but I'm doing okay. I would have returned your calls earlier, but I haven't been given much access to my old life."

Mae had so many questions, but they were stuck in her throat.

"Can I see you?"

"I'm allowed visitors this weekend for the holidays," Corinne said. "I know it's a busy time, though."

"No," Mae said quickly. "It's okay. I can make time for a visit."

"My family's coming Sunday. You could come on Saturday?"

"Okay, yes. I'll be there."

"Mae?" Corinne said before hanging up. "Come alone."

Chapter Forty

MAE DROVE DOWN A WINDING, tree-lined road covered with snow. A small wooden sign had been nailed to a thick stump just ahead of her. *The Ranch This Way*, it said. And, *Private*.

At the entrance was a canopy of pine trees, and beyond that was a piece of land with a big red house in the middle of the open yard. Picnic tables sat out front and people in coats and hats with work gloves and wheelbarrows walked back and forth, stopping to chat with the others sitting at the tables.

Mae thought it looked like a little compound. It wasn't at all what she expected. She thought she would find pale faces and slow bodies—not healthy, ruddy people. They all looked so energetic. Evelyn had described Alice and Corinne as broken, but this wasn't what broken people looked like. She picked up her phone from the passenger seat to check directions again. Did she have the right place? When she glanced up, Corinne exited the front door of the red house, appearing as if on cue. She took a seat at one of the picnic tables alone.

Her hair was tied back loosely at the nape of her neck. She had on clothes that were much more casual than she usually wore, and yet, they still gave off an air of money. They were the kind of jogging pants that were made of expensive material and tailored in all the right spots to be cute and flattering at the same time. Her ski jacket fit her perfectly. She put her hands in front of her mouth and blew into them, then shoved them into her pockets.

Mae parked and got out of the car, pulled a hat on her head, and raised a hand when Corinne glanced in her direction. Corinne's smile was so faint Mae couldn't see the flash of brilliant white teeth she was used to.

"Hi," Mae said as she approached the picnic table.

Corinne didn't stand up. "Sit," she said. "It's good to see you."

Mae sat across from her and looked down at her hands, a rush of awkwardness settling over her. Now what? She hadn't come with much of a plan.

"How have you been?" Mae asked, and then swallowed, embarrassed. Bad question to start with.

"I've been better." Corinne looked around her and then leaned in slightly, as if someone was listening to her speak. "This place is great but exhausting. I think that's how they keep you healthy. You're too damn tired to have dark thoughts."

Mae tried to smile, but it felt inappropriate. "I was worried about you. What happened? How did you get here?"

Corinne looked like she was considering the question,

as if she was wondering how any of themgot here. "I was getting stressed out and upset over everything, all the time. At the kids, at my husband. It wasn't fair to them; they didn't do anything." She placed the edge of her forearms on top of the picnic table and squinted into the wind. "I found out about Alice."

Mae froze. Her heart sped up. "What do you mean? About her—" She couldn't bring herself to say it.

Corinne lowered her head. "I already knew she was found dead." Her voice was choked, and a tear edged the outside of her eye. She wiped it away. "I found out what happened before that. I thought it was all so weird that Alice went missing, and almost nobody was concerned. I had my suspicions, so I went to talk to Leah."

"I wish we had talked about it."

Corinne nodded. She closed her eyes and took a deep breath in.

"What did you say?" Mae asked.

"I told Leah I knew about Alice, about how her mental health was teetering on the edge of breaking, but I couldn't find Alice anywhere. I wanted to ask her how I could help."

Mae shifted in her seat. "And what did Leah say?"

"She tried to play dumb. Like she had no idea what was going on, but I could see it was an act. Her indifference scared me. She was trying to pretend it was nothing. I started thinking Leah had a bigger role in everything."

Mae nodded, taking it all in. "What did you actually find out about Alice?"

"Nothing completely concrete, unfortunately. But I think Alice knew something about Leah, and I think Leah wanted to keep her quiet. The next thing I heard, Alice was missing. And now ..." Corinne shook her head. "She was weighed down by whatever it was, I guess. She couldn't see a way out. It's all so confusing, but it's really frightened me."

Corinne was right; there were still so many holes and gaps. It was impossible to make sense of.

"I'm sure Leah is somehow involved," Corinne continued. "I'm still trying to figure that out, but I had to protect myself and my family in the meantime. So, I came here without telling anyone at first. I needed to be alone."

A chill ran down the middle of Mae's back, and she pulled her coat tighter around her. She told Corinne about talking to Grace and the article, and about Drew losing his job. There were so many little coincidences. Her mind went to the visitation and Jeff.

"What do you know about Tessa Neele?" Mae asked.

Corinne shifted in her seat. Her head tilted to one side. "She used to live in the neighborhood. Her kids went to Riverpark. I didn't know her really, just that there was a horrible accident with her daughter. She moved away after that. Why?"

"She came to Alice's visitation, but I didn't get a chance to talk to her. Alice used the name Tessa Neele to check into the wellness center she was at. Why would she do that? And a few days ago, Jeff gave me this." She took out the clipping and showed Corinne. "I can't understand the connection. Alice and Tessa. Tessa's daughter."

It was all so tragic and awful, but none of it lined up for Mae.

Corinne read it and then shrugged. "I don't know. It

doesn't make sense to me either. I guess she was back because she knew Alice?"

A woman came to the table and put a hand on Corinne's shoulder. She had a bouncy bob and wore a flashy Christmas sweater with a reindeer on the front. Her voice was calm and soothing. "Corinne, you need to report to Farm Crew soon."

Corinne nodded, but her gaze was still focused on Mae. The woman stayed there, hand on Corinne's shoulder, frozen in place, looking down at Corinne with that same smile across her face. Mae shivered.

Corinne looked up. "Okay. I'll be there."

The woman's smile only faltered for a moment before she turned and left, her hair bouncing as she walked.

"They like to pretend they're all earthy and granola, but they're strict as hell here," Corinne said quietly.

"I saw the text message between you and Leah," Mae said. "Leah said you knew what you had done."

Corinne closed her eyes briefly and sighed before speaking. "It was one of Leah's scare tactics. I guess it worked."

Mae ran a hand through the tips of her hair. She pulled a handful of it over her shoulder and fiddled with the ends. "Do you think she did that to Alice?"

"I think she did something," Corinne said. "And I think she wants to keep it quiet. I want to know the truth, but I have to protect myself and my kids, too."

It was still a little mild for December, but Mae zipped her coat all the way up to under her chin and shoved her hands into her pockets for warmth.

"Are you going to be okay?" Corinne leaned in and touched the side of Mae's shoulder.

Mae shook her head. She still had trouble putting it into words. "I don't understand the women in Burlington."

Corinne placed her crossed arms on top of the table in front of her. "I know, same with me, but I've had a lot of time to think. I've realized they're lonely, insecure, unhappy women. They'll never admit that to anyone, though."

Mae's jaw clenched. "Are you going to come back home soon?" She couldn't imagine returning to the Riverpark schoolyard alone, unable to trust anyone and having no allies around her.

"No. I went over in my head a million times what I had done wrong, but eventually, I realized it's not me. It's all them, and I'm not ready to come back to that. I miss my kids and my husband, but I need some time." She looked at Mae. "I want to help. I want to figure this out, but I'm scared about what might happen. I don't want to lose everything." Corinne's voice was edging on erratic, her eyes flashing.

"Hey—it's okay," Mae said.

"I lost my family once," Corinne explained. "Growing up, my brother got into drugs and fell apart. My parents were absent after that. Everything just came undone. I need to keep my family together now. I need to do whatever I have to do."

"Of course," Mae said.

Corinne stood up. She smoothed down the front of her jogging pants and rolled her shoulders like she could shrug off her past. "Come with me for a second."

They walked around the grounds, past the main house and toward an old barn. Behind it was a view of the most stunning rolling hill, filled with snow-covered evergreen treetops that went on and on as far as Mae could see. A path wound around the grounds, dotted with buildings. Some were rickety-looking little shacks that looked like they had been there forever. Others were rustic but homey.

"It's beautiful here," Mae said.

Corinne nodded. "I love how simple it is."

Mae saw a group of three women with a bucket heading into a doorway that had a sign that said *Repairs* over the top.

"When I first got here, they told me that their core belief is that recovery can only begin in a community. Everyone has to do their part, and everyone is respected." She put her hands into her pockets and smiled. "I like that."

"Sounds like summer camp," Mae said.

"I guess it kind of is. Except work is the main thing here. It's the primary medium of therapy. Each week, we choose between work in the woods, farm, shop, or gardens." They resumed walking again, and Corinne pointed out the different spots as she told Mae about them. "In the woods, you're expected to chop down trees, split wood, build rock walls, and make maple syrup. When you're in barn you take care of all the animals: chickens, pigs, sheep, goats, turkeys, llamas. Shop crew builds furniture, and there's also a full-service auto repair shop. In the garden, you're busy planting, harvesting, and making pesto to sell at the local Farmer's Market in the summer."

"Wow. That's a lot."

"Five days a week. All day." Corinne nodded sharply. "Can you believe anyone from Riverpark is doing that kind of stuff?"

Mae laughed. They came to a stop and sat on a bench situated along the path.

"The thing is, everyone here learns to care for something that's bigger than themselves. The therapists tell us that goes a long way in caring about yourself." She placed her hands on her lap and pointed her face up to the sun. "I can see it. I mean, I've made friends here already, and I can feel my walls coming down, you know? I have a hard time trusting people, but I'm working on it. It's easier here."

"That's great," Mae said. She was struck by how sad and hopeful that was at the same time.

Corinne turned to face forward like she was thinking. The sun was peeking through the trees in front of them, creating lines of shadows and illuminating the ground.

"I have to tell you something." Corinne paused for a beat. "I sent you that anonymous note."

"You did?" A jolt of shock went through Mae. "Why didn't you just call me?"

"I was getting more and more nervous at the time, and I didn't want Leah to find out. I didn't want to risk them knowing, but I wanted to warn you." She turned her head. "I never imagined it was going to go that far with Alice."

They sat in silence. Mae tried to digest everything. They hadn't spoken this way before, with such honesty.

"I didn't know anything," Mae said finally. "How could I have not noticed?"

"Women like Leah are very good about masking who they are. It's easy to miss when you're mixed up with them. You need to find your community, Mae. The people willing to do the work with you. Focus on them."

Mae glanced over in time to see a glimmer of light illuminate the top of Corinne's head, shimmering through her hair and on the edge of her cheek.

"Let me know what you find out about Leah," Corinne said. "And be careful, okay?"

Chapter Forty-One

In the dark of the evening, after the girls had gone to bed, Drew came into the living room where Mae was sitting. She flicked through the TV with a glass of wine, looking at the screen but not seeing a thing. Her head was too far away.

For days, Mae wavered between wanting to forget what was going on and needing to know more. She wanted to be a good human being and find details about Alice, but she also wanted to just be Mae. Wife, mother of two. Who else was she now? When you got to a certain age, Mae noticed, you crossed over from defining yourself by what you like to do (I play soccer, I like to draw, I'm outdoorsy) to defining yourself by what you have to do and the people around you (I'm a lawyer, I'm a journalist, a mother, a wife).

When Mae was growing up, she heard her mother talk about this endlessly—knowing who you were as a woman.

You had to know who you were to know what you wanted and how to get it. Mae came from a long line of women who were strong, sure of themselves, and wanted the best. It mattered so much to Mae's mother that Mae have more than she had, and after having kids, Mae understood. As a parent, you work so hard to try and give your family the best; you want the most for your kids, and you want them to aim higher and have it all. Mae was so certain she had made the right choices. That was how she ended up here. Although now, with things going the way they had with Alice and Evelyn and Corinne, Mae wasn't sure of anything. Did she make the right choices? It was impossible to know.

"Ready for visitors tomorrow?" Drew asked, standing in front of her now.

"I guess." Everything was ready for Christmas, at least.

There was a pause while Drew's eyes remained on her. He looked at the television.

"What are you watching?"

"Nothing."

He tilted his head and raised his eyebrows.

"What?" Mae said.

"I'm concerned about you."

Mae put her wine glass to her lips and took a long sip. "I'm fine," she said after.

"Are you?"

"What's that supposed to mean?"

"I found this." Drew held something up in his hand. Her notebook.

"That's personal!" Mae snapped. She went to stand

and grab it but stopped herself. What was the point? He probably read it all, and there was nothing secret in there. It was just the facts.

"Why are you keeping notes about Alice?"

"Because I want to do something. I need to help somehow," Mae said.

Drew sat beside her on the couch and handed it to her. "I know I've been preoccupied with finding a job, and it's been busy with holiday plans, but I want to know what's going on. You can talk to me."

"I've been thinking. Maybe you were right," Mae said. "Maybe we should move."

Drew was silent for a long time. "I thought we agreed not to make any hasty decisions."

"I don't know what to think anymore." Mae's voice was rising. It came over her like a wave. She was irritated at everything, but mostly at her indecision. One moment, she had everything she ever wanted, the next, she wasn't sure of anything.

"Let's sleep on it," he said. "But you're right. Maybe we should go home."

Home. It was such an odd concept now to Mae. She hadn't felt at home anywhere for most of her life.

She slumped, her shoulders rounding in on her body. When she started to cry, heavy, deep sobs, she realized it was the first time she had cried like this since Alice died.

Drew grasped for her hand, one of his arms wrapping her body into a tight hug.

"It's okay," he said. "We'll figure this out together."

She didn't believe him that it would be that easy, but

she let herself come apart then, like a million little pieces of her body releasing themselves out into the air until she was weightless and felt nothing.

Chapter Forty-Two

It was good to have family around. Her parents and Drew's family came for Christmas dinner, and Mae let herself be preoccupied with cooking and presents and conversation over too much food. She didn't bring up Alice, Drew's job, or anything else heavy. It was a nice breather.

A few days after the hubbub had died down, Mae woke one morning and showered, got dressed, and had a cup of coffee like she always did. After running a few errands alone, Mae sat in her car and searched for publishing companies. Her eyes locked on what she needed.

The drive was short, thanks to light traffic. Mae parked on the street in front of the tall, grey building. It had a bright red sign at the entrance and was covered with windows. She made her way to reception and paused at the front desk only briefly before telling them who she was hoping to see. On the way here, she hadn't considered the fact that Jeff might not be in so soon after Christmas. He might not even see her. She pushed the thought away. Determination brought her this far. She wasn't going to crumple and fall apart now.

Jeff appeared a few minutes later. He wasn't smiling.

"Come with me," he said. Mae followed him wordlessly to a big office with giant windows and a tidy desk. "Have a seat." He gestured at the small couch and took a seat on a large chair.

"How were your holidays?" Jeff asked.

"Good, thanks. And yours?"

He nodded.

"I might as well cut to the chase," Mae said. Her determination wavered only for a minute before it came back again when Jeff's face softened. "I want to know what's going on. The truth. Why did you tell me about Tessa? Why did you give me that hint to lead me to her story?"

Jeff's head dropped. He pinched the area between his eyebrows. "I knew you would come and ask. I'm not surprised by the fact that you're here now. It's just that this is—it's hard to talk about."

Mae waited. She scrunched her fingers into a ball on her lap.

"Tessa used to live in Burlington, in the neighborhood. Her kids went to Riverpark. She was very—" he searched for the right word. "Outgoing." He shifted in his seat.

Whatever that meant wasn't especially clear. She watched Jeff sighing and shifting in his seat and waited for him to continue.

"She didn't fit the mold, I guess you could say. She was

so different from the rest of the women. A lot of people really liked her. Some more than others."

"I don't understand," Mae said.

"She moved to town a single mother, and she stood out from day one. She was different, so confident, and she didn't fall in line or follow along with the rest of the women here. She did things her way. A lot of people found that really ... interesting. Some of the husbands, too. There was one in particular who took an interest in her."

"Who?"

Jeff pursed his mouth and studied Mae as if he wasn't sure if he should continue. "Evan."

Her breath hitched. "What? They had an affair?"

Jeff shook his head. "No. He wanted to, but Tessa wasn't interested. It didn't really matter though. Once Tessa went to Evelyn and threatened to tell everyone if he didn't leave her alone, it got ugly."

"I still don't understand what any of this has to do with the story or why you told me," Mae said. She thought of the newspaper clipping. *A child was pronounced deceased at the scene. Our thoughts are with the family and community regarding all the kids that are involved.*

"Some really awful stuff happened. A few of the women targeted Tessa. They sent her threatening notes, followed her around town watching her, they trashed the inside of her car. Then the rumours about her started." Jeff ran his hand over his chin, his frown growing deeper.

"And nobody did anything? Everyone let it happen?"

He shook his head. "It went too far. Way too far. The kids at school knew something was going on, and they all started taking sides. A few of them were bullying Tessa's daughter on a regular basis. The principal and a bunch of parents tried to stop it." His voice trailed off.

"But?" Mae said.

"There was a horrible accident."

"The drowning?"

Jeff nodded, his face grey. "A bunch of kids followed Tessa's daughter down to the creek and taunted her. Someone pushed her, and then they left, but they had no idea. They couldn't have known she wouldn't be able to get out. They would never." His voice broke. "They were kids. It was an accident."

A chill went through Mae from the top of her head down to her toes. It didn't sound like an accident. When Ruby was little, she fell into a swimming pool once. Mae was right there; she jumped in and grabbed Ruby before anything could happen. But that feeling, the sheer terror that ripped through Mae in the split second that Ruby was underwater, the whiff of death, even the mere hint that something could take Ruby away from Mae was enough to terrify her. She couldn't begin to imagine how Tessa could cope.

"What happened after?" Mae said.

"Tessa couldn't recover." Jeff rubbed his hand over the back of his neck, scratching. "The parents around here tried to cover it all up, wash it away. Evan even tried paying Tessa off to disappear and stay quiet. I don't know what happened exactly, but she and her son moved. We never heard from them again."

Mae's mind flashed with the envelope full of money for Alice.

"Why are you telling me all this? I still don't get it."

"Leah was kind of involved."

Mae's limbs tingled. Corinne was right.

"She had a role, but she wasn't the one orchestrating it all," Jeff said quickly, as if he felt the need to keep explaining.

"Who was?"

"It was always all Evelyn. That's why Evan tried to keep Tessa quiet."

Mae took a deep breath in. Her ribs hurt.

"The thing is, I know Leah's not that kind of a person. I know she regrets everything, but I'm not sure Evelyn does," Jeff continued.

"Then why didn't Leah do something about it?" Mae asked. This was why she had come here, she needed answers, but she still didn't know what was true and what wasn't.

Jeff looked directly at Mae. "Why do *you* let them act the way they do and keep going back for more?"

Mae flinched. It hadn't been put so bluntly for her before. "You can't compare me with what they did. I've never even come close."

Jeff nodded and waved his hand at her. "I know. I know."

They sat in silence for a while, Mae's mind turning and turning.

"The truth is, I don't know why Leah allows some things to happen; I don't know why she needs these friends, but I know she's scared of being alone, of not being liked. I also know she's a good person."

Mae's eyebrows raised.

"She is," he said firmly in response. "You don't know

her well enough yet. She's a good person," he repeated. "But I'm not blind. I can see she needs validation. She has some issues she needs to work out."

"Wait." Mae shook her head. This still wasn't making sense to her. It was so much to take in. "Why would Alice use Tessa's name at the wellness center?"

Jeff paused and took a breath in. "She knew about Tessa and Evan and what happened at the creek."

"Everyone did. It was in the paper."

"She knew one other thing that only a few of us knew." He looked down, pain in his expression as clear as day.

"What?"

"Evelyn convinced her kids to target Tessa's daughter. She told them lies to make it seem like Tessa and her daughter were bad people, that they were mean and dangerous. She started it all, and that never came out in the reports. It's been covered up."

Mae's vision narrowed, her peripheral vision going dark. She stood and stumbled, falling back down into her seat again. "How can you live with yourself?" she said. Alice mustn't have been able to.

Jeff's face fell.

"Why did you tip me off? Why involve me?" Mae asked.

"I wanted to warn you. You seem like a good person, Mae."

"Why would you need to *warn* me?"

"Because," Jeff said. "You're the next target."

Chapter Forty-Three

ON THE WAY back from Jeff's office, Mae called Drew first to fill him in on everything, and then she called Corinne, hoping to catch her on a day when she was allowed to use her phone. When Corinne picked up, Mae breathed out deeply, trying to steady her voice. She explained what had just happened with Jeff and everything she had learned.

"Wow," Corinne said. "It's Evelyn, not Leah?"

"Seems like it," Mae said. "He said I'm next." Her entire body was weak, her limbs shaky.

"What does that mean?" Corinne asked.

Mae stopped at a red light. "He said Evelyn likes to be in control, and I was too much like Tessa in some ways. Tessa didn't go along with what the rest of the Riverpark Moms wanted." Mae thought about her own actions. She wasn't proud of how long it took her to see the truth.

"What are you going to do now?"

"I'm going to tell the cops everything I know about the cover-up."

"Hasn't it been too long?" Corinne asked. "Can they even do anything about it?"

Mae hadn't thought about that. She frowned. "At the very least, I can get a restraining order. I have to do something. I have to protect my kids, and Evelyn needs to be stopped."

"She does," Corinne agreed. "What about Leah?"

"I don't know about her yet," Mae said. "She might be okay."

"What?" Corinne's voice was riddled with disbelief. "They're all the same, Mae. You should distance yourself as much as you can from Leah. Forget second chances."

Mae said nothing, but part of her agreed with Corinne. The things the women did here were not what regular, good people did. As she sat waiting for the light to change, Mae saw around her for what felt like the first time: the clumps of mud edging the sidewalk, the dead brown grass next to it, the pieces of garbage littering the boulevards here and there. This area was supposed to be perfect, but it was ugly when you looked close enough.

"I wish you could be here with me. I've got nobody I can trust," Mae said.

"I'd like to be there for you, but to be honest, Mae, I don't know if I have it in me. I'm so worn out. I have to think about my family."

Mae told Corinne she understood and hung up. Then she drove home as fast as she safely could to see Drew.

DREW WAS IN THE KITCHEN, chopping and slicing vegetables for dinner. He put the knife down and wiped his hands on the tea towel next to him as soon as she appeared in the doorway.

"Let's call the police," he said. "And then let's call a real estate agent. We've got to get out of this place."

"Who do you know in real estate around here?" Mae's mind was already flooded with details. How quickly could they sell? What would it take to expedite the closing time?

Drew shook his head as he resumed chopping, only this time in an erratic, rushed way. He scraped bell peppers from the cutting board into a bowl with the edge of his knife. "I don't know. I can ask around."

"Drew. Be careful." Mae gestured at the knife. He was so wound up. "Who would you ask?"

She stood on the other side of the counter from him, her palms down on the cool surface. They should be careful about everything now. They shouldn't talk to just anyone and risk having the wrong person find out they were planning to get the hell out of there.

Mae glanced at Ruby and Isla in the living room, relaxing on the couch. When she was searching for something in town soon after they first arrived here, Mae googled Burlington and discovered there were twenty-nine places named Burlington in the United States. It struck her that this place, the town she was living in, wasn't so unique. She had no idea what the other Burlingtons looked like or what kind of schools and parks and restaurants they had, but she was certain that no matter where you lived, these women and problems were anywhere and everywhere.

A small seed of doubt sprouted in Mae. Maybe wanting to leave so quickly was rash. If Mae could help the next person who would inevitably be on Evelyn's list, or whoever else had a list in this messed up town, maybe she should at least try before running. The responsibility nagged at her.

"I'll find someone to ask," Drew said. "The point is, we need to leave."

"I know. You're right."

Drew looked up from breaking up the lettuce. His brow was furrowed. "Why do I feel a 'but' coming?"

Mae needed to think. She needed to figure out how to approach it before bringing it up to Drew. "No, but," she said. Not yet, anyway.

Her phone vibrated on the counter. She picked it up.

Where are you? We need to talk.

It was Evelyn.

Mae could see that what she had been trying all along wasn't going to work. No, blending in and making nice was all wrong. Mae needed to stand out now. In fact, she wanted to stand out, and she finally had the nerve to do it. She picked up her phone and typed back.

We have nothing to talk about. Leave me the hell alone.

Chapter Forty-Four

In the car the next day, Mae was focused on taking Ruby to a movie. Her children needed normalcy, they needed her, and that was where her attention had to be until she could figure out exactly what to do. Isla didn't want to come, so she stayed at home with Drew, slouched into a ball on the couch, reading one of the many new books she got for Christmas.

When Mae glanced in the rear-view mirror, she could see wisps of Ruby's hair around her temples—the kind that refused to be tamed into a ponytail. Ruby was looking out the window, quieter than usual today.

As Mae moved out of the driveway, a light on the dashboard flashed at her. She would have to tell Drew about it after the movie. If they didn't leave now, they'd miss it. When her phone buzzed with a notification, Mae's eyes flicked down to where it sat in the center console. She should have put it away in her purse, but it became second nature to have it within reach at all times. A text message flashed across her screen and then disappeared again. Mae caught sight of Evelyn's name. She leaned over and pressed her finger on the round button on the front of her phone to make the screen light up again.

Leah wants to talk with you.

Mae's eyes snapped back up. Her pulse sped up. Anger started bubbling, simmering up underneath the surface of her skin, swirling in her chest, but the anger was directed at herself.

She had given Evelyn so much power—and all the Riverpark Moms—and for what? They didn't care. The truth was, they didn't care about Mae at all. Suddenly Mae couldn't understand why she had allowed them to make her feel any of the things she felt around them—less than, not enough, even the good feelings she had.

Mae wondered what life would have been like if they had never come here. She might still be living in a starter home, taking a commuter train to a day job, living a simple life. It was plain, but she wouldn't have had to worry about lies and rumours and getting caught up in dangerous secrets. What the hell had she gotten herself into?

She looked down at her phone as it lit up again with a few more words.

Leah wants to talk with you. I shouldn't even be warning you but—

Mae ignored it. She pressed on the brake as the car rolled down the hill her house sat on top of, but something was different. The car kept going. Mae looked down at her foot and then back up at the road again, instinctively pumping on the brakes, but nothing happened.

"What the hell?" She frantically jammed her foot

down, over and over, while the car picked up, faster and faster, hurdling forward.

"Mommy?" Ruby's voice came from the back seat, laced with confusion and fear. Mae's eyes snapped from her foot to the road in front of her. They were going faster now. She couldn't stop it. Her breath hitched. What could she do?

She pushed her foot down harder, pressing it to the floor, desperate to stop and not understanding what was happening until it was too late. The other car was coming straight at her from the right. It was only when they had smashed into her, and Mae's car went careening around in a circle, that Mae caught sight of the tree now in front of her.

The crunch of metal, the sensation of spinning, of being whipped around, the disorientation. It was only a few seconds, but it felt like much longer. When they stopped moving, the silence in the car sent a lurch of fear up through Mae's body and into her throat. There was a searing pain in her legs. Her head throbbed.

Ruby.

"Ruby!" Her name came out of Mae's mouth in a choked breath. Mae struggled to turn her body around, frantically straining against her seatbelt to see her daughter. But she couldn't.

She couldn't see anything at all because everything went black.

Chapter Forty-Five

When Mae woke up, she was in a strange, stiff bed. Her body hurt when she tried to move. Every muscle, her skin, her eyelids. There was a beeping noise and shuffling of feet. Mae looked around. She was in a small room with a big window overlooking the water. Outside, it was raining and dreary.

"Mae? Do you know where you are?" An unrecognizable voice. "You're at the hospital. You were in a car accident."

Mae looked up at a woman in a long, white coat. She was standing over Mae, jotting down notes on a clipboard. She placed a hand on Mae's leg, a soft touch. Mae shook her head frantically when everything started to come back. She ignored the pain in her throat, croaking out a word.

"Ruby!"

"Your daughter's stable. She's on another floor. Your husband is with her."

There were machines hooked up to Mae's body and an

IV needle in her hand. She looked down and saw dried blood crusted and caked into her nail beds.

"Stable? What happened? Why aren't I with my daughter? I want to see Ruby. I need to see her now!"

"You will, I promise. You've been in a serious accident, Mae. You need to be careful."

Mae tried to move, but the aching stopped her. It was everywhere, dull and constant. Her head hurt. "What do you mean stable?"

The doctor frowned and placed a hand on Mae's leg again.

"She's very resilient, but your daughter is going to need time to recover. So will you."

Mae winced and then heaved her body to the side of the bed so she could throw up.

What have I done?

After a while, the doctor spoke in a gentle voice. "Rest, okay? You're going to need it. We'll take you to see Ruby as soon as we can." She left the room, indicating to a nurse that they needed a mop and fresh sheets in there.

It was visceral, the need Mae had to be with Ruby, to hold her soft body and smell her familiar little-kid scent. Lavender shampoo and fresh air. Mae was sick and distraught, and the doctor didn't seem to understand. There was no way she could rest.

DREW CAME BY. It could have been a few hours later, but Mae wasn't able to tell. Her head was foggy from the pain medication.

"Mae," Drew whispered. He leaned forward and kissed her gently, resting his forehead on hers. His face was pale except for the purple bags under his eyes.

"Thank God. Mae." He said her name again like he needed to hear it.

"How is she? Is Ruby okay?" Mae asked. She could remember now. Bits of the accident were coming back to her. Ruby had looked so tiny in the back seat. She was sitting in a booster seat; Mae had insisted Ruby stay in it until she was taller, but she looked so small to Mae. It was only a flash of a memory, but Mae could see Ruby then, her shoulders up by her ears, her arms stiff and straight as her palms sat on the armrests of the booster seat. Her eyes were wild when they looked at Mae. A single thread of blood had been trickling from the top of her head down the side of her face.

"She'll be okay," Drew said. "She just needs a bit of time."

"Why can't I see her?" Mae was growing frantic.

"You will, but you're both going to have to stay overnight. Maybe a couple of days to recover."

"Where's Isla?"

"At home with your mom. I didn't know what to expect, so I didn't bring her."

Mae's heart seized in her chest. "I want to get out of here."

A nurse came in then, swiftly checking over Mae's chart, changed the IV bag, and smiled at Drew and Mae.

"The doctor has you scheduled to go for some scans, and then we've got to check them out. It'll be a while yet." She smiled again before leaving the room.

"I'm so glad you're okay," Drew said. He looked at her for a long time with red, watery eyes. "You scared us. What happened?"

She could remember more now. The hill, the other car, the screech of the tires. And her phone. She was looking at her stupid phone, trying to read the text about Leah. Mae felt sick again. The embarrassment was thick as mud. These women had too much power.

But—the brakes. She remembered the brakes now. The way she jammed her foot down so many times, and nothing. They hadn't been working. It all happened too fast for her to think about it, but she distinctly recalled how useless it was when she tried to stop.

"My brakes. I think they were messed with."

"What?" Drew said. "No, this was all a bad accident." His eyes had widened, and the purple bags underneath looked darker now.

"Where's my car?"

"It was towed to a shop for repair."

"Ask about the brakes. They didn't work. Something flashed on the dashboard, too. Something isn't right."

Drew's eyebrows folded together, and his lips made a tight, white line across his face. He stayed that way for a while like he was thinking, but it was painful. Eventually, he stood and touched Mae's leg under the blanket.

"Okay, I'll find out, but you need to promise me you'll rest." His voice cracked. He leaned over and kissed her forehead again. "Sleep. Please. I need you." He gazed into Mae's eyes for a long time, and then he straightened upright. "I'm going to check on Ruby. I'll let you know how she is. In the meantime, you need to trust that rest is the best thing for you."

Mae wanted to wrap her arms around his waist, to settle into the groove of his shoulders and neck where she usually fit, but instead, she watched him leave, unable to move from her spot in bed.

She tried to loosen her shoulders and relax her body, but she couldn't. Her head pounded when she closed her eyes. The brakes were messed with. She knew it. And now it was hard to trust anything or anyone.

Chapter Forty-Six

MAE WOKE SOMETIME LATER to the sound of shuffling around in her room. A nurse, she suspected. When she opened her eyes, it was Leah.

"This has gone too far," Leah said.

Mae tried to sit upright, but her body ached at the movement. She twisted her head toward the door, searching for a doctor or a nurse.

"What do you want? Why are you here?" Her throat was dry and scratchy, and her voice came out hoarse.

"I know you've been asking around again." She frowned. "And then I heard about the car accident. It's too much."

Mae still couldn't move very well, but her eyebrows lifted.

"I realize we've never warmed up to one another, and you don't have much reason to believe me, but I promise I'm not that bad." Leah sat down on a chair beside the bed. "Evelyn, on the other hand—Evelyn is a psychopath."

Sweat formed at the back of Mae's legs, just behind her knees. Her mind tried to think of the right words but couldn't. Leah kept talking.

"She tries to cover up by being so nice at times. Makes you feel like you're friends. She's so good at that."

Mae nodded slowly. Evelyn did do that. Mae believed they were becoming friends back when they first met.

"I thought we were so close, so I gave her the benefit of the doubt, but after everything that's happened lately, I'm learning that Evelyn isn't anyone's friend. She's always looking out for herself."

"I still don't understand," Mae said. What was happening? What was Leah trying to tell her?

"I know. For a long time, I couldn't understand why someone would be awful and hurtful with nothing much to gain from it. Now I think some people have it in them. To hurt."

"What the hell, Leah—" Evelyn was standing in the doorway, her eyes flashing.

A jolt of surprise went through Mae. She tried to shift in bed again. It was still so painful to move.

Leah shot up from her seat. "I'm sick of this. Everything has gone too far now. You're out of control."

Evelyn moved through the doorway and stood on one side of Mae. She glanced down at her. "You okay?"

"Oh, come on, cut the act," Leah said.

"I don't know what you're talking about." Evelyn put her hands into the pockets of her jacket. She had an air of indifference about her.

"Of course you don't," Leah said. "You don't know anything about Tessa or Sarah, do you?"

Evelyn's eyes flicked down to her feet only for a second.

"Tessa's daughter's name was Sarah," Leah said. "And Alice. Our friend. They're gone. Now Mae's in the hospital. She almost died, too."

Evelyn stiffened. "That's got nothing to do with me." Her voice was hard, like steel.

"Grab your phone and search *brake lines cut in Burlington*," Leah said to Mac.

Mae's heart sped up.

Evelyn shut her eyes so tight it looked like she was in pain. Her voice was small when she finally spoke. "Shut up."

Oh god, her brakes. Mae knew it. She moved her hand over the bed, her eyes darting to the table next to her. Where was her phone? She needed to call Drew. Now.

"You know what you'll find?" Leah said to Mae. "You'll find four reported cases of brake lines being cut in the neighborhood. Just before you moved here, police officers went door to door distributing leaflets, warning people to check their vehicles while they searched for clues, but they never found any possible motive." She turned to Evelyn. "I thought you were done with shit like that. You swore."

Evelyn lifted her chin into the air. "I was done. Until shit started up again."

Mae's body went cold. She couldn't think. She tried to sit up again, to move. "Cutting brakes? What the hell? You cut mine?"

Evelyn shrugged; she actually shrugged like this

wasn't a big deal. "I can't stand when things are out of my control."

"You can't blame your mother forever, Evelyn." Leah crossed her arms, standing stiffly at the edge of the hospital bed.

Evelyn's head snapped around. *"Don't* talk about my family or my life. You don't know."

"Then tell us. Tell her everything," Leah insisted, gesturing at Mae.

Evelyn sighed. "Listen, people only really care about you if you're the best or the most liked. Everyone tries to pretend they accept all differences, and they like to say they're all caring and loving, but I've seen it over and over again: when you're perfect, everyone likes you more. Everyone listens to you. I want to be listened to."

"That has nothing to do with you destroying other people's lives," Mae said. "What you did to Tessa—" She paused as a shiver went through her spine. "What did you do to Alice?"

"I was patient. I put up with a lot." Evelyn said. "Alice was always complaining, always saying she couldn't live with herself, knowing what happened with Tessa's daughter. She said she was going to tell everyone to get it off her chest. She was going to ruin my life, take away everything I have, just so she could feel better."

Mae blinked. "Do you hear yourself?"

Evelyn kept talking like Mae hadn't said a word. "Alice had no right to tell anyone about it, to rehash it. She wanted to unload her guilty conscience. All I did was try to contain her before it got out of control."

"You threatened her," Leah said. "You terrified her until she felt like she had no other options."

Evelyn frowned. "That's not my fault. She did it to herself."

Leah turned to Mae. "Evan tried to pay Alice off. When that didn't work, Evelyn wouldn't let up with the threats. Just like last time."

"Last time?" Mae said.

"When you did it to Tessa," Leah said, looking directly at Evelyn. "And what about when you did it to me?"

Mae's eyes shot to Leah.

"I was a target a long time ago. I forgot my place, I suppose. Evelyn made sure I fell in line."

Mae's breath caught in her throat. "Why would you take it? Why stay friends with her?"

"I wasn't strong enough then. I used to think your only worth was in how much other people liked you. I'm not proud of it."

Mae's mind flashed with a memory. "But you threatened Corinne." Leah couldn't be trusted either.

"What are you talking about?"

"You sent Corinne a text telling her you know what she did."

Leah's face contorted with confusion briefly before she dipped her head back, her face pointing up at the ceiling. When she looked back at Mae, her expression was flooded with understanding. "That was meant to *help* her. Did she think it was a threat? I tried to tell her that I knew she suspected things weren't right. I wanted to be on her side for once."

"Are you done? I've had enough of this accusing shit." Evelyn crossed her arms over her chest. "I don't need it."

Mae felt dazed, but not enough to stop her from finally sitting up in bed. She ignored the pain. "You killed Alice."

Evelyn's head darted around like she was looking to see who heard. "Alice ended up dead, but it's not my fault. I tried to help her. How could I know she was going to do what she did?"

"You texted her and told her not to come back. You told her she was nothing," Leah said.

"She was weak. She would have done it no matter what I said or did. And you both need to watch what you say. These are serious accusations." Evelyn shifted her weight from one leg to the other, her hip jutting out to one side. She looked directly at Mae. "Do you think you have some kind of power here?"

Mae could see it now. It was right in front of her, in the way Evelyn carried herself, in her eyes. She was the weak one, and it terrified her. Watching Evelyn now felt final to Mae.

"Stay the hell away from me and my family."

"What?" Evelyn's voice was incredulous, like nobody had ever requested that of her before. A hint of desperation appeared on her face and then disappeared. "Stay away from you? Who do you think you are?"

Mae knew now that Evelyn needed her. She needed Alice and Corinne and Lisa, too. She needed someone to direct her anger and insecurity at, or she would fall apart. And as long as she had them, nothing would change. There was only one thing Mae could do.

"Get out. I'm calling the police."

Before Evelyn could say anything in return, Mae spotted her phone behind a bouquet on the side table, picked it up, and dialed.

Chapter Forty-Seven

"STOP. DON'T DO THAT." Evelyn's tone was abrupt and sharp. Her face went white, almost grey. Tears formed in her eyes. Leah stood on the other side of the bed, mouth open and frozen in place.

"Jesus, Evelyn."

"Stop it!" she repeated. "You will *not* say a word about any of this to anyone." She gripped Mae and tried to rip the phone out of Mae's hand, but Mae's instincts took over. She lunged at Evelyn from her place in the hospital bed. Pain. Blinding pain shot through her body from the sudden movement, but Mae managed to yank Evelyn backwards by the arm and get her phone back.

Evelyn moved toward Mae and raised her arm up and backwards, her hand balled up and sliced through the air, barreling toward Mae.

Thud.

Mae's cheek and eye socket stung. A biting pain, like a thousand wasps. Her hand shot to the side of her face. She had never been punched before. There was so much she had never experienced before Burlington. Before Evelyn.

"Evelyn!" Leah rushed around the bed, but a nurse who heard the commotion came thundering into the room.

"What on earth?" she said. "You can't do this here."

You're right, Mae thought, relieved finally. *You can't do any of this here, Evelyn. You can't.*

Evelyn's body went slack as the nurse took her out of the room. Mae hobbled back to bed and collapsed. She touched the side of her face gingerly and then ran her hand over the top her head, through her hair. When she pulled her hand away, a clump of hair came with it. One of the extensions had come loose, and the tape that had attached it to her head was gummy and sticky.

Leah looked down at Mae. "I'm—I'm sorry."

"About what?" Mae asked.

"Everything."

Mae felt herself falling, even though she was already reclined in her bed. She was suddenly so sleepy, so drained. Her eyelids hurt. It had been so long since she ate, and her stomach felt hollow.

"I have to go," she said to Leah. "I have to see Ruby." But the next thing she knew, her eyes were closing, and she was falling asleep.

WHEN MAE WOKE UP, her room was empty. Soon after, the same nurse came back.

"Are you okay? I made everyone leave. You needed rest after all that. You've been through a lot."

Mae mumbled that she was fine. "Can I see my daughter? Please. I need to see Ruby." She looked closely at the nurse, noticing for the first time that she was young. She must have been in her mid-twenties. Her thick hair was swept up into a ponytail, and some of the hair at her temples had escaped, wispy and loose like wings. Just like Ruby.

"Your scans are due back any minute. Then you can go." The nurse touched Mae's leg and looked down at her with compassion. "I promise." Mae looked at her name tag. Hailey.

"I like your name," Mae said.

"Oh, thanks." Hailey smiled. "Me too."

———

WHILE WAITING for the scans to come back, Mae spoke to the police. She told them everything she knew from start to finish, and then, once she was done, she let it all go. Her mind was focused on something else. After Mae was cleared to be discharged, Drew came and got her, and Mae finally got to see Ruby.

Mae needed to comfort her daughter more than she needed anything else at that moment. The instinct had been there since the girls were babies, when they would cry and Mae would feel the urge to hold them, like she couldn't stop herself. Ruby stood when she saw Mae, her mouth widening into a deep smile. There was bruising on the side of her face, shining purple and yellow, which made Mae recoil with shame when she first saw it. Then her shoulders softened as she stretched her arms out and held her baby, her Ruby. It was like water after a drought, the way it felt when she held Ruby's small body.

In the parking lot, after they were discharged, Drew took Ruby by the hand and opened up the back seat door of his car for her. He helped her get in and buckled her in gently and delicately, like he was handling glass. He leaned in to place a soft kiss on the top of her head. Then he turned to Mae.

"How's your face?"

"I'll be fine." She would be. A bruise would heal. Mae tried to look past Drew, through the car window. Ruby's face was pale and wan. Drew placed a hand on Mae's arm and pointed his face in front of hers, searching for a quick kiss.

"Let's go home."

———

THAT NIGHT, Mae took off her clothes in the bedroom and put on her pajamas, brushed her teeth, and wiped her mouth on the towel hanging on the shower rod. Casual things. Like everything was perfectly normal in Mae's life and she and Ruby hadn't almost died in a car crash.

After the girls had gotten ready for bed, Isla settled into her bed like a bird in a nest, surrounded by her stuffed animals and blankets. Drew sat next to her on the side of the bed, one leg propped up on a sequinned pillow as he read a book.

"She's waiting for you," Drew said, pointing his chin toward Ruby's room.

Mae nodded at Drew and then went to Isla. She

leaned down and kissed her smooth forehead. "Night, sweetie. I love you."

"Night, mommy."

She continued down the hallway to Ruby's room and stood at the edge of the doorway, hesitant. "Hey, you. Ready to go to sleep?"

Ruby looked up at Mae from where she lay in her bed. She pulled her blanket up and tucked it underneath her chin, shimmying and shifting her body until she was comfortable on her side. "Can you lie down with me?"

Mae would never say no to that request. She had given up that fight long ago—there had already been so many years of long bedtimes with Ruby and Isla—and now she didn't mind. When Ruby was a toddler in her big kid bed for the first time, the only way to get her to stay in it and fall asleep was to lie next to her. At nine years old, Ruby was used to someone being there, and tonight especially, Mae wanted to be with her, too.

Mae crawled into bed and rolled onto her side, placing her hand under her cheek, a slight bend in her knees. She moved her body down until she was face-to-face with Ruby, their eyes lined up with one another. Ruby's were already closed. A sliver of light slid into the room from the hallway, allowing Mae to see the crescent of freckles sprinkled across Ruby's nose. Her thick eyelashes fluttered on her cheek as her breathing grew low and steady. Mae watched Ruby's face, studying each feature that made up her daughter. Her thick eyebrows, her rounded cheeks, the wisps of hair that fell over her forehead. Ruby's plump lips parted for a minute as sleep took an even deeper hold.

"I'm sorry," Mae whispered.

A sound came from outside the room: Drew closing the door to Isla's bedroom. It was just enough to startle Ruby momentarily, as if she was on the brink of deep sleep and was interrupted. Her eyes fluttered open and flitted to Mae's, confused for a moment, until they focused and locked on Mae. Then a realization washed over Ruby's face. It was like she remembered where she was, for only a split second, and Ruby's small mouth formed a broad, open mouthed smile, her eyes crinkling before they fluttered closed again. She released a small breath, the smell warm and minty, like toothpaste. Mae felt her chest open up and ache with the kind of love she had felt ever since first holding Ruby. And then she watched her daughter drift off to sleep again as her eyes filled with tears.

Chapter Forty-Eight

THE DAY after leaving the hospital, Mae spoke to the police again. Evelyn was arrested for the brake cutting and charged with attempt to do bodily harm and vehicle tampering. She was questioned about her involvement in Alice's death, but soon after, she was released on bail. Evelyn had tons of money, which meant the best lawyers would be involved. Who knew what would happen while she awaited the trial? It was painful for Mae to have no answers, but she worked through it little by little. Each day, she righted the wrongs she could.

Shortly after the holiday break, and after the news about Evelyn being arrested started to die down, Mae stood outside of the school waiting for the girls when she spotted someone she had wanted to speak to for a while now.

"Hey," Mae called. She quickened her pace. "Lisa."

Lisa turned and glanced at Mae with a hint of curiosity. "What do you want?"

"I was wondering," Mae pushed a piece of hair behind her ear. "I was hoping we could maybe go for coffee sometime?" Mae asked.

Lisa stood still for a moment and then only nodded her head, a small gesture. It was enough.

———

Now, Mae sat at her laptop and opened it up. She only stopped writing recently; she hadn't lost the ability to tell a story yet, and thanks to an agreement she worked out with Grace, Mae was going to write a collection of articles about the fraught and complicated lives of mothers for Grace's publication.

They already agreed to some ground rules—no dishing or gossip, no naming names. Instead, she would explore motherhood, the expectations, the pressure, and the tenuous relationship the women around her had with one another. Maybe she would discover something about herself. But first, she was going to tell Alice's story.

Mae set an office up for herself in the corner of the master bedroom, just under the window where enough natural light would come in. She downloaded an app that played background noise—white noise, beach sounds that were designed to help you focus—and most days, she wrote. She wrote about Alice without identifying her, and she examined the diverse identities of motherhood within Burlington's social sphere. She explored the hierarchy of men and women in the town. She gave voice to women who couldn't speak. It felt right.

The screen of Mae's phone flashed with a message.

You ready? I'm out front.

Mae closed her laptop and grabbed her jacket on her way out the front door.

"Let's go," she said as she slid into the front seat of Corinne's car.

Corinne had been back for a couple of weeks by now. She showed up on Mae's doorstep one day and said she was ready to heal. Now that Evelyn wasn't around all the time, the two of them were calmer and more relaxed. They spent as much time together as they could.

Corinne drove the winding roads until they arrived at their destination. She put the car into park and glanced sideways at Mae. Mae smiled. They didn't need to say anything. In fact, most of their visits here were silent.

They walked for a few minutes before they arrived at the gravestone. Mae brushed some snow off the top.

"Hey, Alice," she said.

Corinne put her hands into her coat pockets. They stood shoulder to shoulder, talking to their friend until the sun dipped below the trees. Once they said their goodbyes, Corinne and Mae made their way back to the car in the dim light of dusk, feeling lighter than when they first arrived.

Everything else in Mae's life remained similar; with Evelyn on house arrest and Corinne back, she and Drew decided to stay in Burlington. Drew had found another job, the girls continued to go to Riverpark, and Mae started meeting up with Lisa for coffee after school drop-off a few times a week. They had a lot in common, and Mae liked getting to know her. Sometimes Leah joined them, but not often. That was still raw and new. Mae was being careful, and so was Leah.

It took some time for Evelyn to no longer be at the center of everything. The news about her buzzed on the lips of all the parents at pick up and drop-off. She was being charged with a serious offense, one that all the money in the world couldn't make go away. Maybe Evelyn would have to finally own up to what she did to Alice.

In the meantime, until the trial was over, the court had ruled that Evelyn could leave her house only to take her kids to school, so she appeared in the schoolyard every so often and floated around, unchanged, trying desperately to make women want to orbit around her. Although, without Mae or Lisa or Corinne to try and control, Evelyn had lost something. Every time Mae saw her in the schoolyard, she mattered less and less.

She was simply there, existing on the periphery.

Chapter Forty-Nine

FOUR MONTHS later

THE MORNING AIR was warm on Mae's skin, even though the sun wasn't shining. She had a tank top on for the first time that spring, and her body felt light, weightless. Hope came along with the changing of the seasons.

Mae cracked a window open wide in the kitchen to allow more air in as she went from one place to another, putting dirty dishes into the dishwasher, and filling up water bottles for the girls to take to school. She had already made their lunches and only had to dry her damp hair before she would be ready to walk. Ruby and Isla sat at the island in the kitchen on tall stools, finishing their cereal while their legs dangled underneath them.

"Is your homework all done?" Mae asked Ruby. Ruby nodded without looking up, her shoulders hunched over her bowl, her eyes cast down on the book she had flat on the counter in front of her, one hand pressing it down in place.

A breeze came in through the window and tickled the edges of Mae's arms. She breathed in and then, with a long blink, let it back out again slowly, satisfied.

When it was time to leave, after brushing teeth and hair and zipping up backpacks, the three of them left the house and made their way down the nearly empty sidewalks to school. Most trees were blooming now, some with soft, pale pink flowers, others with small buds, some with big leaves already. Mae looked up at the canopy over her head and marvelled at the massive size of the branches attached to thick trunks. God, they were stunning.

On the way, Ruby and Isla talked together. Mae half-listened but mostly let her mind wander. Her mood was as light as the air. It could have been the leftover endorphins from her early morning run, but Mae suspected it was something else. It was the warm air, the budding trees, and the sound of her daughters' voices. It was everything, in fact.

They took their time getting to school, walking with their heads down to examine the ground underneath them. Isla stopped suddenly and crouched down into a squat. "Guys, look!"

Mae stopped. Isla was bent over, her eyes focused on a stretch of sidewalk beneath her. There was a tiny, baby blue robin's egg sitting at the edge of the sidewalk where it met the grass of someone's lawn.

"There must have been a nest somewhere around here," Ruby said. She bent over at the waist to examine the shell closer, too.

"It's perfect," Isla said. Mae knew Isla meant that it was still intact and hadn't cracked.

"It is," Mae agreed.

Isla reached out a hand to pick it up and let it roll into the middle of her palm.

"Leave it." Ruby chastised her sister.

"I'm just looking." Isla kept her eyes on the egg. It was so small and delicate. A thin, smooth shell decided the fate of a life. A small life, but a life, nonetheless. "I can't wait to see the baby bird that hatches out of it." Isla smiled down at the egg.

Mae reached her hand forward. "Here. Let me." She picked it up carefully, with delicate hands. Mae knew it wouldn't survive the conditions—animals, weather, people walking by. There was little chance, but she didn't say anything. Instead, she placed it at the base of a tree, nestled into a patch of long grass, hoping it would help. Maybe it would make a small difference.

"Let's go," Ruby said.

Mae stood still, watching Isla and Ruby resume walking ahead for a moment. The outlook they had, the incredible amount of hope. It was stunning and beautiful enough to stop her in her tracks and hold Mae in place. Then she brushed a piece of hair out of her face and followed them the rest of the way to school.

The End

Acknowledgments

This book would not have been possible if it weren't for the many, many incredible people I feel lucky to have in my circle. I can't thank you all enough for helping my biggest dream come true.

Firstly, thank you so much to Alex and Tina at Rising Action Publishing for helping me craft my book into something I'm incredibly proud of. The amount of work you put into everything is astonishing and I'm very grateful to be a debut author with you. I want to say an extremely special thank you to Alex for believing in me and my book and for being the first one who helped me realize my dream. You are a true rock star.

To my OG writing friends and early readers Jennifer Millard, Julie Green, Erin Pepler and Lauren Roberts. Thank you for going on this journey with me.

To the best writing group a person could ask for, the SPs (if you know, you know). You are such a talented group; I feel so lucky to be considered a part of it. Thank you for helping me to become a better writer, and thank you to Amanda, Anne, Maren, Elise and Greg for reading early versions of this manuscript and giving me excellent advice. And to Liz Kessick, I will be forever grateful for your advice and your support through every step and stage.

To my two very special writer friends who I met after this book, Georgina and Lydia, I love the way we work together. Thank you for your support.

To Michelle Meade for the excellent feedback and advice. You are wonderful to work with.

Thank you to Nat Mack for designing a cover that receives many, many compliments. It's so stunning and eye-catching and I love it so much.

To all my friends who have always believed in me, cheered me on and asked about my book: thank you so much. I love you all. You really know how to make a person feel special. And a very special thank you to Sarah Langley for crying in coffee shops with me for over 20 years now. When it comes to friends, you are the best as they come.

To Melissa, for being so supportive from the first day you met me. And to my brother, Chris, for being one of my biggest fans. Your support and love have meant so much. I guess I forgive you for the nickname Booger McFats. For my dad who gave me the good advice, "You've got to have a murder in this book." You weren't wrong! And for my mom. There's no way I could do you justice in a few short words, so instead, I write you into every book I can. You're *so good* at being loving and supportive, and you're the best grandma three girls could ask for. I'm lucky to have you in my life.

For my husband, Andrew—the muse for all my good husband characters. I work every little bit of you into all my characters because I love everything about you. (Even when you eat your salad with a spoon.) Thank you for being able to sleep through my early morning writing sessions in our bedroom. And thank you for holding down the fort when I need to escape.

And, finally, for Anna, Lauren and Paige. You make it so easy for me to write about motherhood with emotion and depth because you will forever be the best thing that has ever happened in my life. I love you so much and I promise you that my face will always light up when you walk into a room.

About the Author

Heather Dixon is a member of the Women's Fiction Writers Association, a managing editor of a non-profit website, and a mother of three daughters (and a 90-pound Bouvier). She lives just outside of Toronto, Ontario. *Burlington* is her first novel.

Burlington
Book Club Questions

1. Mae struggles to find her place among the women in the new neighborhood. Do you think female friendship gets complicated in adulthood? Does it get harder to establish and keep friendships?

2. What was your reaction to Mae as she began to spend more time with Evelyn and the other Riverpark Moms? Why is she drawn to Evelyn? Did you understand her motivations? Did you sympathize with her or were you frustrated by her?

3. Mae thinks a lot about the expectations she feels are put on women and mothers in Burlington. For example, the need to be wealthy, to be a perfect mother and wife, and to make everyone happy. Do you think this was an exaggeration or do you think these kinds of expectations still exist for women and mothers? Who places these expectations on women?

4. After the car accident, while they're lying in Ruby's bed, Mae tells Ruby she's sorry. What do you think Mae is sorry for? How do you feel about adults apologizing to their young children?

5. What did you think of the story Mae tried to tell Grace for the magazine? Do you think the outcome would have been different if she were able to edit it or write some of it herself? Who do you think had the right to tell the story— the person being interviewed or the publication putting the story out?

6. Near the end of the book, Ruby and Isla find a robin's egg on their walk to school. Mae says "It was so small and delicate. A thin, smooth shell decided the fate of a life. A small life, but a life nonetheless." What do you think she means?

7. What were your impressions of Alice? Do you think her death was caused by someone? Was it caused by something specific that happened? Evelyn says, "She did it to herself." What did you think when she said that?

8. What do you think of Leah? Were you sympathetic to her? Could you see yourself being friends with her? As the novel progresses, do you feel differently about her?

9. Are there any lingering questions about the book you're still thinking about?

10. What did you think of the ending? Did it end the way you thought it would?